this
thirty
some
thing
life

About the Author

Born in Southampton, England, in 1975, Jon Rance is the author of the romantic comedy novel, *This Thirtysomething Life*. He graduated with a degree in English Literature from Middlesex University, London, before going travelling and meeting his American wife in Australia. He's currently working on his second novel, *Happy Endings*. He drinks a lot of tea and spends far too much time gazing off into space.

Please visit his website at www.jonrance.com or connect with him on Twitter @JRance75.

this
thirty
some
thing
life

jon rance

HODDER

First published in Great Britain in 2013 by Hodder & Stoughton
An Hachette UK company

1

Copyright © Jon Rance 2013

The right of Jon Rance to be identified as the Author of the
Work has been asserted by him in accordance with the Copyright,
Designs and Patents Act 1988.

A CIP catalogue record for this title is available from the British Library.

ISBN 978 1 444 77749 9

Printed and bound by CPI Group (UK) Ltd, Croydon, CR0 4YY

Hodder & Stoughton policy is to use papers that are natural,
renewable and recyclable products and made from wood grown
in sustainable forests. The logging and manufacturing processes are
expected to conform to the environmental regulations of the
country of origin.

Hodder & Stoughton Ltd
338 Euston Road
London NW1 3BH

www.hodder.co.uk

To my darling wife, for a million things more than I could ever write about in a book and for putting up with my 'man-tention span'. I love you.

january

SUNDAY, January 1st, 2.00 p.m.
New Year's Day

In the kitchen. Emily upstairs. Cloudy overhead. I think it might rain.

Less than a day into the bright sparkly new year and already I'm in the dog house with Emily. What have I done wrong? Your guess is as good as mine. All I know is that she's acting very strangely and she's definitely in a strop about something. I heard the toilet flush about fifteen minutes ago, but otherwise silence. I'm afraid to go up there.

Possible reasons why she might be mad at me:

1. I may have done something awful last night which has yet to filter back into my consciousness. Was I that drunk? Possibly. I did throw up in the front garden, use the bath as a toilet and I somehow managed to fall asleep with my trousers on backwards. All bad signs.

2. She might be annoyed I haven't cleaned out the shed yet. She's been asking me to do it for months, but based on her current stroppiness, this feels like something much worse.

3. Period? She does get very hormonal when Aunt Flo comes for her monthly visit. Must check the period calendar.

4. Could she still be mad at me vis-à-vis buying the classic Star Wars figures on eBay? Emily doesn't understand that they're a family investment. She just thinks I bought some old toys off the internet. I tried to explain that I could take them on the *Antiques Roadshow*, but she said, 'I don't care

about the fucking *Antiques Roadshow*, Harry. You spent five hundred quid on figurines!'

5. Some completely irrational Emily thing like the time she didn't talk to me for three days and called me a, 'useless, immature, emotionally redundant fuckwit, who wouldn't understand the meaning of romance if it kicked me in the testicles'. Admittedly, I forgot our wedding anniversary, but still, I think she went a bit over the top. Yes, she'd spent a good deal of time making that photo album, the mix CD of our favourite songs and the six-course meal, but did she need to take out that ad in the local paper and offer me in exchange for a better model? The worst part was she didn't get a single bloody reply.

4.00 p.m.
Emily still upstairs and presumably still pissed off. Will she ever come down? Am I brave enough to go up? It's the first day of January and already this year's looking as depressing and gloomy as a Charles Dickens novel. I feel like I'm living in an actual Bleak House.

4.40 p.m.
I'm going over the top. Actually, dearest diary, I'm going upstairs, but running towards a barrage of German artillery doesn't feel like a bad alternative compared to facing Emily when she has the hump. I already checked the period calendar to see if she is premenstrual (negative) and I made her a cup of tea. As Mum always says, 'Start the New Year as you mean to go on.' Based on the first twelve hours, it's going to be a difficult one.

5.30 p.m.
Having a cigarette by the back door. Emily upstairs getting ready. It just started to rain.

I went upstairs with my PG Tips peace offering and she was in bed reading a book. I placed the tea on her nightstand and said lovingly, 'There you go, Em, a nice cup of tea.' She didn't say anything and continued reading her book in a cheerless silence. Not wanting to take this lying down, I did. 'I'm sorry.' I didn't know what for, but best to apologise anyway. Whatever I'd done wrong, she was making it perfectly clear it was going to take a lot more than tea and apologies to get back in her good books.

Eventually, when the cold shoulder had become bloody frosty, she slammed her book shut, rolled over and fixed me with a Himalayan stare. Her deep, dark Irish eyes gave me a look that said, 'This is bloody serious, Harry, and don't even think about making one of your stupid, asinine jokes. This is major, big-picture stuff and you'd better bloody well pay attention.'

'I want to have a baby, Harry.'

'But, Em, we've already talked about this.'

Twice last year she brought up the subject and both times it ended with the same result. I'm not ready. I don't know why exactly, but I'm not ready to give up what we have. Maybe I'm being selfish, but I love our life the way it is. I love the fact that if we wanted to we could spend the weekend in Dublin, Dubrovnik or Düsseldorf. Admittedly, we haven't done much mini-breaking over the last few years, and I have no real desire to spend any amount of time in Düsseldorf, but it's nice to have the option.

Unfortunately, Emily didn't care about weekend mini-breaks. She'd had enough of her career. She used to love her job, but now it weighed her down and she was ready for a change. She was ready to start a family and be probably what she always dreamt of being, a mummy.

'Well, I want to talk about it again. I want a family. I'm ready.'

'But . . .'

'But what? Give me one good reason why we can't.'

The truth is I didn't have one good reason. I didn't have any number of reasons, good or otherwise. Is being selfish a good enough reason? Probably not. Is being afraid to grow up a decent argument for not having kids? Definitely not. What about inexplicable fear? I should probably have told her how much I loved her and explained I definitely wanted a family one day, because I do. I want to have kids, do things like the 'school run', possibly buy a people carrier and wear slippers around the house. I want all of that, but not yet. I couldn't confess any of this to Emily though and so I said the first thing that came to mind.

'Because what about our trip to Italy? We said we'd definitely do that before we had kids.'

'And we can, Harry. We can go in the next couple of months, I promise. Please just say you'll think about it. It's important.'

I took the easy way out and agreed to think about it. This led to a cuddle and a kiss. Women are so sneaky. Men are so weak. Why does starting a family scare me so much? Why when everyone around us is making babies with all the ease and excitement of the von Trapp family am I putting it off for a fantasy holiday once mentioned over a drunken Valentine's meal? I fear I might be on the verge of some sort of early mid-life crisis.

And to rub salt in an already gaping wound, we're having dinner tonight at Steve and Fiona's in Worcester Park. Not only do they have three kids, but also the audacity (or stupidity) to give them all names beginning with the letter J (Jane, Joseph and James). How mental is that?

MONDAY, January 2nd, 9.00 a.m.
Bank holiday

On the sofa. Eating a bacon sandwich. Emily still asleep. Cloudy.

What a truly awful night. Steve and Fiona are expecting another baby. A fourth J to add to their jumble of Js. When are they going to stop? They told us over the guacamole dip. There must be something in the water (or perhaps the guacamole dip) in Worcester Park.

We have known Steve and Fiona since university and they used to be our regular going out partners. They used to be normal until about seven years ago when they announced they were pregnant. At first it wasn't too bad, I was even mildly happy for them, but gradually, as they added to their collection of Js, rumblings of change began to sweep across our relationship. Steve and Fiona couldn't go out anymore so we always had to go to their house for dinner, which would usually end before eight o'clock with both Steve and Fiona asleep on the sofa. Twice we threw a blanket over them and sneaked out. They also (very quickly it seemed to me) became walking clichés of exactly the type of people who have kids. They went from a snazzy four-door Audi to a boxy people carrier. They both gained enough weight that they were only physically attractive to each other. They started dressing as though clothes were merely canvasses for their children's vomit and the last time we went to their house for dinner, Steve said to me (and I'm not making this up), 'Daddy has to go pee pee on the potty wotty!' It was the last straw. Baby talk had crossed the line.

Of course, their announcement led to the inevitable questions about when we were going to start trying for a baby.

Cue glares of disappointment and despondency from Emily. I was prepared for this, but what followed completely threw me. Steve and I popped out to the garden for a cigarette. Actually, I popped out for a cigarette while Steve came to remember what it was like to smoke (Fiona made him quit when they had their first J). I was finally relieved to get some peace and quiet when Steve said, while inhaling my second-hand smoke:

'So, Harry old boy, what's the problemo?'

'Excuse me?'

'Why don't you want to have kids? Kids are brilliant!'

They had pulled Steve in too. It was a bloody conspiracy. He was one of them. A woman in man's clothing!

'I'm not ready yet, that's all.'

'I wasn't either, but now I'm having number four and I couldn't be any happier. They change your life, they really do.'

'So does going bald and I'm not ready for that either!' I exclaimed and went back indoors.

The rest of the night was a complete and utter disaster. Hint upon bloody hint about having kids. At every opportunity they would pass me one of their Js to play with in the hope I'd suddenly see the error of my ways and proclaim, 'I'm ready to have a family!'

Why does every parent in the world think you can't be happy until you have kids? I don't ring them up at eleven o'clock every Sunday morning when I've had a glorious lie-in to gloat. I don't text them every time I'm at the pub having a few pints, while they're at home changing nappies and I don't brag about how much sex we have, knowing they probably haven't done it for months. Parents are like the bloody Jehovah's Witnesses of your thirties: hounding you to succumb to the almighty power of parenthood. Back. The. Fuck. Off!

10.30 a.m.
New neighbours next door. I had a quick peek out of the window when they were moving in and it's a terrible thing to even think, I know, but they had the whiff of terrorists about them. Mrs Crawley from number four (head of the neighbourhood watch committee) was immediately outside in her front garden having a good old nose. No doubt she'll call an emergency meeting. Unfortunately, I'm on the committee.

Off to Canary Wharf to meet best mate Ben for lunch. Hopefully this will cheer me up.

3.00 p.m.
In the kitchen. Watching a squirrel run around the garden. Feeling a wee bit tipsy after lunch with Ben. (Why do I always start using Scottish vernacular when I'm drunk?)

It was great to spend an hour with someone who didn't only want to talk about the power of procreation. We talked about football, the good old days and his latest adventure to Peru. We smoked, drank and I had a very nice lunch before Ben had to get back to work. Although, before he headed off, I told him about the baby conversation I'd had with Emily and he said, 'It's perfectly natural, mate. You've been married for what, six years now? She's in her thirties. It was bound to happen eventually. If you're not ready to be a father, you need to figure out why and soon because, trust me, when it comes to babies, women get very impatient. Bloke at work, Rupert Strang, only been married for five minutes and he just got divorced. His wife wanted a baby and he didn't. Admittedly, the devil was also screwing his assistant, but still, you get my point.'

I did.

I'm watching a squirrel run around the garden and I'm

wondering if I'm being a bit unreasonable. Maybe Ben's right. It is a natural progression and we aren't getting any younger. Should I give Emily a child whether I'm ready or not? Will I ever be ready? Sometimes I think it would be easier to be a squirrel because all he has to worry about is his nuts. Perhaps we aren't that dissimilar after all.

TUESDAY, January 3rd, 10.00 a.m.

In the study. Listening to The Beatles. Emily at work. Blustery showers on their way from the north (according to the BBC weatherman).

Last night when Emily got home from work, I made her a sumptuous dinner of citrus-seared tuna with crispy noodles, herbs and chilli (thanks Jamie Oliver). She seemed impressed. I opened a bottle of Italian red and attempted to have a proper conversation about starting a family. I was open, honest and everything she claims I'm not. I told her about my lunch with Ben and watching the squirrel, which to be honest, seemed to confuse her, but she listened intently and when I'd finished she said very calmly, 'Harry, don't freak out, but I'm pregnant!'

'What? I . . . err . . . don't understand, Em . . . how?'

'About three weeks ago. We both had our work Christmas parties.'

'Not ringing any bells.'

'I came home drunk. You were eating a lamb kebab.'

'Oh, right, yeah, the lamb shish . . .'

'That's what jogged your memory? Anyway, I forgot to take my pill that morning and we were a little lax with the condom.'

'Shit.'

'I took the pregnancy test on Saturday and it was positive.'

'Are you sure though because pregnancy tests are notoriously hard to read? Blue lines, pink lines, single lines, double lines, who can really tell?'

'It said pregnant, in words.'

'Oh.'

'I'm definitely pregnant, Harry. You're going to be a father.'

There is nothing in the world that can really prepare you for those words. You're going to be a father. You, Harry Spencer, aged thirty-two, will soon be responsible for a little baby being. My whole life flashed before my eyes and I even surprised myself because no sooner had the words left her mouth than I started to cry. I wasn't expecting that and I don't think Emily was either. The tricky part though is I'm not entirely sure what sort of tears they were. It's hard to categorise because I was certainly happy, but I was also scared, terrified and my mouth suddenly got very dry. However, after the initial shock had slowly downgraded to just surprise, I had a question.

'But if you were pregnant all along, why were you asking me if I wanted to be a dad? Why the whole guilty baby parade at Steve and Fiona's? Why didn't you tell me straight away? I'm confused, Em.' For the record I still am.

'Because I knew it would be a big deal and I thought if maybe I could get you used to the idea first . . . I'm sorry, Harry, but you know what you're like.' (Yes, brilliant.) 'Are you happy about this?'

She had asked the question. It had to be asked I suppose and to be honest, I was. I didn't think I'd be quite so delirious about it, but the reality was very different than the nightmare in my head. Maybe I was ready to be a father after all. I looked at her and smiled.

'Of course I'm happy about it, Em. We're having a baby.'

We kissed, hugged, she cried, I stopped, until gradually the horror of the situation slipped into my mind. I'm going to be a father forever. What if I fuck it up? What if I'm an awful dad? What if I don't love them as much as I'm supposed to? What if . . . I could go on, but while Emily was snuggled firmly into my neck, her tears of joy trickling slowly down my shirt, I couldn't let go of the fear. It took me three attempts to pass my driving test and I studied hard for that, but this didn't come with a learner's manual and I only had one chance to get it right.

'Are you going to be ready?' Emily said or something along those lines because I'd slipped into a man-coma. Emily was talking (her lips were moving anyway), but I was locked inside my own little world, until she suddenly brought me back with a click of her fingers.

'Harry, are you listening to me?'

'Sorry, I was thinking.'

'I know this is a lot to digest, but it's not the time to have a mid-life crisis.'

'Who's having a mid-life crisis? I'm not having a mid-life crisis.'

'Because the last thing I need at the moment is you losing touch with reality. You're going to be ready aren't you, Harry?'

Am I going to be ready? Obviously not. Am I having a premature mid-life crisis? Quite possibly. I didn't know what to say. Unfortunately, while I was thinking about it, I slipped into another man-coma and before I knew what was happening, Emily was clicking her fingers again.

'Harry, Harry . . .'

'Yes, sorry?'

'I said I'm going to need you for this. I can't do this on my own.'

'I know and I'm going to be here for you every step of the way.'

'Promise?'

'Promise.'

1.00 p.m.

Still awaiting the blustery showers from the north. Eating a packet of prawn cocktail crisps. Squirrel outside taunting me with his carefree happiness. Pain in my side.

In an attempt to delay the onset of middle-aged spread and prepare myself physically for the rigours of fatherhood, I attempted to do some sit-ups and almost fainted. I've had a sharp pain in my side ever since. I looked up the pain in my side and it could be anything from a stitch, kidney tumour, shingles, to an impending heart attack! Fantastic. I tried working out and it could lead to an early death.

I also made a list of pros and cons about having a baby:

PROS

1. Babies are cute and generally considered to be a good thing.
2. It will make my mother the happiest mother in the whole world.
3. It will make Emily the happiest wife in the whole world.
4. It might even make me happy.
5. We will have someone to take care of us when we're old and miserable.
6. I will have someone to mould in my own image.
7. It might be fun.
8. I'm not getting any younger.

CONS

1. They're expensive.
2. Changing nappies.

3. Lack of sleep.

4. It would severely hamper our freedom.

5. No more weekend lie-ins.

6. What if it destroys our sex life?

7. What if it destroys our marriage?

8. I don't feel anywhere near ready.

9. I'm too young.

10. At the moment we have a good life. We have two steady jobs and a nice house in a good part of London. Am I ready to put all of that in jeopardy for a baby?

11. Lastly (and most importantly I think) every couple we know with kids are the most boring people on the face of the planet. All they ever want to talk about is their bloody kids, e.g. 'Last week Angus did his first banana-shaped poo, it was too adorable.' Am I ready to become that dull? Am I ready to openly discuss poo with my nearest and dearest?

The cons won 11–8. Not a good sign. Bugger.

9.00 p.m.

Emily in bed. Still no sign of the mysterious blustery showers from the north. Having a last cigarette of the day by the back door. Side throbbing.

Strange banging noises coming from next door. Maybe they're making a bomb! What should you do when you think your new neighbours might be potential terrorists? I'm tempted to do nothing, but what if they are terrorists and they blow up the Houses of Parliament? I'll always be the bloke who could have stopped them, but didn't. My ugly mug will be on the front pages of every newspaper in the country: 'HISTORY TEACHER IN BOMB PLOT BUNGLE!' I can already see the disappointment on my parents' faces.

WEDNESDAY, January 4th, 2.00 p.m.

At Starbucks. Sunny. Still no sign of blustery showers from the north. Pain in side getting worse.

I spoke to my parents this morning vis-à-vis grandchild on the way. Both parents were very excited, especially Mum. It took about fifteen minutes before she stopped simultaneously crying and squealing, while Dad chipped in with his usual stoic cameo, 'Nice work, son.' They're popping up for a visit this weekend. Maybe I should have asked Emily if we're telling people. I'll mention it tonight. I'm sure it's fine.

7.00 p.m.
We aren't telling people. I casually mentioned over dinner that I'd told my parents and she went ballistic. Apparently, although she never mentioned this to me, she had a big plan to invite both of our families over for an official announcement party. It was going to be like the opening ceremony for the Olympic Games. I apologised, but she was unmoved and hasn't said a word to me since.

I may have to make an appointment to see Dr Prakish about the pain in my side. It's getting worse. I don't want to die because of sit-ups.

Interesting development regarding the so-called blustery showers from the north. Tonight the weatherman didn't even mention it. The outlook for the next five days is good to fair. I've lost all faith in weather people. Not a great evening. To make matters worse, tomorrow's the first day of the new term. Not looking forward to teaching again after the Christmas break. Roll on half-term.

THURSDAY, January 5th, 10.00 p.m.

In the lounge with an empty bottle of wine, six empty cans of lager and two empty packets of crisps. Emily in Buckinghamshire. All quiet on the Wimbledon front.

What a day. First day back at school was a disaster. I forced Year Ten to watch a video and half the class fell asleep. Gavin Haines was snoring so loudly that the kids who were awake couldn't hear the television. I would have woken him up, but to be honest, I just didn't have the energy. Year Eight got the medieval slide show (minus commentary).

At lunchtime I had a cigarette with Rory Wilkinson (Art) and told him all about my marital strife.

'Still, at least now it's happened, there's no going back, eh,' said Rory.

'But what am I supposed to do? I just don't know if I'm ready for this.'

'Well you can either spend the next nine months in a mood about it or you can accept it and get ready to be a dad.'

'They're my only options?'

'You could run away but I don't think that's much of a choice. Although Paul Gauguin did some of his best work after he left his wife and moved to Polynesia,' Rory said. He added, 'Although he died of syphilis.'

'Cheers, Rory.'

I spent the afternoon thinking about my conversation with Rory. I decided I don't want to spend the next nine months in a mood or die of syphilis. I need to show Emily that I can change, grow up and be the husband/father she so desperately craves. I'm finally ready to be that man. I was excited to get home and tell her, but my enthusiasm was short-lived because when I got home from school she wasn't here and instead I found a note on the fridge. I'd been Dear John-ed.

Harry,
I realise you didn't mean to be a thoughtless, callous idiot when you told your parents about the baby. I also realise you're scared stiff about being a dad, but this is something we have to do together. It's make or break time and I need to know you're going to be there for me and our baby. I've gone to my parents for a couple of nights. I hope this will give you some time to think about things.
I love you.
Emily x

I was incredulous. I rang her up straight away but her dad answered. Derek's an ex-copper and quite bloody scary. He's six feet tall and about the same width and spent thirty years patrolling the streets of East London. He isn't to be messed with. The conversation didn't go well.

'Hello, Derek, is Emily there?'

'She is.'

'Can I speak to her?'

'Not at the moment.'

'Why?'

'She seems upset and wants to talk to us.'

'About the baby?'

'Baby, what baby?!' Fuck. She obviously hadn't told them yet. She was going to hate me.

'Well . . . umm . . . shit.'

'Is Emily pregnant?' This is when I heard Emily in the background. 'Emily wants a word.' Fuck.

'What the fuck is wrong with you?' Emily screamed down the line.

'I . . . err . . . sorry.'

'Aggh!' said Emily and hung up the phone.

That was five hours ago. Since then I've finished six cans of lager, half a bottle of wine and a packet of cigarettes. I watched England's tragic exit from Euro '96 on penalties to Germany on YouTube (why Gareth Southgate, why?) and I listened to the Baddiel and Skinner classic, 'Three Lions on a Shirt'. I also listened to an entire James Blunt album. It's been an emotional night. I'm pathetic. The only good thing is that because I'm so drunk I can't feel the pain in my side anymore.

4.00 a.m.

Woken up by a loud drilling noise from next door. Maybe I should pay them a visit. I need to see inside their house before I call MI5. I don't want to waste the taxpayers' money if they're just making home improvements. Suicide bomber or DIY enthusiast?

FRIDAY, January 6th, 9.00 a.m.

At home. Eating a sausage sandwich. Emily still in Buckinghamshire. Pain in side worse than ever.

I had an erotic dream last night about the girl who lives at number seven. She's only about eighteen, but drop dead gorgeous. We were in the garden shed, which was really messy (must clean out the shed) and she was naked, but when she pulled my underwear down I had no penis! All I had was a smooth area like an Action Man figure. Then my old maths teacher Mr Rogers walked in wielding an enormous knob and they went off together. What could that mean?

I called in sick today. I couldn't face school with my marriage in tatters. I tried calling Emily this morning but she was still asleep (according to her mum). I'm meeting best mate Ben at twelve. Hopefully he'll have answers.

1.00 p.m.
Canary Wharf. Just finished a very tasty steak and kidney pie. Ben outside on the phone. Emily still in Bucks.

Ben is organising a big lads night out. I explained everything and he said what I needed was, 'A break from all the drama and to get really, really pissed!' I think Ben might be a genius. He's on the phone now summoning the cavalry. This will be my first big night out in a long time. Tonight is going to be wonderful. No worrying about having a baby, upset wife or living next door to potential terrorists. Tonight is all about being with the lads, getting drunk and having fun. Just like the good old days!

SATURDAY, January 7th, 11.00 a.m.

Home (just). Head hurts (a lot). Side hurts (more than head). Morning sickness (where did that come from?). Emily asleep upstairs.

I AM NEVER DRINKING AGAIN! Quite possibly the worst night of my life. It started well with a few pints in Covent Garden, but once we got to the club it all started to go pear-shaped.

We were on the dance floor making absolute fools of ourselves. Simon (Bano) Bannister (professional shark) was doing his best to pull every girl in the club. Richard (Ritchie)

Dennis (professional accountant and contender for the world's most serious individual) was giving some poor girl advice on her investments. Ben was chatting up a girl at the bar and I was slaughtered and barely able to stand up. Then, at about midnight, trouble erupted. It turned out one of the girls Bano was dancing with had a boyfriend. It also turned out he'd just walked in with a couple of his mates. Long story short, we heard shouts and then the next moment we saw Bano flying across the dance floor. The next hour was pandemonium, but the outcome was that we were all arrested and spent the night at a police station. This, unfortunately, wasn't the worst part of the evening.

For some reason, when asked for a contact, I gave Emily's number and when light broke through the cell window in the morning, there was Emily and her dad waiting to take me home. I have never been so embarrassed. The car ride home was silent. When we got back, Derek left (with a menacing stare) and Emily said (in that scary way of hers when I can't tell how mad she really is), 'I was hoping you were going to use these two days to grow up. I didn't expect to have to come and get you from the police station. To say I'm disappointed is an understatement. I'm going upstairs to bed. Don't even think about trying to join me.'

And to make matters worse, my parents should be arriving within the hour to celebrate their first grandchild. Brilliant.

7.00 p.m.
In the shed. Smoking a cigarette. Emily having a bath. Parents probably somewhere on the M3.

My parents (God bless them) turned up with balloons, a giant teddy bear and party poppers just as Emily came walking down the stairs. Perhaps I should have warned them about the situation. It was too much for Emily, who ran back upstairs crying. I had to sit my parents down and explain that Emily was having a hard time and was a bit emotional. I left out the bit about me being a callous bastard and getting arrested.

'I told you we shouldn't have brought that stupid giant teddy,' said Dad.

'Let me talk to her, Harry, she needs a woman's touch,' said Mum. I tried in vain to stop her but my mother is a very determined woman.

'Right then, we're going to the pub,' said Dad and off we went.

Dad got a couple of pints and we sat by the window. I didn't want to talk about the baby and so that only left football or him as topics open for discussion. I chose the latter.

'How are you and Mum?'

'Don't ask.'

'I just did.'

'Your mother's in a stinker of a mood.'

'Why?'

'Goodness knows.'

'Did you ask her?'

'And have my head bitten off? No thanks.'

Sometimes it's easy to see why I'm the emotionally redundant, typical bloody man that annoys Emily so much. I come from a family where best case scenario, we can ignore anything that might vaguely resemble a conversation, and worst case scenario, we might have to talk about something slightly important. Not feelings or emotional needs but something similar. We're the human equivalent to ostriches.

After a few minutes of awkward silence, Dad and I retired to our happy place (football), where we could talk for hours without the distraction of having to discuss anything remotely personal or important.

MONDAY, January 9th, 7.00 p.m.

What's happening to me? Admittedly, I've been going grey for a while now, but it always felt like something that was happening gradually. A bit like global warming. Suddenly, however, I've got huge clumps of grey sprouting up everywhere. It seems the salad days when I could use Emily's tweezers to pluck out the occasional stray grey are but a memory. Now the only solution is hair dye, but do I want to go down that road? Surely it's best to grow old and grey gracefully.

I also have more pressing hair issues to deal with. My nose seems to be under the impression that more is definitely better. Unfortunately, my ears also seem to have jumped on the hairy bandwagon. The result is that I spend at least five minutes every day in front of the mirror manscaping all of the excessive hair from my various extremities. This is the first sign that middle-age is definitely looming large. At the moment I'm winning the battle, but soon, one day, I'll wake up and the forest of unwanted hair will be beyond my control and then I'll be my father. Ironically, while I'm sprouting superfluous facial and body hair like it's going out of fashion, the hair on my head is retreating faster than a platoon of well-trained Italian soldiers. Just my luck!

TUESDAY, January 10th, 8.00 p.m.

In the shed. Eating a scotch egg. Emily watching TV. Pain in side excruciating. Must make appointment to see Dr Prakish tomorrow.

I had one of my episodes today. I don't know the official term but Emily calls it my 'man-tention span'. I was reading an article in the newspaper about tri-sexuals and Emily started asking me something. I should have told her I was reading or put down the newspaper and listened, but instead I attempted to do both. Big mistake. I was trying to find out what tri-sexuals were and then the next moment Emily was standing over me.

'Well, what do you think?' I obviously hadn't heard her question but I didn't want her to know so I replied.

'Whatever you think is best, baby.' This was my second mistake.

'And what did I ask you?'

I looked up from my paper but what could I say? I hadn't heard a word she'd said and I was no nearer to finding out what tri-sexuals were. I was firmly in a lose/lose situation.

'Sorry.'

Emily was fuming.

'You never bloody listen to me.'

'I do.'

'No you don't. You hear but you don't listen. I'm sick of being ignored, Harry.'

'But, Em, I love you.' This was my third mistake.

'If you loved me, Harry, you would listen to me.'

She, of course, had a point.

I still have to find out what tri-sexuals are and I'm in the dog house with Emily (again). A truly unsuccessful evening on every level.

WEDNESDAY, January 11th, 4.00 p.m.

Doctor's waiting room. In pain.

Today the pain got worse. I left school as soon as the bell rang and rushed to the doctors. The pain is searing, burning, numb and sharp. I might be dying. I hope Dr Prakish can save me.

6.00 p.m.

Back home. Dr Prakish said that I'm fine. I explained what had happened and that I had a searing, burning, numb, sharp pain in my side.

'Give it to me straight doctor, am I dying?'

'Mr Spencer, if you didn't smoke, drank much less, ate a healthier diet and exercised regularly, you would be fine. As it is, you're just very unhealthy and doing a couple of sit-ups made you feel as if death was converging on you. I would suggest a complete lifestyle change. More salad, less booze, quit smoking and walk for half an hour every day.'

I think I might have to start looking for a new (more sympathetic) doctor.

FRIDAY, January 13th, 7.00 p.m.

Today, on my way home from school, I popped into the newsagents to buy a magazine and found myself embroiled in the philosophical debate that has haunted man since the beginning of time. Intellectual stimulation or tits? Or in this case, *GQ* or *Loaded*?

I'm in my thirties now and so I should be buying *GQ*. It

has better articles, great advice on fashion, health and fitness, but on the other hand, *Loaded* has a lot more tits.

If I purchased *GQ* I would enjoy it, but a part of me would feel empty, while if I bought *Loaded*, another part of me would feel neglected. So, not wanting to disappoint any facet of my psyche, I decided to get them both. What is life without intellectual gratification and what is life without tits?

I also found out what tri-sexuals are. They're people who will literally try anything. The Urban Dictionary says:

A person or persons actively engaging in sexual intercourse with anyone or anything, be he, she or it, animate or inanimate.

Inanimate? How does that work? Hello mug, fancy a quick shag? Fruit bowl, any chance of a threesome with the television? Very odd.

SUNDAY, January 15th, 1.00 p.m.

In the kitchen. Waiting for Yorkshire puddings to cook. Emily watching TV. Pain in side still loitering with intent. Squirrel in the garden eating an olive (it seems we have Wimbledon's only bourgeois squirrel).

Emily had morning sickness for the first time today. She looked bloody miserable, poor thing. It was, however, a good chance for me to show her how sensitive and caring I was. I asked from the other side of the bathroom door if she was alright and needed anything.

'Do I fucking sound alright?' she shouted back.

'Love you,' I replied supportively, but all I heard was Emily throwing up last night's dinner. That's the last time I push the boat out and buy free-range organic beef. It's much too expensive to not stay down.

I went to see my octogenarian Granddad at the old folks' home yesterday and the first thing he said when I walked in was, 'It's so hard not to be a racist these days, Harry.' When I asked him what he meant he replied, 'I was talking to this darky fella. From Africa he was. I mentioned I thought Sammy the Paki had stolen my apple. Next thing the darky fella said I shouldn't use the word Paki because it's derogatory. I told him Sammy was from Pakistan and a thief. Things aren't what they used to be, Harry. It's not like the good old days.'

Granddad is always going on about the good old days, like there was a magical period of time when people would stand on street corners and give out money. When you could buy a house for a shiny penny, a car with a cheeky smile and there was a good old knees-up at the pub every night. Sort of like Eastenders but without the drama and violence. The only problem with the good old days is that no one actually knows when it was, where it was and if it even existed.

'How's everything going apart from the racism and theft, Granddad?'

'I need to have sex, Harry. I need to feel the pleasure of a woman's touch before I die.'

'Emily and I are having a baby.'

'Sex, sex, sex!' Granddad said before Sammy (the Pakistani fella) walked past eating an apple and all hell broke loose. Granddad had to be restrained by two staff members. 'I didn't fight in two world wars to have my apple stolen by a bloody Pakistani!' Granddad shouted across the lounge as he was escorted away. For the record, he didn't fight in either war.

As I was leaving the home I heard someone shout, 'Spirit of the dam busters!' And I'm sure it was Granddad.

MONDAY, January 16th, 10.00 p.m.

In bed. Eating a pork pie. Emily asleep.

I got the dreaded text from Mrs Crawley today: 'NW meeting. 8pm. My house. Urgent!' I've been expecting this since our new neighbours moved in, but when it finally appeared in my inbox my heart sank.

Mrs Crawley, despite her kindly Miss Marple demeanour and religious leanings, is something of a suburban tyrant. She takes her role as head of the neighbourhood watch committee to ridiculous lengths, which does mean we live on one of the safest streets in South London, but as Emily always says, at what cost?

The meeting lasted an hour and consisted of her talking about the new neighbours without actually mentioning the new neighbours (heaven forbid she is perceived to be a racist). She said things like:

'Recent changes need to be noted with regard for the on-going safety of our street.'

'It's been brought to my attention, due to recent activity on the street, that we need to be more diligent than ever.'

'We must, at all costs, be sure we not only watch those that appear to be, shall we say, up to no good, but those that live right under our noses.'

When Brian from number fourteen innocently asked, 'Are you talking about the new people who moved in next to Harry?' Mrs Crawley looked appalled.

'Of course not, Brian, what made you think that?' Then

Jon Rance

she made more tea and gave everyone a single digestive biscuit.

After the meeting, I felt even guiltier about mistrusting my new neighbours because of their race and appearance. I'm not a racist bigot like Mrs Crawley. I'm going to make more of an effort to get along with them.

Emily was sick again today. She was in bed and asleep by eight o'clock. Poor thing.

TUESDAY, January 17th, 7.00 p.m.

At home. Eating bangers and mash. Emily nibbling on a sausage (unfortunately, not a euphemism).

Begin rant.

We had to use the ladies' toilet at school today because of a blockage in the gents. No doubt Bill Jenkins (Maths) was to blame. That man has the bottom of the devil. Still, it was quite an eye-opening experience. The ladies' toilet is lovely. They have pretty, pink towels, pictures of quaint English countryside scenes on the wall, they have hand lotion, hand moisturiser, the cubicle actually has toilet roll (and how soft it was) and they have a little box of potpourri next to the basin. I had no idea the female staff had it so good in the lavatory department.

Going into the gents is like visiting someone in an East European jail. Hard sandpaper towels, grey paint peeling off the walls, there's never any soap, there's always one half-square of toilet roll left (who uses half a square of toilet roll?) and the smell. The thought of having to pee or worse starts a spiral of thought which can take up an entire morning of teaching. Do I really have to go? Can I wait? Just bloody well clench up and keep it in.

We're intelligent human beings. We're responsible for educating the next generation of industry leaders, artists and sports personalities, yet we have to defecate like monkeys in the rainforest, while the ladies get their girlie bits pampered like bloody royalty. It isn't right. Just because I'm a man, it doesn't mean I don't enjoy a bit of potpourri and hand moisturiser from time to time.

Rant over.

WEDNESDAY, January 18th, 6.00 p.m.

In the bathroom. In shock. Emily in the bedroom laughing.

I've been going to Dave's Barber Shop for the last eight years. Dave is middle-aged, a bit camp and possibly gay (although married with two kids) and does a great haircut, quickly, cheaply and with very little conversation. An average Dave appointment goes something like this.

'Alright, Dave.'

'The usual, is it?'

'Yes please, Dave.'

'Right.'

Then Dave goes about his business until it's time to pay. I always give him a two-quid tip and then he says, 'Thank you, thank you, bye, thank you, bye, thanks,' about eighty times. On quiet days, I can still hear him outside on the street thanking me and bidding me farewell. It's probably the most comfortable relationship in my life. However, today when I went to Dave's there was no Dave and in his place was a spotty youth.

'Where's Dave?'

'Holiday, innit. I'm the trainee, Troy.'

'Troy the trainee?'

'Yeah, izzit.'

Then Troy the trainee went on to explain what he'd like to do to my hair. He seemed keen to shave most of it off. I thought about leaving and returning when Dave was back, but something about the desperate look on Troy's face made me sit down in the chair and let him loose with the scissors. Thirty minutes later and I was looking in horror at his handiwork.

'Whatdoyerthink?' said Troy with a proud look on his mottled face.

Basically, it was a fucking shambles. He had shaved parts, cut other parts and none of it seemed to match or be level, but I didn't have the heart to ruin Troy's grand vision.

'Yeah, great, perfect, just what I was after.'

I gave Troy the trainee a two-quid tip and then left. Troy didn't say thank you or bye once. I left with a feeling of emptiness and embarrassment, which wasn't helped when I got home and Emily started laughing at me. For the record, she still is.

WEDNESDAY, January 25th, 4.00 p.m.
Burn's Night, Scotland

At school. Raining. In need of a cigarette.

Miss Simpson (Dictator Headmistress) called me into her office today. She was concerned I seem distracted (I am). She lectured me on being professional, taking time off 'nilly willy' and the importance of classroom discipline. She said she'd received a complaint from a parent. When I asked her what the complaint was she said, 'Certain students are being allowed to literally sleep through lessons and their snoring is upsetting the other pupils.'

I lied and said to the best of my knowledge, no student had ever fallen asleep during class. She gave me a look of such vile contempt that I actually felt physically violated.

The pupils call her Miss Hitler, which is especially pleasing to me, being a history teacher. She said she'd be keeping a careful eye on me. When she said this, she narrowed her eyes until I could hardly see them anymore.

8.00 p.m.
On the sofa. Eating a cheese and onion slice. Emily lying next to me. Watching the telly.

Will my future son/daughter look like me? Will they have my looks and Emily's brains or vice versa? Will they be a ginger? Emily's grandmother was a redhead. Maybe it's a recessive gene. I'll have to Google that.

FRIDAY, January 27th, 9.00 p.m.

Having a cigarette by the back door. Emily asleep upstairs. Drilling noise from next door. Almost a full moon tonight.

I had a drink with best mate Ben in The Alexandra tonight and he had some staggering news. He's fallen madly in love with an Aussie girl and they're leaving for Australia in less than a week!

'I'm in love, mate. I think she's the one.'

I'm in complete shock. He's always been the single one. A confirmed life-long bachelor. He was never going to settle down, get married, have kids and do all the normal stuff. While I was busy creating a sensible suburban existence in south-west London, he was off bungee jumping in New Zealand, scuba diving in Australia and hiking the Himalayas. A part of me has always been jealous of his freedom and exciting lifestyle, but now he's going to be just like me. It doesn't feel right. I need to live vicariously through Ben, but if he's doing the same mundane shit as me, it isn't going to work.

'I never thought I'd see the day. She must be something special.'

'It was love at first sight. I've never felt this way before. She's going back to Australia next week and I'm going with her.'

'But what about your job? What about your flat? What about me? Are you coming back?'

'I don't know. I just know I need to go. Work's giving me some time off. My flat will be fine and I think you'll be OK.'

'We'll see about that.'

I can't believe Ben is abandoning me in my hour of need. He invited Emily and me to his flat tomorrow night to meet Katie.

SUNDAY, January 29th, 10.00 a.m.

Drinking tea in the garden. Emily still asleep. Squirrel up and about. All quiet next door.

We had dinner at Ben's flat last night. Katie is exactly what I expected. She's tall, beautiful, interesting and I fell madly in love with her in about five seconds flat. Her life story reads like an action adventure. Mountain climbing, skydiving, scuba diving, iron woman competitions and surfing.

Fitness oozed from her body like the smell of laziness seeps from mine. She's gorgeous, funny, intelligent and absolutely perfect for Ben. It doesn't mean I'm happy about him traipsing halfway across the globe though. Who will I go for drinks with now? When I said this to Ben he replied sarcastically,

'In case you've forgotten, mate, you're about to be a dad. You'll have about as much use for pubs as I have for talcum powder.' Then he laughed hysterically. I'm glad the smug bastard is going to Australia.

MONDAY, January 30th, 6.00 p.m.

In the lounge. Eating a Pot Noodle. Emily lying on the floor in pain. Raining.

I came home from work to find a stack of baby-related books on the coffee table. Here's a selection:

50,000 of the Best Baby Names. It makes you wonder which names were omitted. Adolf would be one I assume.

The World's Best Baby Names. A second baby name book seems a tad excessive. Do we really need names from North Korea and Iran? We're unlikely to call our child Chung-Hee Spencer or Farzad Babak Spencer. I imagine we'll probably stick to something a bit more traditional.

The Bloke's Survival Kit for Being a Dad. This jovial-sounding book was, I assume, purchased for me. I flicked through and even I was offended by the level of immaturity it presumes all men possess. I mean, seriously, it had a chapter called, 'Babies v Beer – You think it's all over, it is now!'

'You expect me to read this rubbish?' I said to Emily.

'Fiona said Steve loved it. He couldn't put it down.'

'But Steve's a moron.'

'Just read the bloody book,' Emily replied and it seemed a bit churlish to argue with a pregnant woman lying on the floor in pain. Admittedly the pain was not baby related. She twisted her ankle coming down the stairs, but she's still carrying our child and is, thus, untouchable.

TUESDAY, January 31st, 8.00 p.m.

Full moon. In the study. Emily asleep. Drinking wine alone.

I don't know if it's because I'm about to become a dad, or because Ben is leaving, or maybe it's just the wine, but I'm feeling a tad wistful. Emily went to bed at six o'clock because she was knackered. She didn't even eat dinner.

I've been going through my box of memories and reminiscing about my good old days. I found some old photos of me as a young boy with really awful clothes and a dodgy haircut (the late eighties wasn't a good time for me).

I also dug up my old sixth-form yearbook. I skimmed through until I found pictures of Ben and me. We were trying our best to look cool and aloof, but obviously we looked stupid and inane. Ben had one of those half-goatee chin beards, which he thought made him look interesting and intelligent. Ironically, he was interesting and intelligent, but the half-goatee chin beard made him look like a bit of a knob.

Then I stumbled across a picture of my old girlfriend, Jamie O'Connell. God she was beautiful. Slender body, long blonde hair, sparkling blue eyes and breasts that seemed to literally defy gravity. Bouncy yet firm, pert but well rounded, large, but somehow just the perfect handful. She was also the first person I'd ever met who'd really travelled and who knew about obscure indie bands and not because she wanted to sound cool, but because she genuinely loved music. She had read just about every novel ever written and watched every film, including the black-and-white French ones (and not just because they're occasionally a bit mucky). She created style instead of following it, spoke her opinion without ever preaching and while we were trapped in a sort of post-secondary school whirlpool of identity crisis, she knew exactly who she was. She somehow managed to be strong, vulnerable, sexy and intellectual all at the same time.

How she became my actual girlfriend will always remain something of a mystery. She was like a sixth-form Brigitte Bardot, while I looked bloody awful with my slightly long hair (curtains, as we called them) and extra-large glasses (they literally covered half of my face). She was also Scottish, which made her even more exotic and desirable, but some-how (sheer luck I'd imagine) I managed to woo her. Jamie was my first love and like all first loves I thought we were going to be together forever.

I start wondering about the girl I loved so much. Is she married? Does she have children? Where does she live?

In a moment of inquisitive melancholy, I manage to find her on Facebook. Unfortunately, her page is blocked and so I have no choice but to request we become friends. I doubt whether she'll even remember me. She's probably married to a rock star/actor/millionaire/model and living it up in the south of France. C'est la vie.

4.00 a.m.
I woke up in a terrified, sweaty panic. I'm going to be some-one's father! They're going to call me Daddy and expect me to know how to mend things, know about photosynthesis and take them fishing. I don't know how to fish. I went once when

I was seven. I don't know how to change a plug and God knows about photosynthesis. Something about light, carbon dioxide and plants, but I don't know. How can I possibly be a good father if I don't know about photosynthesis?

february

WEDNESDAY, February 1st, 8.00 p.m.

In the lounge. Eating a bowl of cereal. Emily asleep. Raining cats and dogs.

I was called into Miss Simpson's office again today.

'Mr Spencer, why when you were in here a few days ago being lectured on class discipline are you here again?'

'I'm as baffled as you.'

'Pupils fighting in class?'

'Well, yes, but . . .'

'There are no buts, Mr Spencer. Why were two of your pupils brawling in class?'

'It was a silly misunderstanding.'

Actually, it wasn't silly or a misunderstanding. Robert Mitchell (class moron) got a blow job from Gary Brown's girlfriend around the back of Tescos. It wasn't a big deal and I quickly resolved the situation. I was more annoyed to learn my pupils were getting more oral action than me. Especially Robert bloody Mitchell.

'It isn't good enough, Mr Spencer. I don't want to have any more of these little chats. Do I make myself clear?'

'Crystal.'

'Now be on your way.'

She's the devil and quite clearly hates me. I'm for the chopping block.

THURSDAY, February 2nd, 10.00 p.m.

In bed. Emily asleep and snoring loudly. Dribbling with rain.

Emily and I had an argument over breakfast this morning. We were at the table when I spotted an absolute bargain in the newspaper.

'Look, Em,' I said pointing at the newspaper excitedly. 'A 1966 Volkswagen camper van, partially restored, needs a bit of work, but otherwise in good working order. Need to sell quickly. Best offer accepted. I think we need this.'

'We don't,' she snapped, not even looking at me or the newspaper.

'This was our dream remember? When we first met. We said how amazing it would be to get a camper van and travel around the country, maybe Europe, maybe the world.'

'And it would have been good ten years ago, Harry, but it's too late now.'

'Why is it too late?'

'Because we're having a baby.'

'Even more reason to get it. The kid will love it. Holidays in the camper van. It will be our thing. People will say, 'Oh, look, there go the Spencer family off in their camper van again, lucky devils.'

'No.'

'Just like that.'

'Yes.'

'Why?'

Emily stopped eating her toast, closed her book and looked at me with that look. The look that said beware. The look that said, 'Stop talking, shut up and listen!' The look that scares the bejesus out of me.

'Because this is another entry on the long list of Harry's wonderful ideas that will end up in the shed.'

'What's that supposed to mean?'

'The radio-controlled airplane you bought two years ago: how many times did that make it off the ground?'

'That's a bit unfair because it broke during take-off and I haven't had time to fix it yet.'

'The skateboard, roller blades, windsurfing?'

'Well, yes, but . . .'

'And where is your windsurfing board at the moment?'

'It's in the shed, but . . .'

'Along with the calligraphy set you so desperately wanted.'

'It's nice to want to write properly.'

'Model railway world?'

'It would have been incredible.'

'If it had made it out of the box. Don't you see, Harry, this is another one of your great ideas that will end up cluttering up the shed.'

'But this is different.'

'That's what you said about the worm farm.'

'Well a camper van wouldn't fit in the shed!'

'No, it will sit on our driveway for years rusting away, until one day, after the twentieth argument, you'll be forced to sell it. I'm not trying to be difficult, but we don't need this. You always get these silly ideas in your head, which was fine when it was small silly things and we didn't have a baby on the way, but it's time to grow up and stop buying crap because it's your pipe dream of the day.'

'But this is for the both of us.'

'Like the tandem bike you bought on eBay?'

'Well, yes, I grant you, that didn't work out.'

'And what makes you think this will? It needs work and you know nothing about cars. You can't even change the oil in the car we have.'

'I could learn.'

'You could but you won't. The answer's no.'

'And that's your final answer?'

'Yes.'

'Fine, but remember the next time you want to buy another pair of shoes you'll wear once and then throw in the back of the wardrobe that we had this conversation.'

'Fine,' said Emily and we finished our breakfast in silence. I really must clean out the shed.

FRIDAY, February 3rd, 8.00 p.m.

In the shed. Emily asleep. Smoking a cigarette. I just heard whispers over the fence from next door.

A sad day. Ben and Katie left for Sydney. We had a quick drink in The Alexandra last night to say our farewells. Will I ever see Ben again?

Emily's arranged to have Steve and Fiona over for lunch on Sunday with their brood of Js. We're going to tell them the good news. No doubt they'll be over the moon because now we can join their soppy circle of sadness. It feels like the end of an era. Goodbye best mate and drinking buddy, hello annoying family from hell and their litter of kids.

SATURDAY, February 4th, 4.00 p.m.

Emily in bath (as in bubble, not the city). Still raining. Eating a chicken and ham pie. No sign of squirrel. All quiet next door. No reply regarding friend request from Jamie. BBC weatherman claims more rain on the way from the west. Can I believe him?

I went to visit Granddad today and he was in unusually high spirits.

'I met a girl,' he said as soon as I walked into his room. 'A younger woman, Harry.'

'Oh, really, Granddad.'

'Seventy-one and she still has most of her own teeth!' he exclaimed with pride.

'That's great, Granddad.' Then he announced they were going on a date!

SUNDAY, February 5th, 10.00 a.m.

In the kitchen. Listening to Radio 2. Peeling spuds. Emily lying down. Bright, blue skies (no chance of rain). Still no response from Jamie.

Why are weather people never right? It's probably the only profession in the world where you can be wrong most of time and still keep your job.

Squirrel outside with another squirrel and they seem to be quite amorous. Good for them. Steve, Fiona and their brigade of ankle biters will be here at noon. I'm not looking forward to it. I've spent most of the morning child-proofing the house. As a result, all of the alcohol is now in the shed.

6.00 p.m.

In the shed. Having a cigarette. Drinking a cocktail (Sex on the Beach!). I might as well enjoy the fact the alcohol's now in the shed and I finally get to use the cocktail recipe book I got two Christmases ago. Steve, Fiona and ankle biters just left. My nerves are frayed.

I plied myself with red wine and then we told Steve and Fiona our good news. They went berserk. At one point Steve screamed like a little girl, while Fiona kept yelling, 'OMG! OMG! OMG!'

They already have us down at a birthing class, family therapy session, pre-birth playgroup and something (if I heard them correctly) which sounded like a week away together to Cornwall. Emily did most of the talking, while I just smiled a lot and said things like, 'It's unbelievable. Really exciting. Doesn't seem quite real yet.'

Emily was in her element and spent ages talking to Fiona about baby names, types of nappies and a whole hour about the importance of breastfeeding. Steve even popped out to their car to get their spare breast pump and gave us a demonstration (on himself!). Emily got out the calendar so we could see how many days our new babies are going to be apart. Apparently, they're going to be within a month of one another, which is obviously fantastic news.

Luckily, I spent most of the time preparing lunch and so I managed to avoid most of the baby talk. I did, unfortunately, get stuck with Steve while I was trying to sneak in a cigarette outside.

'It's great news, old boy.'

'We're very excited.'

'You know there's this book . . .'

'*The Bloke's Survival Kit for Being a Dad*?'

'Yes, how did you know?'

'I have a copy.'

'Oh, it's a must read, really quite, you know, true. I think us blokes need a little bit of extra help, don't you?'

'I suppose.'

'And if you have any questions, anything, just let me know. Even the delicate stuff.'

44

'Thanks.' I didn't want to ask what kind of delicate stuff he was talking about.

'And we have that week in Cornwall, which will be absolutely immense.'

'Right, yes, wait, what?'

'We're going to Newquay for the week in May. We're thrilled you're coming. The kids can't stop talking about it.'

'Yes, of course, can't wait.'

Emily had pulled a fast one and agreed to go on holiday for an entire week with Steve, Fiona and their clan. I must stop this disgrace. How could she do this to me?

The next few hours passed extraordinarily slowly. I played with the kids for a while, mostly to get away from Emily, who still didn't know I knew about Cornwall. Eventually they all left and I came outside for a cigarette and a cocktail (Irish Car Bomb!) to compose myself before I confronted Emily about our sham of a holiday to the West Country.

8.00 p.m.

According to Emily, we had a conversation about Cornwall last week and I agreed to it! I find this very hard to believe. I have no memory of the conversation in question. Is Emily using my 'man-tention span' against me?

'I don't remember any conversation about Cornwall, Em. I think I'd remember.'

'Last Wednesday, we were having dinner.'

'What did we have?'

'I don't know. Pork chops I think.'

'Nothing's coming back to me.'

'Surprise, surprise.'

'OK, yes, I grant you, my memory's a bit . . .'

'Shit?'

'Yes, but I think I'd remember a whole conversation where

I agreed to go to Cornwall for the week with Steve, Fiona and their gaggle of Js.'

'You'd think so.'

After our conversation I started to wonder if maybe she's right. Had we had a conversation about Cornwall? Is it possible that my 'man-tention span' is getting worse and I'm losing whole chunks of my life without even knowing it? What else have I agreed to? Time to pop out to the shed for another cocktail.

MONDAY, February 6th, 7.00 p.m.

God I'm ugly. We have an unfortunate full-length mirror in our bathroom. Unfortunate because I just saw myself getting out of the shower and the years haven't been kind. My sparkling blue eyes are now a sullen grey and my once fairly trim body is looking more rotund and disproportionate every year. Why do I only gain weight around my midriff? The result is skinny arms, pencil-thin legs and a Buddha-style belly.

People say that as men get older they get sexier and more dignified (e.g. George Clooney, Sean Connery). Well, trust me, there was nothing sexy or dignified about what I saw in the mirror. I must try and get in shape.

TUESDAY, February 7th, 8.00 a.m.

At school. Emily at work. Still no reply from Jamie.

I woke up this morning and felt as sick as a dog. I threw up in the bathroom. Then Emily woke up and she threw up in the bathroom. I think I might have sympathy morning sickness. What's happening to me? Am I turning into a woman? That's the last thing I need at the moment.

1.00 p.m.

I had a chat with Rory at lunchtime today.

'I think Miss Simpson hates me,' I said.

'She hates everyone.'

'Really?'

'Well, most people. She seems to quite like me. The other day she commented that my Year Eight sculpture project was a great example of out of the box thinking. I wouldn't be worried though.'

'Right.'

'Unless she starts making sudden appearances in your room. Then you can start panicking. Remember Doug?'

'Dirty Doug?'

'Dagenham Doug.'

'With the dogs?'

'Yes, well, just before he was fired, she started turning up in his room, watching him and taking notes. Next minute he was gone.'

'I'll watch out for that.'

5.00 p.m.

Miss Simpson made a sudden appearance in my room this afternoon and took notes. I am for the high jump.

11.00 p.m.

Emily got home from work and said she was craving Indian food. We went to our local Indian, The Spice of Wimbledon, where Emily ordered the chicken madras! For the record, she normally orders the korma and asks for it extra mild. I spent

Jon Rance

the next hour watching her sweat and dribble her way through the second-hottest curry on the menu. When we got home she demanded sex.

'I want to have wild, animal sex, Harry,' she said astride me, her face alight with lust and passion.

This would normally have me as stiff as a guardsman outside Buckingham Palace. However, for some reason, all I could think about was Miss Simpson. Needless to say, it wasn't so much animal sex but minimal sex. Emily dismounted, a very unhappy, sexually frustrated passenger. What is wrong with me? I complain when we don't have sex, but can't perform when we do. Typical.

WEDNESDAY, February 8th, 5.00 p.m.

In the shed. Eating a chocolate orange. Drinking a cocktail (White Russian!). Emily lying down.

Jamie accepted my friend request! She remembers me. She wrote me the following message.

Harry, it's been too long. I miss you! I've spent the last few years in Scotland, but I just moved back to London. I'm a nurse now if you can believe it. Would LOVE to catch up soon. Take care, Luv Jamie XO

I replied instantly.

It has been too long. I miss you too! I'm still in London and would LOVE to catch up soon. Take care, Luv Harry XO

I wrote that and then instantly started obsessing about it. How can we possibly just catch up? It's not as if we can meet for a friendly drink. Emily, you don't mind if go out for a casual, friendly drink with my ex-girlfriend, who I haven't seen in fourteen years, do you? Of course she would bloody mind.

And wouldn't it just be awkward? It's been fourteen years. After we had caught-up and reminisced about the good old days, what else would we talk about? And what if there was still some sexual tension after all these years? Do I want something to happen with Jamie?

I'm talking bollocks. There's no way we can meet in person. It's mission impossible and I'm definitely not Ethan Hunt or for that matter Tom Cruise. I'm Harry Spencer. I'm thirty-two going on forty-two. I'm out of shape, running out of time and definitely out of luck when it comes to meeting ex-girlfriends for a friendly drink. I need to stop thinking about it. She probably won't reply anyway.

Emily said our first baby doctor appointment is on Thursday at five o'clock. Apparently, she told me a while ago, but it must have slipped my mind.

5.30 p.m.
Still in the shed. Drinking a cocktail (The Churchill!). Moving the alcohol to the shed was a genius idea.

Lots of whispering and lights next door. I peeked through the fence. I couldn't see much, but what I did see was quite alarming. I saw five men digging a hole! It must be for a body! They were acting very suspiciously and one of the men looked across and I'm convinced he saw me. It was dark, but I quickly dashed back into the shed. They're definitely up to something, but what can I do about it? I'm afraid if I don't do something, they will commit terrible crimes against innocent civilians, but if I do something, they will commit terrible crimes against me.

8.00 p.m.
I was wrong about Jamie. She did reply.

So glad you wrote back. I just moved to Greenwich and I don't know many people here so it would be wonderful to see a friendly face. I had a quick peek at your photos – I see you're still as handsome as always. Your wife's a lucky lady. Here's my number, give me a call and we can go for a drink or something. Can't wait to hear from you. Luv Jamie, XO – 07858 902654

Oh Lordy! What am I doing? Why did I find Jamie on Facebook? I was just reminiscing about my lost youth, why did I have to act on it? Why did she have to write drink or 'something' which leads me to imagine that 'something' is actually sex?

I'm literally caught between my pregnant wife and my former lover. Emily's lying there, tired, carrying my child and watching a rerun of *Only Fools and Horses*, while Jamie is toying with me on Facebook. What should I do? What can I do? I can't meet Jamie for a drink without lying to Emily. If I lie to Emily about meeting Jamie, then I'm at the top of a very slippery slope. I don't want to be That Guy, but a part of me is curious to see Jamie again. Confusion rains down on the house of Spencer. Off to the shed for another cocktail.

THURSDAY, February 9th, 6.30 p.m.

In the lounge. Drinking tea. Emily taking a shower. No appetite.

We just got back from the baby doctor and I think I can speak for the majority of men when I say I really don't appreciate other men staring at my wife's vagina. Especially when they say things like, 'Oh yes, that really is a splendid vagina.'

I had reservations about going to a male obstetrician in the first place, but Emily said Fiona had recommended him very highly. I protested, but Emily said a great obstetrician was something to be cherished. I mean, seriously, they're all looking at the same vagina with the same level of education, how different can they be? Unfortunately, my protests were noted and ignored and so off we went to see Dr Proops (yes, seriously).

The minute we got there and I felt like my protests were vindicated because Dr Proops looked like an old perv. He had a moustache, which if I'm not mistaken is the first sign of a dirty old perv. He may as well have been masturbating underneath a trench coat. Why do women always assume that because a man's wearing a white coat, he's not a filthy old git?

Then secondly (and I'm not making this up) he stuck three fingers up Emily's vagina and said with a smarmy smile, 'That's three fingers.' Why is he turning Emily's vagina into a drinking game? I was disgusted. And this perv of a man is going to deliver our baby!

But then a miracle happened. We heard their heartbeat for the first time and everything else melted away. It was the single most incredible moment of my life. Emily and I held hands and looked at each other in amazement and suddenly

I didn't care that Dr Proops was a man and seemed to enjoy staring at Emily's vagina a bit too much. For the first time since I found out, I felt like a dad. It felt real and suddenly I started to cry. Emily was crying too, while the beat, beat, beat of our baby's heartbeat provided the backing track. It was a glorious moment.

7.00 p.m.

I just had a very unexpected phone conversation with my mother.

'How did it go, dear?'

'How did what go?'

'The doctor's appointment, of course.'

'How do you know about that?'

'Emily told me last week.'

'When last week?'

'She gave me a call. Unlike my doesn't-tell-his-mother-anything son, she has the good grace to let me know when huge events are occurring in our life.'

So Mum and Emily are having secret conversations behind my back. What else are they sharing? Fashion tips? Recipes? Top ten most annoying things about Harry? Menstrual cycles? Does Mum still have a menstrual cycle? Why am I thinking about that?

'Sorry, Mum.'

'So, how was it? How's Emily? How's the baby? Did it go alright? How was the doctor? Was it a man or a woman? I have a woman, she's lovely, very soft hands.'

'It was fine.'

'Fine, that's it, fine? I want details, Harry. Did you hear the heartbeat? What did it sound like? Are you nervous because you know what you get like when you're nervous? Remember when you started secondary school? You almost threw up in your cornflakes and your driving tests, I can't even talk about that. Luckily your father was there.'

'It was great, Mum. We heard the heartbeat and I'm fine.'

'Because Emily mentioned you were a bit . . .'

'A bit what?'

'You know.'

'No I don't know. That's why I'm asking.'

'You know how you get under pressure. Just like your father. You close up, Harry. You don't talk and spend more time playing bloody golf.'

'I don't play golf.'

'It doesn't matter what it is, Harry, you need to talk to Emily. Make her feel loved. Let her know you're going to be there for her when it matters and you aren't going to wet your trousers again.'

'Why would she think I was going to wet my trousers? Did you tell her about that?'

'It may have slipped out.'

'Jesus, Mum. One time I accidently wet myself and suddenly it's all over the bloody news.'

'It's OK, dear, it happens to every little boy. Admittedly, you were fifteen, but it happens.'

'Mum, can we not talk about it please.'

'Does it still hurt?'

'Mum.'

'Sorry, Harry.'

'Do you and Emily talk on the phone often?'

'Oh, not that often really. Once every couple of weeks.' Blimey. What else have they shared over BT friends and family? 'In fact, she's on the other line right now. I have to go.'

'Mum . . .' but she had already hung up. She had to talk to her daughter-in-law and, apparently, it was more urgent than talking to me – her only child. I think I need to have a conversation with Emily about this.

FRIDAY, February 10th, 9.00 p.m.

In the kitchen. Smoking a cigarette. Emily and her 'splendid vagina' asleep upstairs. Drinking a bottle of Sauvignon Blanc.

I attempted to have a conversation with Emily about her relationship with my mother over dinner tonight.

'I hear you and Mum talk on the phone quite a bit.'

'I suppose,' Emily said casually while eating her tuna niçoise salad.

'I'm just not sure it's such a good idea though ... you know.'

'Why? I like talking to your mum.'

'I know, but she can be a bit ...'

'A bit what?'

How could I explain to Emily that I didn't want her and my mum getting together for their fortnightly Harry-bashing session without sounding like a complete and utter twonk? This was one of those moments that required the utmost tact and sensitivity.

'A bit overbearing.'

'I don't think that at all. I think she's lovely.'

'Well, yes, she is lovely, obviously, but ...'

'But what, Harry?'

'Look, Em, I'm just thinking about you, that's all. I love my mother dearly, but sometimes she can be a bit of a nutter. It starts with a few casual chats here and there and before you know it, she will be calling every day and asking about your nipples and giving you advice on stretch marks.'

'That's fine though. I don't mind.'

'Really, you're happy with that?'

'Yes, because she always wanted a daughter and . . .'

'Excuse me?'

'Well, yes, isn't it obvious?' Actually, no. It does explain the photograph she always brings out on my birthday of me as a little lad in a pink dress and make-up. Although, she always said I did that to myself, but now I'm not so sure. 'She needs a bit of girlie time and I'm happy to oblige.'

What could I say? It would be a bit churlish of me to cause a stink about my mother's desperate desire to have a daughter.

'Is this about the time you wet yourself? Because your mum explained everything.'

'Oh, for fuck's sake, why does she always have to bring that up? It wasn't a big deal.'

'Of course not, baby,' Emily said with a giggle. 'It happens to every fifteen-year-old boy.'

This is why I don't want them talking. We finished our tuna niçoise salad and Petite Mange Blanc bread in silence.

SATURDAY, February 11th, 8.00 a.m.

In the lounge. In pain. I might throw up. Emily still asleep. Squirrels outside playing together and looking happy. As Madness once sang, 'It must be love'.

I made my second attempt at delaying the onset of middle-aged spread, but I fear I may have made things worse. I woke up at six-thirty and decided to go for a jog (big mistake). The last time I went for a jog I was fifteen and it was cross-country running at school with Mr Hilliard (our cross-dressing PE teacher). I've never been much of a runner, although I did think I could probably run a mile without almost dying. Sadly, I was wrong. I was in my new Lycra shorts (never pretty). I had my iPod on, my pedometer on and I got my jog on.

I started slowly and got to the end of our street (about two hundred yards), before I turned onto Wimbledon Hill Road and started towards the High Street, and this is where things started to unravel. At first it was a slight pain in my side, which quickly became an excruciating pain in my chest and the next thing I knew, I could hardly breathe. I looked at my pedometer and it said 0.25. I had only run a quarter of a mile!

I staggered home, fell onto the sofa and I haven't been able to move since. I'm officially pathetic. I need to face facts. I'm probably going to die young and my chances of running the London marathon are disappearing by the hour.

8.30 a.m.
No sympathy from Emily. She said if I spent as much time exercising as I did eating junk food, not paying attention to her and smoking, I wouldn't be on the verge of death. She's as bad as Dr Prakish. Obviously she doesn't care if I live or die. It's a terrible indictment of our marriage. I thought hearing our baby's heartbeat had brought us closer together, but sadly it seems to have been but a fleeting moment.

10.00 a.m.
Email from Ben.

G'Day! In Sydney. It's bloody hot. Life is good. We're living in Glebe, a trendy suburb, with a friend of Katie's. Going to the beach, surfing, going out and enjoying life. Have I told you how

amazing, incredible and absurdly wonderful Katie is yet? I'm in
love mate. Miss my drinking buddy though. Maybe you and Emily
could get out here for a holiday. Not sure when I'm coming
home. Love to Emily. Speak soon. Ben & Katie x

I'm glad he's happy, but I wish he were here. He would know
what to do about Jamie. Still exhausted from my quarter-mile
run. Maybe I should send Jamie a picture of me naked. That
would definitely put her off.

11.00 a.m.
I was trying to think of something special Emily and I could
do for Valentine's Day and then I had an epiphany. We're
going away for a night of fun, frolics, fellatio (hopefully) and
food in Cambridge. We leave after lunch. I just booked the
hotel. Emily will be so excited.

It will also give me a break from our potential terrorist
neighbours, the Jamie situation and it may help rekindle
the flames of passion with Emily. We went to Cambridge
just after we started dating and hopefully we can recreate
that magic again. And she says I'm not spontaneous or
romantic.

12.30 p.m.
In the shed. Smoking a cigarette. Drinking a last-minute
cocktail (Screwdriver!). Emily packing for Cambridge.
Still in some discomfort after my attempted run (alcohol
should help).

I told Emily about Cambridge over toasted cheese, gherkin
and tomato ketchup sandwiches (Emily's choice).
    'Oh, Harry,' she said, grabbing me around the neck.
    'And the best part is we're staying at the same hotel.'

'The one by the river?'

'We leave in thirty minutes, you'd better get packing.'

Emily got all excited, gave me a kiss and ran upstairs. It's the happiest I've seen in her months. I hope after my run I'll be able to perform in the bedroom. My groin's feeling awfully tight.

SUNDAY, February 12th, 10.00 p.m.

Home. Emily asleep upstairs. In the lounge. Nibbling on a piece of mature cheddar I found at the back of the fridge.

We had an incredible time in Cambridge. The hotel was just as I remembered. The weather was perfect. We went punting along the river Cam, had a lovely meal, walked along the backs, visited a few pubs and had a truly memorable couple of days. I even managed to perform in the bedroom (despite tightness of groin) and we came home a hundred times happier than when we left. Cambridge was a rousing success.

However, after I kissed Emily goodnight and came downstairs to check Facebook, my pleasure quickly turned to torment when I read this note from Jamie.

So disappointed I haven't heard from you yet. Call me. I'm bored and lonely and in need of a bit of Harry time. Luv Jamie XO

What am I doing? She is bored and lonely and what does she mean by 'Harry time'? If Emily knew what was happening in the world of Facebook, I'd be in serious bloody trouble. I fear my tight groin and I would be kicked out onto the street. Why am I dabbling in the illicit world of past partners when I should be focusing on my pregnant wife?

However, despite my fear of being caught, I'm also aroused, excited and a little bit curious. Is she flirting with me? Does she still want me? I know it's wrong. I know it's reckless and could ruin everything, but like so many men before me and I'm sure after, what my brain has in common sense, my penis more than matches with pure, unadulterated stupidity. I decide to write back.

Sorry, been away for a few days. Bored and lonely sounds like a terrible combination – you poor thing. I would love to help you but it's difficult. I'm not sure my wife would appreciate me having a drink with another woman – especially one as attractive as you. I hope you under-stand. Luv Harry XO

I tried to set the tone somewhere between apologetic rejection and flirtatious banter. I don't want to jeopardise my marriage for a quick frolic in the sack, but I also quite enjoyed the rush of adrenalin after so many years of being in a stable relationship. It's like suddenly hurtling down a hillside after driving on the flat for mile after mile. I feel, for the first time in donkeys' years, alive.

TUESDAY, February 14th, 6.00 p.m.
Valentine's Day

In the kitchen listening to Oasis. Emily putting her feet up. Having a cigarette. All quiet next door.

Emily and I carried on with our weekend of happiness today. She woke up in a glorious mood (neither of us feeling sick) and she even brought me breakfast in bed. Just had a scrumptious dinner of grilled lamb kebabs with pistachios and spicy salad wrap (thanks again Jamie Oliver) and we're going to watch a bit of telly before bed. And I'm on a promise.

No surprise visits from my evil headmistress today. I replied to Ben and told him, in no uncertain terms, that he'd better come home or else. No sign of anyone next door. No reply from Jamie and I found a ten-pound note in the school car park. Everything is right with the world. All in all a great Valentine's Day.

10.00 p.m.

Emily delivered upon her promise in the bedroom (new technique was outstanding), but then the sly minx dropped a bombshell. She told Steve and Fiona we'll watch their tribe of Js on Friday night so they can go out for their wedding anniversary. I would have protested, but I was in a heavy, post-orgasm coma. I could barely move, let alone complain. Had she given me the promised fellatio as a sweetener to the Steve and Fiona news? Why are women so devious? Why do I become such a useless lump of jelly after every orgasm? Why does the idea of watching three children scare the crap out of me?

THURSDAY, February 16th, 6.00 a.m.

In the kitchen. Emily still asleep. Still dark outside. Morning chorus in full swing.

I was woken up by a loud noise from next door. Emily didn't bat an eyelid. It sounded like a scream. Was I dreaming? I came downstairs and it's been quiet ever since. I'm too afraid to go outside into the garden and peek through the fence. Its half-term next week and I'll be home alone. I must get out of the house otherwise I'll be a sitting duck.

7.00 a.m.
Still quiet next door. What am I going to do? I can't keep living like this. I think I need to go and see Mrs Crawley. She has always been a discomfort in the deepest part of my rectum, but maybe she can help save me from Al-Qaeda. They may be potential terrorists, but Mrs Crawley is an old lady with nothing to lose. I'm going to send her a text and request an emergency meeting.

Just saw the two squirrels playing together in the garden. They're obviously in love. It's nice to see them so happy.

1.00 p.m.
Good news! Mr Heath (Geography) has been sacked! I mean, obviously, it isn't good news for Mr Heath, but we're having leaving drinks for him on Friday. No one knows why he was fired, but to be honest, none of us were surprised. Mr Heath has been living on borrowed time for a while. He's constantly trying it on with the younger female staff members and there have been (unsubstantiated) rumours of relationships with students over the years. He's a great geography teacher, but for someone with his map-reading skills, he seems to have real trouble keeping track of his penis. This could save me from babysitting Steve and Fiona's tribe. I just need to break the news to Emily.

6.00 p.m.
'Seriously?' Emily wasn't happy.

'It's a quick drink. I'll be home by seven at the latest.'

'But Steve and Fiona are dropping the kids off at six. I thought this would be a great trial run for us and now you're going to be drunk.'

'Hardly drunk, it's just a quick drink with work.'

'And remind me again, how did the last quick drink with work end up?'

'That was different.' It wasn't.

'You always do this, Harry.'

'Do what?'

'Let me down. Just when I think you're finally starting to grow up, accept responsibility, you disappoint me.'

'It's just a quick drink.'

'But that's the problem, Harry. It's always just a quick drink with you, isn't it?'

'I don't know what that means.'

'It means you're a dickhead!'

8.00 p.m.
Text from Mrs Crawley. We're meeting on Sunday at two o'clock.

FRIDAY, February 17th, 10.00 p.m.

In the kitchen. Smoking. Emily asleep. Cream crackered.

Oh what a night. It started at the pub. Despite Emily's protests, I decided to go for a quick drink with work. Sexual predator or not, Mr Heath deserved a decent send off. The Bell and Whistle pub was heaving with teachers. Mr Heath was in high spirits. He was also drinking spirits and trying to get off with Miss Beaumont (sexy first-year French teacher). I was chatting with Rory and generally having a good time, except for the little voice in my head which kept reminding me that Emily was mad at me. I tried to ignore it, but a couple of pints later and the voice was getting louder and louder. I felt guilty. Really guilty. Terribly guilty. Really fucking guilty. Emily was right. I did always let her down. How many quick drinks had there been over the years that had ended up as all-nighters? Lots. Many. Copious amounts. Emily needed me and I was going to be there for her. Luckily, I still had time to make it home before Steve, Fiona and their pack of Js arrived.

Once home, I apologised profusely. Emily and I kissed and made up. Everything was right again and I felt good. Then, of course, the kids turned up and that was when the shit really hit the fan.

I think most women (with the exception of Miss Simpson, my evil dictator of a headmistress) have some degree of parental ability, maternal instinct if you will. Men, on the other hand, have absolutely none and we need time to learn and grasp every skill required to become decent, trustworthy parents. When Steve and Fiona finally left (after giving us detailed medical and dietary instructions for each of their Js) and it was just Emily and me, I had absolutely no idea what to do with them. Luckily, Emily did.

The trouble when you're not used to taking care of a single child is that three is a bit of a stretch. It's like going from a Ford Fiesta to a Ferrari. Without proper instruction, it's destined to be a disaster. The kids in question were six-year-old Jane, three-year-old Joseph and fourteen-month-old James. I had a feeling I'd do best with Jane and so we went off upstairs, while Emily stayed downstairs with the remaining Js.

Things started relatively smoothly. Jane was reading a book and she told me all about it and we read a couple of chapters together. It was fun. However, after about half an hour, she wanted to go back downstairs and so we did. Emily found a colouring book the kids loved and for a magical hour, it felt like we had our own little family. I looked at Emily, she looked at me and I could tell she was thinking the same thing. We could do this. We could handle a child of our own. But like most things in life, the moment you start thinking everything's going swimmingly, it's bound to start going completely and utterly tits-up. And it did.

It started with James. He was annoyed, hungry, needed his nappy changed, just fancied crying, honestly, we didn't know. We tried everything, but the little bugger just kept wailing. Then Jane thought it would be a good idea to open up the cabinet and pull out all of our good china (wedding present from Emily's parents) and in the process she chipped two plates. Then, while I was running towards Jane, trying to prevent one of our most valuable assets from turning into a Big Fat Greek Wedding, Joseph decided to go and play hide and seek. Unfortunately, he was the only one playing. Ten minutes later, Emily had finally calmed James down, Jane helped tidy up her mess and it was only then we realised we were missing a child.

'Where's Joseph?' Emily said looking around in a panic.

'Shit!' I said.

'What's shit?' said six-year-old Jane.

'Fuck!' I said.

'What's fuck?' said Jane.

Now, bearing in mind our house isn't that big, you would think we'd be able to find a three-year-old boy fairly easily. Wrong. Five minutes went by, ten minutes, twenty minutes, and by thirty minutes, Emily and I were in a blind panic. We ran around the house. We looked high and low and we even searched the back garden, but nothing.

'We lost him,' said Emily, and the fear of what we'd done flashed across her face.

'Don't panic, Em, he's got to be here somewhere,' I said, but deep down I was terrified.

How could we lose one of their kids? They definitely wouldn't let us babysit again. That was the least of our concerns though, because if we didn't find him soon, we'd have to call the police and worse than that, we'd have to call Steve and Fiona. However, five minutes later, just as Emily had finally broken down and was crying into my shoulder, Joseph ran back into the room with a huge smile on his face. 'Here I am!' he shouted with joy. He'd been playing hide and seek and had definitely won.

For the next hour we didn't let any of them out of our sight. When Steve and Fiona returned, nothing was said about Joseph's vanishing act, although as they walked out of the front door I heard Jane say, 'Daddy, what does fuck mean?' We said goodnight and closed the door quickly.

SATURDAY, February 18th, 3.00 p.m.

At the park. Emily lying next to me on picnic blanket. Birds singing, sun shining. Life is good.

I went to see Granddad at the old folks' home this morning. I told the young girl on reception I was there to see George Spencer and she smiled.

'What now?' I asked. This wasn't the first time I'd seen that particular smile.

'Your granddad's been quite the talk of the home this week.'

'What's he done now?'

'I probably shouldn't tell you this, but it isn't so much what he's been doing, but who, if you get my drift.' My grandfather, the dirty old bugger, must have finally got laid! I couldn't wait to see him.

I eventually found him with his new girlfriend (seventy-one-year-old Audrey, who has most of her own teeth) in the garden. They were all over each other, like a pair of overly sexed teenagers. I was partly happy for him and partly disgusted.

'Harry, this is Audrey. Audrey, this is my grandson, Harry.'

I said I was pleased to meet her. However, as she tried to get up to say hello, one of her breasts fell out. I'd never seen such an old breast before and I was quite taken aback. Unlike Emily's wonderful, firm, good handful, it was saggy, wrinkly and looked like an old piece of fruit. Granddad didn't seem to mind though.

'Excuse me,' said Audrey, popping the offending breast back in again. 'I stopped wearing a bra, Harry. No point at my age you see, but occasionally they do fall out.'

'I hear you two have been causing quite a stir around the place,' I said, sitting down and doing my best to wipe the last ten seconds from memory.

'Miserable buggers are jealous. If my girl and I want to have sex in the middle of the afternoon, then we will. I fought in two world wars, Harry. I think I've earned the right to have a bit of nooky when I fancy it.'

For the record (once again) he didn't fight in either war. For a start, he wasn't born until 1928 (ten years after the end of World War One). He was also only eleven when Hitler's Germany marched into Poland and subsequently started World War Two. Still, despite these irrefutable statistics, Granddad will argue tooth and nail until the day he dies that he fought in both world wars. You have to admire his determination, if not his factual knowledge.

'I think it's fantastic. You go, Granddad!'

Looking back, I can't believe I actually said that. I'm the last sort of person to say something so street, especially in relation to my granddad shagging his seventy-one-year-old girlfriend. I'm happy for him though. He deserves his last shot at happiness.

Nan died five years ago, slowly and painfully over six months until the cancer took her last breath. Granddad didn't leave her bedside for a moment and when it was all over, the once wry, witty, gregarious man I loved so much looked beaten. But now the old spark is back. This is his last hoorah and good bloody luck to him.

As I left, I turned around to wave goodbye, but Granddad and Audrey were in the middle of what looked like some pretty heavy petting. Granddad was on top of Audrey and I couldn't see his hands, which in my world of secondary school teaching is equivalent to at least a week's detention. I smiled as I made my way towards my car.

8.00 p.m.
Finally a response from Jamie.

Harry, you silly boy, of course I understand. I'm disappointed because I really wanted to see you again and it would have been lots of fun! Still, if you ever happen to be in Greenwich give me a call. I would love to see you again.
Luv Jamie XO

So, unless I just happen to be in Greenwich anytime soon, I suppose that's it then, which is probably a good thing. I'm partly relieved and partly disappointed. My brain's relieved and my penis is disappointed. I think if I'd actually met up with Jamie, it may have been the other way around. I think it's probably best left the way it is. I wrote back a last message.

Thanks for being so understanding. It would have been fun to catch up in person, but at least we still have Facebook. I hope all goes well in Greenwich and I'm sure you'll make lots of friends soon. Luv Harry XO

SUNDAY, February 19th, 3.00 p.m.

In the shed. Sunny. Eating a slice of Battenberg cake. Emily visiting her parents. Squirrels frolicking.

Just back from the emergency meeting with Mrs Crawley. It was the first time I'd met with just Mrs Crawley and, suffice to say, I hope it will be the last.

Mrs Crawley is a widow – her husband died a few years ago (I would imagine she either poisoned him or he poisoned himself) and so now her whole life revolves around being nosy, making wild speculations, complaining to the council and generally being a nuisance. Apparently, she has two children and a few grandchildren, but I've never seen them visit.

When I arrived, she already had my new neighbours hanging at the Tower of London. She would have been a brilliant judge during the witch-hunt trials. The first thing she said when I walked in was, 'I knew from the moment I saw them they were trouble. I don't know why we let them in the country in the first place.' I stressed we shouldn't get carried away and that we didn't know anything for sure, but she was having none of it. 'This isn't the time to sit on our hands and do nothing, Harry. We could have terrorists on our street and it's our job to stop them. During the war . . .' she started and I could feel a long, dull story coming on.

'I think it's probably the police or MI5's actual job,' I ventured, but this seemed to encourage her.

'And you think, without a trace of evidence, that the police or MI5 would traipse all the way down to Wimbledon on a hunch? Nonsense. We have to provide the evidence. We, Harry, as in you and I, must spy on them until we know for sure what we already know.'

'Which is?'

'That we're in the middle of a jihad!'

I left her house convinced of two things.

1. Mrs Crawley is barking mad.

2. My new neighbours definitely aren't terrorists.

I should never have got her involved. I did agree to spy on them, but only to appease the old bag. Honestly, what was I thinking? I'll pop over to see Ali with a peace offering and end this madness.

TUESDAY, February 21st, 11.00 a.m.
Shrove Tuesday

Half-term week. In the study. Drinking tea. Smoking. Blustery outside. Emily at work. Squirrels playing in the garden. All is well in Wimbledon.

Ah, the joys of half-term. I didn't wake up until almost ten this morning. I took a leisurely stroll to my local newsagent, where I purchased a copy of the *Guardian* and twenty Marlboro Lights. I made a fresh pot of tea and a bacon sandwich before I retired to the study to contemplate my life.

Since January I've tried to get fit and delay the onset of

middle-age spread twice (unsuccessfully), been convinced my new neighbours are terrorists (probably untrue), babysat three children and lost one (returned unharmed), eaten my body weight in unhealthy snacks (actual weight not known), been to Cambridge (brilliant), been to see Miss Simpson twice (not brilliant), seen one seventy-one-year-old breast (definitely not brilliant), reconnected with currently single, sexy ex-girlfriend (almost disastrously), had multiple fights with Emily (mainly my fault), become a father (scary but exciting), been to baby doctor (weird but exciting) and I've seen two squirrels in my garden. It's been an eventful year thus far and sitting here in my study on a relaxing, half-term morning, I have to say I'm rather happy.

1.00 p.m.
At The Alexandra pub on Wimbledon Hill Road.

I felt terribly guilty after my meeting with Mrs Crawley and so I thought I'd pop around to see Ali with a peace offering. After a brief search through the alcohol stash in the shed, I found a nice bottle of wine (a gift from Emily's rich but strange Uncle Vernon). I took the wine next door, rang the doorbell and waited. A few minutes went past, no one answered and so I rang again. Eventually, just as I was about to admit defeat and leave, the door opened and Ali stood in front of me looking a little flustered.

'Harry Spencer, from next door,' he said a little too loudly. I heard whispers behind him and I'm sure I saw a shadowy figure pass by.

'Yes, hi, Ali, how are you?'

'Good, good, yes, yes, very good, very good,' he said before he added, 'and you?'

'Great, thanks. I'm on half-term.'

'Yes, yes, of course, of course.'

'Right, well, anyway, I wanted to give you this,' I said handing him the bottle of wine.

'Thank you, Harry, thank you, very much, but I'm afraid I must decline. I do not drink alcohol.'

'Oh, I'm sorry, I didn't think.'

'It's not your fault I choose not to let alcohol pass my lips. It's a religious belief.'

'Right, well,' I said and we just sort of stood there for a moment.

I heard more whispers behind him, but I couldn't see past Ali. I caught a quick whiff of something strange-smelling and then I heard a crash inside the house. Ali turned around and I had a quick look past him. The house was bare. There was no furniture inside and I saw another man squatting next to a camp stove. Something was definitely amiss.

'I have to go. Thank you again, thank you,' Ali said, handing me back the bottle of wine.

'Is everything alright?'

'Fine, fine, yes, yes,' Ali said and then he closed the door.

As I walked away, I knew something was definitely not right about this. I didn't want to believe that Mrs Crawley was right, or that my new neighbours were perhaps part of a terrorist cell, but what else could I believe? Then, as I was walking to the pub, I decided I needed to get a closer look at what's going on next door. I need to get inside the house.

SATURDAY, February 25th, 2.00 p.m.

At Mothercare with Emily.

Emily wanted to come shopping for baby stuff. We looked at prams (four hundred quid), types of nappies (I had no idea there was so many varieties. Apparently, one size doesn't fit all), clothes, bottles, breast pumps (ruined by Steve), types of food (organic pear, artichoke and mint risotto – they're going to eat better than us!), baby name books (seriously?), cots (v. v. expensive) and many other things. I don't know if we can afford a baby, especially with my job being in such a precarious position.

However, another part of me, the paternal, happy-to-be-a-father side, also enjoyed it. Emily was beaming as we walked around looking at all the baby paraphernalia. It also got me thinking about being a father and I think one of the main differences between men and women is that for men, being a father isn't something we think about until we are. As kids, girls are urged to play with dolls, encouraged to cook, pretend to play mummies and daddies, while boys climb trees and dream about being the next David Beckham.

It isn't their fault they crave kids because we make them that way. I realise it's also biological. They simply can't help but want children, while men simply can't help but freak out about it and reminisce for their lost youth. Babies make women dream of the future and men long for the past. Neither of us can help who we are or what we need. The brilliant thing though is that somehow it works.

SUNDAY, February 26th, 11.00 a.m.

In the shed. Eating baklava. Slightly chilly. Squirrels shagging.

The squirrels are really going at it! At first I wasn't sure if they were playing or fighting, but after a moment it all became quite clear. It's pleasing to see them so in love. Soon we will have baby squirrels running around the garden. I took a picture of them doing it with my phone and sent it to Ben.

MONDAY, February 27th, 6.00 p.m.

In the study. Eating a toasted cheese sandwich. Windy.

I often wonder how I'm going to die and, honestly, I hope it isn't something ridiculous. You hear all the time about people who get killed falling off roofs, being hit by stray golf balls or accidently electrocuting themselves while shaving in the bath. I don't want to die like that. I want to shuffle off this mortal coil in a dignified manner, while recounting stories to my great-grandchildren about the good old days. I don't want my obituary to read, Harry Spencer died suddenly at age forty while over celebrating a strike at the bowling alley.

I think we all deserve a decent death. I want to be able to say goodbye to everyone, tell them I love them and that it's going to be okay. I don't want a policeman to turn up and tell my nearest and dearest, 'Sorry, but Mr Spencer was running for the bus, he tripped over his shoelaces, hit his head on one of those Golf Sale signs and died on the spot.' That's no way to go.

TUESDAY, February 28th, 7.00 p.m.

In the study. In shock. In deep shit. In over my head. In trouble. In pain.

Jamie sent me another message on Facebook. Only it wasn't just a message. She also sent me a photo of herself in just her underwear! I'm in shock. The photo is, quite literally, mind-blowing. She's gorgeous. She always was, but now she's absolutely stunning. In the photo she's on a bed, on all fours, looking at me in only a pair of white knickers and very small bra. I opened the message about fifteen minutes ago and I haven't been able to think clearly since. Under the photo there is a short but very clear message.

I wanted to show you what you're missing! Luv Jamie XO

What the fuck am I going to do? Jamie is ridiculously sexy and for some reason, wants to get it on with me. Why did she have to do this? I was happy. I was content. But now all I can think about is having sex with the girl in the photo. My head hurts, my balls hurt and I think I might need some Harry alone time. I'm in a vast chasm of trouble. Bugger.

march

'Here's how it's going to work,' Emily said. 'We write down ten names each. Five boys and five girls. Then we compare. We both have to agree on a name and if we don't it's vetoed. Understood?'

It's actually much harder to think of baby names than you'd imagine. I knew straight away most of the names I liked, but after that I was at a loss. I had eight names, but I couldn't think of any more. Not a single name. My mind was blankness personified. It's hard because every name has a connotation. I loved the name Oliver, but it reminded me of Oliver Norwood, the git who stole my lunch and punched me in the testicles when I was eleven. Also, when you're a teacher, you have a whole separate list of all the pupils you've despised over the years.

Eventually, after browsing through the really big baby name book, I decided on my last two names. Chloe for a girl and Jude for a boy. I looked down at my list and I was reasonably happy. Emily finished hers and we read them out.

Emily: Madison?

Me: Do we live in America? How about Emma?

Emily: Seriously, Emma?

Me: What's wrong with Emma?

Emily: Emma Sloane, my secondary school nemesis?

Me: Oh yeah.

Emily: Elba?

Me: Elbow?

Emily: No, Elba with an A.

Me: It sounds like elbow.

Emily: That's a no then.

Me: It's a no. What about Ella?

Emily: Can't. Katie from work has a daughter named Ella. What about Prudence?

Me: As in Dear?

Emily: If you like.

Me: I like it but everyone will call her Pru and I don't like Pru. Chloe?

Emily: Nah, what about Poppy?

Me: It reminds me of Remembrance Day. I'll need to have a minute's silence every time she walks in the room. Mark?

Emily: First boyfriend.

Me: Jude?

Emily: Third boyfriend.

Me: Jack?

Emily: Fourth.

Me: Seriously?

Emily: Yeah. What about Noah?

Me: Good in an ark situation, naff name.

Emily: Ethan?

Me: Sounds like he'll be a knob.

Emily: Oliver? (I vetoed this for the reason stated earlier. Oliver Norwood: Punched me in the goolies). Alfie?

Me: Do we want to raise a Cockney pickpocket? Gordon?

Emily: It's not a baby name. It's fine when he's fifty, but I can't call our baby Gordon. Oh look, its Gordon the baby.

Me: Fair enough.

Emily: You're going to love this one. What about Sam?

Me: For a boy or girl?

Emily: I don't know, either.

Me: That's the problem. Too unisex.

Emily: That's a no on Sam then?

Me: It's a no. I only have one name left. How about Tom?

Emily: Tom. (She was thinking about it). Yeah, I like Tom.

Me: So we can add Tom to the list?

Emily: Sure. I have one name left too. Lucy?

Me: Yeah, Lucy's good.

Emily: It's on the list?

Me: Sure.

After an hour of researching, writing down and debating, we were left with two names. Tom for a boy and Lucy for a girl.

8.00 p.m.

In the study. Eating a peanut butter sandwich. Emily taking a bath. Looking at the photo of Jamie.

I can't stop looking at her photo. It's mesmerising. I haven't written her back yet because I don't know what to say. What can I say? What should I say? I think what I need to do is have sex with Emily. This will fulfil two needs:

1. It will remind me how sexy and gorgeous she is.

2. It will stop me from feeling so bloody horny and take my mind off Jamie.

Off upstairs to have sex with Emily!

8.30 p.m.

In the study. Frustrated. Trying not to look at photo of Jamie. Emily asleep.

I went upstairs, took a quick shower, got in bed with Emily (naked).

'What are you doing?'

'What do you think I'm doing?' I said, rubbing my naked body against hers.

'I think you're trying to have sex with me, but I feel sick, bloated, I haven't shaved my legs, I'm wearing my big underpants and its cold.'

'I can warm you up.'

'Harry, we're not having sex.'

'How about a blow job?'

'No chance. I brushed my teeth already and I'm not getting up again.'

'Hand job?'

'Harry, I really don't feel good and I'm trying to watch *Mistresses*. Maybe tomorrow,' she said and then gave me a kiss on the nose. On the nose!

THURSDAY, March 2nd, 5.00 p.m.

At home. Eating a Double Decker. Emily still not home from work. Cold and cloudy.

We had a surprisingly lucid and in-depth discussion in class today. Unfortunately, it wasn't about history. It all started with the usually asleep Gavin Haines.

'Are you married, sir?'

'I don't think that's any of your business.'

'Oh, go on, sir, are you?' said Hannah Clifford.

'Yeah, come on, sir,' said Carolyn Flint.

'Well, yes, I am actually,' I replied.

We were supposed to be discussing the causes of World War Two.

'That's good, sir, because Matt Jenkins told everyone you were gay,' said Gavin Haines.

'Why would he do that?' I asked incredulously.

'Dunno, sir, but if you're married you can't be gay . . .' replied Gavin.

'He could be,' chipped in Carolyn Flint.

'I'm not gay, Carolyn.'

'Yeah, I know, sir, but I was just saying, like, you still could be. My dad's brother, yeah, he's married, but he's definitely a bender.'

'Let's not speculate, Carolyn. It's beside the point anyway and nothing to do with the causes of . . .'

'Is she fit, sir?' said Gavin suddenly.

'Who?'

'Your wife, sir, is she fit?'

He was pushing his luck, but everyone in the classroom seemed to suddenly sit up and take notice. I'd never seen them so interested.

'Again, not really appropriate, Gavin, but yes she is quite attractive.'

'Have you got any photos, sir,' said Hannah Clifford.

'Well, yes, but . . .'

'Oh, go on, sir, let's have a look,' said Carolyn.

'Yeah, go on, sir,' joined in Gavin. What could I do? One look at the missus and it was definitely back to history. I showed everyone in class the photo of Emily I keep in my wallet. It's a great photo. It was taken just after we started dating.

'Old, but yeah, well fit,' said Gavin Haines.

Most of the boys nodded their approval, while the girls all said how pretty she was. I have to say it felt good. Not that I need validation from my pupils, but suddenly they didn't just see me as old Mr Spencer, boring history teacher, but Mr Spencer, the teacher with the fit wife. I was suddenly cool.

Jon Rance

FRIDAY, March 3rd, 5.00 p.m.

In the shed. Having a cigarette and a cocktail (White Russian!). Emily getting ready. Still sexually frustrated. Balls the size of freakishly large melons.

We're off to have dinner with our friends Ken and Kara at their flat in Balham. Ken and Kara are the anti-Steve and Fiona. Since university and while everyone else has moved on, grown up and done all of the things we're supposed to do, they haven't changed. They travelled, got jobs in radio (Ken) and PR (Kara) and they still go out clubbing every weekend, smoke weed and hang around with an early-twenty-something bunch.

It should be an interesting night as we're going to tell them we're pregnant. The last time we saw them was before Christmas and we ended up at a club in Islington until two in the morning. I don't envisage that happening again.

11.00 p.m.
In the study. In dressing gown. Cup of cocoa in hand. Just back from Balham. Emily asleep with a hot water bottle. Knackered.

We're officially old. We got to Ken and Kara's flat at around six o'clock. Their flat looks like an IKEA catalogue. I asked Ken about it and he said, 'We did it using the IKEA catalogue. The whole place. It was so easy. We showed them the pages and they came in and did everything.' Ken then proceeded to give us the tour. 'This is the living room, page forty-two. The bathroom, page seventy-six. The kitchen, page one hundred and four. And lastly our bedroom, page one hundred and forty.'

There's no doubt it looked fantastic, but much like the IKEA catalogue, it didn't feel lived in. Everything was tidy, trendy and urban, but you got no sense actual human beings lived there. I have more possessions in my shed (must clean out the shed).

Despite being a year older than me, Ken still looks at least ten years younger. He was dressed in the latest, trendy clothes. He had a stylish haircut (definitely not a Troy the trainee special) and not the slightest hint of grey. Kara looked great too, as if she'd been on one of those makeover shows on the telly. Everything about them shouted, 'Young, metropolitan and cool!'

They served us Spanish tapas, Japanese sushi and Italian tiramisu, washed down with lager from Belgium and Australian wine. Despite Balham not being that far from Wimbledon geographically, it felt like a different world. They played music I'd never heard of by obscure bands from Scandinavia and Canada and dropped names of celebrities that sounded familiar, but I was too old, too out of touch and too un-cool to really know. I spent most of the night nodding like a bloody pigeon. Do we really live in the same city? In the same country?

'We've found this amazing new gastropub, haven't we darling?' said Kara.

'Amazing,' said Ken.

I didn't want to ask, but their faces said I simply had to.

'Oh,' I replied cautiously. Kara took that as the green light to give me the full *Time Out* critique.

'It's post-modern British, Harry. It's amazing.'

'What's post-modern British?' asked Emily.

'They take modern British, obviously, and then they deconstruct it.'

'Right,' said Emily, none the wiser.

'So what sort of food do they serve?' I asked.

'It's amazing,' said Ken unhelpfully. 'They have bangers and mash, pie and mash, fish and chips, bread and butter puddings, real British food.'

'So how's that different from any other pub?' I asked wisely.

Ken and Kara looked at each other with a knowing look before Kara said,

'Because modern British is all about taking simple, peasant food and making it gourmet. This takes modern British and strips it down to its raw ingredients. It's plain, simple, rustic . . .'

'Amazingly rustic,' chipped in Ken.

'So, basically, it's just normal food,' I said.

'But it's amazing, Harry. We simply have to take you there,' said Kara.

'We have to,' said Ken. 'It's expensive but so worth it.'

'How can pie and mash be expensive?' said Emily.

'Because it's post-modern,' said Ken before he added. 'You can literally taste the sweat of the working class in every bite.'

'Sounds delicious,' I said.

After another few drinks it was time for us to share our good news, but before we had the chance, we had to hear about their latest mini-break. Ken and Kara are always on mini-breaks.

'We just got back from Estonia,' Kara said. 'It was magical, you simply have to go.'

'You simply have to,' reiterated Ken. 'It was amazing.'

'Sounds great, definitely, but probably not for a while,' I said. It was time.

Emily looked at me and smiled. 'We're pregnant!' we said in unison.

Bearing in mind the reaction we got from Steve and Fiona, the reaction from Ken and Kara wasn't quite what we expected. The happiness was there, but it lacked the same delivery.

'Kara, get out the skunk. We're going to get fucked!' said Ken.

Whereas Steve and Fiona wanted to share with us their wealth of baby knowledge, Ken and Kara wanted to share their top-of-the-line cannabis. Emily had to decline for obvious reasons, but, not wanting to be a party pooper, I decided to have a toke. Unfortunately, after only one puff, I pulled the world's worst whitey and spent the next hour talking to the toilet bowl convinced Ken's bottle of aftershave was trying to kill me.

On the drive home, Emily and I didn't say much, but I knew we were both feeling the same. We're old now. We can no longer survive in the world of nightclubs, illegal drugs and drinking until two o'clock in the morning. We don't understand the fashion, the music and we certainly can't handle the drugs. We belong in Mothercare, playgrounds and places where middle-aged people with Volvos talk about the congestion charge and school league tables. It's a horribly depressing thought, but we have more in common with Steve and Fiona than we do with Ken and Kara. I suppose this is what it feels like to be grown up.

SATURDAY, March 4th, 8.00 a.m.

In the kitchen. Eating boiled eggs with soldiers. Drinking tea. Emily asleep. Only one squirrel in the garden, looking a bit dejected. Sunny.

I'm going to take Emily out somewhere nice for the day. Hopefully this will reignite the flames of passion and alleviate the pain from my giant testicles.

10.00 a.m.
I told Emily we were going out for the day and she replied, 'Harry, I feel like there's something growing inside of me draining all of my strength and energy and making me feel constantly sick. Oh, wait, there is.'

I have a feeling she was being sarcastic. She's currently lying on the sofa watching telly. I'm in the study looking at the photo of Jamie. My testicles can't take much more of this. Off to take a very cold shower.

11.00 a.m.
I popped by the lounge to see how Emily was feeling.

'It feels like a herd of wildebeest are running around my head,' she said. I asked if she needed anything. 'Some peace and quiet would be nice,' she replied. I took the hint and went out to the shed.

1.00 p.m.
In the shed. Drinking a cocktail (Blue Lagoon!). Eating a Cornish pasty. Emily asleep. Balls painful and even larger. I need to have sex soon. Squirrel looking depressed.

I'm getting worried about the squirrel. The other squirrel seems to have gone and it looks like it's going through some break-up anxiety. It sits in the garden looking around vacantly. It isn't running, playing with its nuts, or doing anything vaguely squirrel-like. I don't know what to do. The squirrel is obviously lovesick.

I'm in need of some male company and fast. Best mate

Ben's in Sydney, which only leaves Rory and Dad as potential suitors. It's depressing that as we get older the pool of friends we have to dip into gets smaller and smaller. During my teens, I had a good bunch of close friends. This got slightly smaller during university and then gradually during my twenties (like my hairline) it seems to have receded even further. It isn't like I don't have the friends, but some have moved away, some I've lost touch with and then there's people like Steve and Ken who, if I'm honest, I don't want to hang out with anymore.

I picked Dad because I needed advice.

'Hi, Dad.'

'Harry, how are you?'

'Good, how's things?'

'Alright, your mother's badgering me about cleaning out the garage.'

'If I pop down, fancy going out for a beer?'

'How quickly can you be here?'

Off to meet Dad for a drink.

11.00 p.m.

In my childhood bedroom. Trying to fit my adult frame snugly into my old, single bed (unsuccessfully). Emily in Wimbledon. Mum and Dad asleep in the next room. Dad snoring very loudly.

Was I a dwarf child? It's the only reasonable conclusion given the size of this bed. I've tried every conceivable (and even some non-conceivable) positions, but I can't seem to keep all of me underneath the duvet.

I got to my parents' house this afternoon and after a brief conversation with Mum – How's Emily? Is she still sick? Why aren't you at home with her? Should I go and see her? Do you think she'd want to see me? Are you ready to be a dad? I'm concerned. Have you thought everything through? Remember Ronnie the rabbit? You wanted him so badly but after a week you were bored of him. Are you going to be bored of your child in a week, Harry? I think I need to call Emily – Dad and I went to the pub.

'I really need some advice.'

'Did you ask your mother?'

'Not really. I need more man to bloke, father to son sort of advice.'

'Oh, right, go ahead,' Dad said. He looked very uncomfortable. I was pushing the boundaries of our relationship.

'I'm finding it difficult with Emily being pregnant. She's always tired, feels sick or asleep. I know it's selfish, she's carrying our child, but I'm feeling a bit dejected. How did you cope when Mum was pregnant with me?'

'Golf.'

'But I don't play golf.'

'Learn.'

'But what if I don't want to learn to play golf?'

'Then you're on your own. Golf is the only thing I know. Without golf your mother and I would've divorced years ago. Golf saved our marriage.' Blimey. Maybe I should take up golf. I could shoot an eighteen every Sunday with Rory. 'Trust me, Harry, take up golf. It may seem silly, trudging around a big field, hitting small balls at a flag, but it's so much more than that.'

'What do you mean? Like something spiritual?'

'Not exactly, but you'll figure it out.'

And with that Freudian masterpiece, the conversation ended. I had my advice. Golf would sort everything out.

SUNDAY, March 5th, 12.00 p.m.

Back in Wimbledon. Emily in Buckinghamshire. Squirrel looking more and more depressed. Sunny.

At last. Ali finally left his house this morning and so I had my chance to take a peek next door. I hopped over the fence and into their garden. I couldn't be sure if anyone else was in the house, so to cover my tracks, I kicked a football over the fence ahead of me. Then if I was spotted, I could say I was just retrieving my ball. I know, genius. James Bond, eat your bloody heart out: 007 – License to Prowl. Name's Spencer, Harry Spencer. OK, I'm being a knob, but you get the idea.

The garden was relatively normal. It had grass, a tree – the usual things. I took a quick peek through the windows. The place was empty. The back room had a sleeping bag, a map (London A–Z, I think) and a torch lying on the ground. The kitchen was bare except for a couple of plastic cups on the side and a packet of cigarettes.

I grabbed my football and was about to head back across the fence, but I quickly tried the back door and it was open. Did I dare go in? This would be a lot harder to explain if I was caught. Footballs don't end up inside. I was breaking and entering. Technically, I was just entering because the door was open. I went in.

I walked slowly through the kitchen and into the lounge which was also very sparse. Just a couple of deckchairs and a small radio. Next I went very quietly upstairs, in case someone was up there. The upstairs was the same as the down. Two more sleeping bags, a wash bag, a towel, another radio, but as I was about to leave, I looked in the last bedroom and suddenly it all became clear. On the wall was a huge map of

London with various coloured drawing pins dotted around. This must be where they planned on attacking. However, as I was looking at the map, I heard a car pull up outside. Fuck! Ali was back. I had to move quickly and I did. I leapt downstairs like a frightened deer (almost falling in the process) and made it outside just in time because as I closed the back door, I heard them open the front. I jumped over the fence and ran inside. I locked the door and fell onto the sofa in a sweaty, heaving, mess of pain, terror and relief. It was then I realised I'd left my ball behind. Fuck!

MONDAY, March 6th, 7.00 p.m.

In the lounge. Trying to tempt Emily into something sexual by giving her a foot rub.

7.30 p.m.
Foot rub had the opposite effect and sent Emily to sleep.

7.45 p.m.
In the study. Emily asleep upstairs. In pain. Need relief.

Part of the problem is that sex with Emily, even before the pregnancy, was getting a bit stale. It isn't anyone's fault per se, we're both guilty. It's just one of those things. Two people + marriage + life + a bit lazy = crap sex. I think it happens to every couple at some point. We used to have great sex. We had unusual sex, outdoor sex, experimental sex, wild sex, but now I'm lucky if I get any sex.

The other part of the problem is that Jamie is gorgeous, brand-spanking new and my memory of having sex with her is that it was phenomenal. We were young, horny, still had great bodies (she still does) and we only did it a handful of times, and therefore it didn't have time to get lazy and crap.

So now, when I look at the photo of Jamie on all fours, looking as sexy as a luxury sports car, I want to take her out for a test drive. I want to see what special features she has. I want to feel the trim. I want to get behind the wheel and see how she compares to my comfy, ten-year-old family saloon. Maybe it's fantasy, maybe it's crazy, but I need to know what she feels like. I know I'll always come back to my familiar, old four-door model, because I like how she runs. I like the way she smells, the softness of the seats and how every scratch, dent and nick carries with it a memory. I'm not ready to trade her in, but wouldn't it be exciting to take the sports car out for a quick spin? I think that's probably enough car/sex analogies for one day. I feel like Jeremy Clarkson reviewing a porn film.

9.00 p.m.
Finally some sexual relief! It wasn't exactly what I wanted, but more like a game of Cluedo. It was Harry Spencer, in the study, with the photo of his ex-girlfriend. Guilty as charged. Balls finally back to normal, but feelings of guilt and disgrace at an all-time high. How much longer can I resist the temptation?

TUESDAY, March 7th, 4.00 p.m.

In my classroom. Eating a packet of pickled onion crisps.

Jamie wrote me another message.

Harry, I want to say how sorry I am. I shouldn't have sent you the photo. When you got in touch all of these amazing memories came flooding back from sixth form and I got a bit carried away. I was so in love with you back then and over the last ten years I've thought about you a lot. I hope you can forgive me and we can stay in touch. Luv Jamie XO

Relief quickly washed over me, followed by a sudden bout of sadness, which was followed by a dose of whimsical self-indulgence and eventually back to relief again. She didn't only want me as a fuck bunny. Maybe we can be friends again. Maybe I can get my life back to normal. I replied.

Sorry I didn't reply before but I was in a state of shock. The photo was incredible. You're incredible. So beautiful and sexy, but seeing you like that made me realise it was just a dream. I'm married. I hope we can be friends too. Please stay in touch. Luv Harry XO

I pressed the send button and I smiled to myself. I'd never cheat on Emily. It was just a fantasy. I closed my computer down and headed home. Everything was going to be alright.

6.00 p.m.
In the study. In deep shit.

I got home to find Emily and Ali drinking tea in the lounge!

'Ali popped by to bring your ball back,' said Emily when I walked in. 'I said it was weird because you haven't played with it for months.'

'That is strange,' I said. My voice sounded weak, feeble and I knew he could see straight through me. 'Thanks.'

'Oh, it's no trouble, Harry, no trouble,' said Ali.

'More tea?' said Emily, getting up.

'Yes, yes, lovely, lovely,' said Ali. Emily was going to leave us alone.

'Harry?'

'Let me give you a hand,' I said, but Emily being bloody Emily wouldn't hear of it and so I was left alone in the lounge with Ali. 'Thanks again for the ball, much appreciated.'

'Honestly, Harry, it's not a problem. Balls are balls. They get lost; it is their way.'

'And where exactly did you find it?'

'It was very strange actually because it was in our kitchen. I only knew it was your ball because it had your name on it.' I'd forgotten I'd written my name on the ball in black marker pen. Nice one, Harry. 'I've no idea how it got in there, do you?'

He was trying to put the frighteners on me. However, as he was trying to telepathically scare the shit out of me (he succeeded), Emily came trotting back in with more tea.

'Tea.'

'Thank you, thank you, but I forgot I have an appointment,' said Ali, getting up.

'No worries, hope to see you again soon,' said Emily.

'I imagine you will,' said Ali to Emily (all smiles). 'Goodbye, Harry,' he said, walking past and giving my shoulder a strong squeeze.

This man is going to murder me. I don't want to die. I'm going to be a father. What the fuck am I going to do? Emily, if I'm murdered and you find this diary please go into one of those witness protection schemes. Do they even have those in England or are they just for big-time Mafia-type people in

America? I must Google that. To be clear though. EMILY, IF YOU FIND THIS DIARY AND I'M DEAD, IT WAS ALI. GO STRAIGHT TO THE POLICE.

THURSDAY, March 9th, 6.30 a.m.

In the kitchen. Eating three slices of toast (two brown, one white) and drinking a large mug of coffee (I need to be alert. Since Ali's visit I haven't been able to sleep). Emily taking a shower. Blustery and cold outside. Second baby doctor appointment tonight.

Emily's mad at me but she doesn't know why.

'It was something you did in a dream.'

'But how can you be mad at me for something I did in a dream?'

'Because it was very hurtful.'

'But it wasn't real!'

Apparently, she can be mad at me for things I haven't even done. She is taking our relationship to a whole new level. I'm at a loss. Should I apologise even though I've done nothing wrong? Will an apology be an admission of guilt? Very confused.

7.00 p.m.

In the shed. Having a cigarette. Emily inside lying down. All quiet next door.

I texted Mrs Crawley earlier to arrange an emergency meeting.

The second baby appointment with Dr Proops was a lot better than the first, mainly because we got to see the baby. Our baby.

It's so strange that a life is growing inside her stomach. They gave us pictures of the scan which Emily hasn't stopped staring at since we left. It sounds terrible because it's my baby, but all I can see is a black blob. Dr Proops showed us where the head was, the legs, arms, etc. and Emily was in tears, but all I could see were black blobs near other black blobs. Am I a heartless idiot?

Emily and Mum were on the phone for nearly an hour when we got back. I listened carefully, but nothing incriminating or inflammatory was said about me. I have to admit, I'm feeling a little bit uneasy about their newly discovered telephone relationship.

10.00 p.m.
In bed. Eating a gherkin with ice cream (is that weird?). Emily asleep. Reading *The Bloke's Survival Kit for Being a Dad.*

I watched Emily getting undressed tonight and her body has started to change. Not hugely and I didn't say anything, but I noticed a few things. Her breasts have definitely got bigger (the tit fairy has come!). Her stomach is getting rounder and she's looking generally a bit puffy, but despite this, I really, really wanted her. There's something quite sexy about a pregnant woman. I can't quite put my finger on why and when I did Emily said, 'Sorry, Harry, I'm knackered. Maybe tomorrow.'

We haven't had sex in ages. I don't know how long exactly, but I think if I can't remember, it must have been a while.

I'm reading *The Bloke's Survival Kit for Being a Dad.* I didn't want to but now I can't sleep, I need something to help pass the time. I'm reading chapter four, 'Sex – The final frontier'. The book says that during the first three months of a pregnancy, the woman will have no interest in sex whatsoever. They're tired, bloated, they feel sick and the last thing they want is to have us rolling around on top of them. This is basically true, but the advice is a little patchy. It ranged from wanking frequently (internet porn is the suggested aid for this), followed by an impromptu visit to Amsterdam, where you can shag lots of reasonably priced but gorgeous prostitutes, and lastly they advised taking up golf (Dad?).

I'm going to pop downstairs and have a bit of Harry alone time with a box of tissues and a hundred million pages of internet porn. It's cheaper than Amsterdam and much less time-consuming than golf.

FRIDAY, March 10th, 11.00 p.m.

Home (just). In the study. Emily asleep. Eating Kentucky Fried Chicken. Really very drunk.

The only way I can deal with my impending death at the hands of al-Qaeda is to get really drunk. I went out with Rory after work for a quick pint, which turned into a marginally slower few pints and then a very long, drawn-out and messy ten pints. Rory really is a top bloke. I think I might love him. He understands me. I also love Kentucky Fried Chicken.

11.30 p.m.
I sent Jamie a message on Facebook.

Jamie, you're gorgeous. A sex bomb! I wish I could do all sorts of things to you. I think about you all day. I even have dreams about you. They always take place in my shed. I wish things were different so I could see what it's like to be with you again. I really want to take you out for a test drive! Good night. Woof! Woof! Harry, XOXO

SATURDAY, March 11th, 9.00 a.m.

In the kitchen. Emily still asleep. Drinking black coffee. Eating a bacon and egg sandwich.

Why do I drink so much? I'm not eighteen anymore. The recovery period for the amount I drank last night will probably be at least three days. My memory's a little vague about what actually happened. All I know is that when I came downstairs this morning, there was a half-eaten bucket of Kentucky Fried Chicken on top of the telly and a pair of unknown shoes by the front door. I remember leaving school with Rory and going to the pub for a quick drink. The next thing I recall is waking up this morning and feeling as though I'd been run over by a bus. My mouth has a distinctly unpleasant taste and my throat feels like a trainee carpenter has sandpapered it.

11.00 a.m.
Emily's mad at me again.

'I don't see why you have to drink so much.'

'I know, neither do I. It's stupid and I'm sorry.' I really am. My head feels like a building site. 'I'm not going to do it anymore.'

'And how many times have you said that?'

'Including today, about fifty, but this time I actually mean it. I feel terrible.'

'Really?'

'Yes, my head hurts, my stomach's spinning like a bad fairground ride and I'm so tired. My body aches.' As I was speaking the realisation of what I was saying occurred to me. This is how she feels every single day. Luckily, before I had time to dig myself further into my own hole, the doorbell rang. 'I'll get that.' Emily stared at me in disgust.

11.15 a.m.
How strange. There was an old man at the door. He was about sixty-ish, with grey hair, a beard and was dressed in trousers, a shirt and a cardigan, but no shoes. I looked at him, he looked at me and then he said,
    'My shoes please.'
    'Excuse me?'
    'Young man, you stole my shoes!' For a moment, I was mystified, but then I remembered the mysterious pair of shoes I saw this morning by the front door. I handed them over. 'Lucky I didn't go to the police,' he said, putting his shoes back on, and then he left!

12.00 p.m.
Fuck! What have I done? I just went online and saw the message I sent Jamie last night. I must have been completely wasted to write such a provocative message. What should I do? Why did I write 'Woof! Woof!'? Should I send an apology and let her know I was just drunk or do nothing and hope she doesn't reply? I'm think I'm going to do nothing and hope it goes away.

I'm never ever going to drink again. Ever. Again. Seriously.

The squirrel's sitting in the garden looking miserable. No reply yet from Mrs Crawley. I've decided to tell Emily about next door. I need to share the burden. I just hope she believes me. She's my wife. I need her support.

2.00 p.m.

I'm completely alone. I told Emily everything. I told her about the house being empty. I told her about the map with the pins in it. I told her that Mrs Crawley and I are spying on them. I told her I think our neighbours might be part of a terrorist cell and when I was finished she said, 'Harry, you're fucking crazy! You broke into their house. You made assumptions based on their race, which makes you a racist and you're conspiring with that barmy old bigot, Mrs Crawley. I can't believe you. What are you playing at? We're having a baby in six months and you're going backwards!'

She stormed out and slammed the front door. I have no idea where she went.

4.00 p.m.

OMG! Jamie just sent me a picture of herself TOPLESS! She's on a bed on her knees looking right at the camera. She's wearing panties, but no bra and her breasts are magnificent. Underneath the photo she'd written.

Something to help with the fantasising Harry. Let me know what you think, BIG BOY!

What is she trying to do to me? I'm done for. It's surely just a matter of time before I cave in and sleep with her.

6.00 p.m.

Still no sign of Emily. I'm getting worried. Has she left me? Is this what separated means? Still in a state of shock, confusion, sexual bewilderment and utter awe at the photo of Jamie.

There are a couple of thing you can do when a girl sends a topless photograph of herself to you.

1. You can destroy the photo immediately. This will absolve you of any blame and stop you from pursuing the girl any further due to heightened sexual awareness.

2. You can keep the photo for a short period of time. Use the photo for sexual activity before you destroy the photo so as not to encourage any further sexual communication.

3. You can keep the photo.

I decide to keep the photo.

SUNDAY, March 12th, 9.00 a.m.

In the kitchen. Eating a full English breakfast. Emily asleep upstairs. Sunny. Squirrel still worryingly depressed. I think it's losing weight and its fur is looking shabby.

Emily came home last night just after eight o'clock. She'd been at Stella's in Kingston upon Thames. They'd had dinner at Jamie's Italian (I ate four olives in the shed with a cocktail). She's still mad at me. Today we're going to her parents' for lunch. I'm nervous to see her dad again because the last time we crossed paths he was picking me up from the police station. My name is mud in the Lamb household. Time to fight back. I'm going to make my famous apple crumble with homemade custard.

8.00 p.m.
Home. Emily upstairs. In the study. In the dog house (again). In the shit (again).

That was literally one of the worst days of my life. It started well. We got to Emily's parents' house around eleven this morning. They were all smiles, cheek kisses and pats on the back. Derek seemed to have forgiven me for my previous indiscretion. Emily's mum, Pam, was in high spirits and wanted to talk about the baby nonstop, while Derek and I raided his Scotch cabinet and smoked cigars on the patio. It was a glorious day. The sun was shining, birds were tweeting, but then Emily's grandmother turned up.

Beatrice Lamb, ninety-something and should have been dead donkeys' years ago. Still, despite the old dear wobbling all over the house with her distinct old-person smell, we all sat down for a lovely lunch. Pam did her lamb (not ironic) and when I brought out the apple crumble everyone ooed and aahed and said how wonderful it was. Great lunch followed by tea in the conservatory. It was going so well. Emily had forgotten she was mad at me and I was actually getting along well with Derek. He even asked how school was and invited me to play golf with him next weekend. I was finally in the family circle.

However, just as the day was winding down, it happened. I was in the garden with Derek. He was telling me one of his stories about his time on the force when I had to nip inside for a pee. Emily was in the kitchen with her mum and she gave me a smile and a wink as I walked by. I made my way along the hallway towards the toilet and this is when I saw Beatrice. She was in the lounge, slumped in a chair and looking, well, finally dead. I don't know what came over me, but I was suddenly George Clooney from ER. I rushed over and listened to her chest. She wasn't breathing. Luckily, being a teacher, I have first-aid training and so the next minute and I was on top of her. I pulled her shirt open before I started mouth-to-mouth. I was really going at it and then the next moment I heard Emily's mum screaming, Beatrice woke up and was trying to push me off and Derek came running in.

'What the bloody hell's going on?' said Derek.

'Harry's trying to rape grandmother!' said Pam.

'No, no, no,' I said, astride Beatrice.

'Rapist!' shouted Beatrice.

'Harry, how could you?' said Emily.

'You filthy bastard,' said Derek.

'I was giving her mouth-to-mouth, honestly. I thought she was dead.'

'I was taking a nap,' said Beatrice.

Derek looked like he wanted to punch me and Emily started to cry.

Eventually, once everyone had calmed down, I explained. They all seemed to believe me, but when we were leaving Derek was giving me the evil eyes again. I asked him if we were still on for golf and he said, 'We'll see.' As quickly as I was in the family circle, I was out again.

TUESDAY, March 14th, 7.00 p.m.

In the lounge with Emily. Watching TV. Eating a Chinese takeaway. Raining.

I'm lying low after the incident at Emily's parents'. I'm staying away from the internet so I'm not tempted by Jamie. I'm staying away from next door so I'm not murdered and I'm doing my best to keep Emily happy so she doesn't leave me. I need to get my life back on an even keel again. One adult with a happy home life, no regrets, no indiscretions, a good career, a nice house in a good part of London, a beautiful wife, a baby on the way and everything to look forward to. As Gordon Ramsay would say . . . 'Done!'

WEDNESDAY, March 15th, 4.00 p.m.

In my classroom. Eating a cheese and pickled onion sandwich. Raining. It was supposed to be dry all week, according to the BBC weatherman!

I had a very interesting lunch with Rory today.

'I think I've been a bit of a knob,' I said.

'How do you mean?' I explained all about Jamie. Rory listened carefully and when I'd finished he said, 'I haven't told anyone this before, but two years ago I err . . . sort of cheated on Miranda.'

'What?'

I was gobsmacked. Rory's the last person to have an affair and Miranda's bloody gorgeous. Rory isn't a bad-looking bloke at all but he definitely got a bit lucky with Miranda.

'It happened at the Basingstoke conference.'

Rory then went on to tell me all about Anna, a graphic designer from Denmark. Anna was giving a lecture while Rory was sitting at the back of the room imagining what she'd look like naked, but not actually imagining he'd ever get to see. Four hours, six pints and two vodka and Red Bulls later, Anna approached him at the bar and they started chatting. Fast forward three hours and Rory and Anna emerged sweaty, naked and dripping in sex from beneath the duvet in her hotel room.

'And I've regretted it every day since.'

'But she was seriously sexy?'

'She made Manet's Olympia look like a bit of a dog.'

'And the sex?'

'Extraordinary. Unbelievable. Mind blowing.'

'And Miranda will never find out?'

'Never. You're the only other person who knows.'

'And yet you still regret it every single day?'

'Every. Single. Day. It doesn't matter how attractive she was. It could've been Heidi Klum or Annette Bening . . .'

'Annette Bening?'

'I've had a thing for her since *American Beauty*. The thing is, Harry, I cheated on my wife and I can't ever take that back.'

'I think I understand.'

'If you're thinking of doing something with this Jamie girl, or if you think you might give in and do something silly, call me.'

'I'd never cheat on Emily.'

'That's exactly what I thought three hours before I did. Call me.'

'Alright, mate, I'll call you. Now seriously, Annette Bening?'

FRIDAY, March 17th, 8.00 p.m.
St Patrick's Day

The day of drinking, debauchery and depravity and I'm watching telly while my pregnant wife is asleep on the sofa next to me . . . There's that scene in *Four Weddings and a Funeral* where the Scottish bloke reads out the WH Auden poem. I don't remember the exact words, but something about stopping all the clocks and letting the mourners come. Well the clock is definitely slowing down and you can bring out the mourners because Harry Spencer's youth is dead!

9.00 p.m.
In the study. Emily asleep upstairs. Still raining. Typing a message to Jamie.

Jamie, I have to stop this now. Whatever this is or could be, it can't. I was drunk the other day when I wrote to you. Not that I didn't mean what I said because you're gorgeous, but I can't cheat on my wife. We're having a baby and it's time to stop living in the past and move on. I'm sorry if I misled you, but this has to stop now. I fear we can't just be friends because you're too sexy and I'm too weak. I'm sorry. Take care, Harry XO

I pressed send, opened a can of Guinness and celebrated St Patrick's Day. Then, with a heavy heart, I deleted the photos of Jamie.

SATURDAY, March 18th, 9.00 a.m.

In the shed. Sunny. The stupid weatherman panicked yesterday and predicted more rain. Smoking a cigarette. Emily still asleep. Squirrel looking very forlorn. All quiet next door. Still no reply from Mrs Crawley. No reply from Jamie.

While the rest of London is suffering from the Irish hangover from hell, I'm feeling as frisky and as lively as a young pup. There are advantages to being an old fart. Emily's still in the land of nod while I'm enjoying the early-morning sunshine. I texted Mrs Crawley again. I'm starting to get worried. Maybe I should pop over and see if she's okay. If she wasn't such a mean, callous old tyrant, I would have gone over earlier, but to be honest, she scares the pants off me.

Off to see Granddad. I hope he and Audrey aren't going at it when I get there. I can't take any more of their wrinkly old-people love, especially when my own love life is stalled and possibly broken down completely.

I just remembered the Oxford and Cambridge boat race is next weekend. Ben's brother Adam is competing for Cambridge and I promised we'd pop along and see him. Adam is even more intelligent, better-looking and taller than Ben. I would hate him except he's so bloody nice. He used to run after me in his nappies when he was a toddler and now he's competing in the most famous boat race in the world.

4.00 p.m.
Granddad's engaged! Granddad and Audrey are getting married in July and he wants me to be his best man!

'She's the one, Harry. I want to spend the rest of my life with her.'

'That's great, Granddad. I'm so happy for you both.'

'Audrey said she isn't going to wear white because she's not a virgin. I told the silly old goat it didn't matter. You're seventy-one years old – you can wear whatever colour you bloody well want.'

'Good for you and I'd love to be your best man.'

'That's splendid, Harry. Your main job's keeping that bloody thief, Sammy the Paki, out of the way. He's had his eyes on Audrey ever since he found out she can still do the splits.'

'Audrey can do the splits?'

'You bet she can,' Granddad said with a sly wink.

Blimey!

TUESDAY, March 21st, 1.00 p.m.

At our staff meeting today, Miss Simpson told us the OFSTED inspectors are coming on Thursday and on pain of life, death and the dole office, we'd better be ready.

'I don't want any hiccups,' she said, looking directly at me. 'Everything must be perfect. Do I make myself perfectly clear?' She was still looking (and I think talking) directly to me.

Ever since my first OFSTED inspection, I've initiated a strategic plan of attack that involves bribery, blackmail and corruption.

Mr Sean Fowler (Year Eight) will be instructed not to talk, raise his grubby little paw or attempt anything other than breathing during class. In return, I won't inform his parents he runs an illegal cigarette scam at school. The little free-market urchin gets cheap (or possibly knocked-off) cigarettes and then sells them during lunchtime. If caught, he would face certain expulsion, but because some of the teachers actually gain from his little operation (free cigarettes for hush money) we have no desire to stop the flow of cheap cigarettes from reaching us.

Mr Simon Alnwick (Year Nine) will be threatened with an extended run on the bench if he does anything else other than stare at the wall during class. Simon's the captain of the school football team, but Alan Hughes (PE) owes me a favour.

If Miss Jennifer Steadman (Year Ten) decides to be anything other than angelic, I'll be forced to inform her parents I found a small amount of what she believed was cannabis in her possession. As it turned out, she had been the victim of a prankster because what she had paid fifteen quid for was actually Italian seasoning.

It may seem a bit unprofessional or even insensitive to bribe my pupils, but if it keeps Miss Spencer from clambering on my back and riding me all the way to the unemployment queue, I'll take my chances.

THURSDAY, March 23rd, 6.00 a.m.

In the kitchen. Tired. Drinking tea and eating toast (one white, one brown, one raisin). Emily moving around upstairs. Sunny.

Today's OFSTED inspection day. I'm going into work early to tidy up my classroom and prepare. I must stop thinking about Jamie and focus on school. It would help if I'd had sex with Emily recently, but I can't remember the last time we performed coitus. I can't even remember what it feels like. Pretty good, I think.

1.00 p.m.

The morning was reasonably good, if a bit hairy at times. An inspector came idling into my room just before ten o'clock, scary clipboard in hand. I had Year Eight and so Mr Sean Fowler (the cigarette mogul) was in the class. I was teaching them about the kings and queens of England and when I mentioned the House of Wessex, I saw a little grin appear on his grimy face and I thought he was going to crack and say something inappropriate. Luckily, when I glared at him, he looked down at the floor and didn't say anything. With Year Eight any word that contains the letters 'sex' is usually open to a few giggles. I usually beat them to it and make a joke myself, but today wasn't the day for fun and frolics. Fortunately, the morning passed without a hitch.

Here comes Rory and he's grinning like a Cheshire cat.

1.15 p.m.

The reason he was grinning like a fool is the rumour on the street (or at least the halls of Wimbledon Secondary) is they're looking for an excuse to fire Miss Simpson!

Apparently, the school is underperforming and they've had multiple complaints from staff members about her management style (fear and mental torture). This could be just the break I need. It seems I don't have to impress Miss Simpson anymore, but just wait until they fire her!

6.00 p.m.
Home. Making dinner. Emily watching TV.

The OFSTED inspectors are gone and everything went swimmingly. Mr Alnwick and Miss Steadman were charming. All of my other kids were a dream. The intelligent ones were even more intelligent than usual (it may have helped that I did a little prepping with them beforehand). There was almost a blip when Gavin Haines from Year Ten almost fell asleep, but I managed to keep him awake by subtly walking past him from time to time and giving him a gentle nudge. Overall though, I'm proud of all of my pupils. As a reward, I'm giving out no homework for the next week. I'm a hero at school.

8.00 p.m.
Unfortunately, not a hero in the bedroom. Emily said she was finally feeling reasonable and that we could have sex, but I was so tired I couldn't even manage a cuddle and kiss before I fell asleep. Just my luck!

FRIDAY, March 24th, 6.00 p.m.

In the shed. Eating a vegetable samosa. Emily still not home from work. No sign of lovesick squirrel. No reply from Jamie.

Email from Ben.

Harry you saucy old sausage, how's things? Katie and I are off up the coast for a month. I quit my job at the bank. I was getting bored anyway. Katie's parents own a small pie shop in Sydney and I've been working there. It's much better than working in a shitty old bank with all the banker wankers. They asked if I wanted to go in with them and make a go of it and I think I might.

I hope all is well with Emily and the baby. Send my love. Speak soon old friend, Ben.

P.S. Say Hi to Adam on Saturday if you see him. I can't believe my little brother is rowing in the Boat Race. He used to eat dog food!

SATURDAY, March 25th, 9.00 a.m.

In the study. Freaking out. Emily asleep. Dark and cloudy overhead (ominous?).

I think something terrible has happened to Mrs Crawley. I popped over to see her first thing this morning. I rang the doorbell but she didn't answer and so I decided to take a look around the back of the house. I peeked through the side windows of her bungalow and saw nothing unusual. I was about to leave when I looked through the French doors and into the lounge and that's when I saw it. It was a mess. Mrs Crawley's house is always spotlessly spick and span. There's never as much as a magazine out of place. However, there were books all over the floor. The pictures on the wall were all askew and the sofa cushions were scattered everywhere. There had obviously been a struggle! She may have been kidnapped, murdered or worse! Maybe Ali had something to do with it. Maybe she knew too much. Maybe I know too much. Maybe I'm next! I rushed home in a panic.

What should I do? Shit! Fuck! Bugger and fuck! I'm fucked. Maybe Mrs Crawley has been fucked. I just don't know. I need to do something. Mrs Crawley needs me. Off to do something.

9.30 a.m.
In the study. Emily on the phone with her dad. I feel sick to my stomach. I woke Emily up and told her everything. At first she called me a 'stupid, paranoid fuckwit', but eventually I persuaded her to call her dad and ask for a favour. I thought if anyone would know who to call, it would be him. I hope he can do something so we can save Mrs Crawley and stop the wave of terror that's fallen upon our street.

10.15 a.m.
Derek agreed to help. Although he said if I was wrong and made him look like a tit in front of the police, there'd be serious consequences. He didn't say what they were, but I got the impression it might involve some form of physical violence.

'You'd better be right about this,' Emily said when she got off the phone. 'Otherwise Daddy's going to be really pissed off.'

I have my fingers crossed something awful has happened to Mrs Crawley.

10.55 a.m.
Two police cars and a van just pulled up outside. It's time to be a working-class hero and stop the terrorists in their tracks. I can see the headlines now: 'HISTORY TEACHER STOPS TERRORIST THREAT, SAVES OAP AND GETS TOP MARKS FROM OFSTED!'

1.00 p.m.

I'm a knob. The police turned up with Derek in tow and went about their business. They went next door, ready it seemed to batter the door down, drag Ali outside and lock him up. Emily and I were watching from behind the curtains in the lounge. It was very tense. Four officers were at the front door and a couple went around the back. It was like watching an episode of The Bill. They knocked on the door and this is when I expected all the action to kick off. Ali might try something desperate. However, much to my surprise, the door opened and after a minute the police walked in very casually.

The danger of an armed siege seemed to be over, so Emily and I wandered outside to see what was going on. Ten minutes later and all six policemen emerged from the house, closely followed by a very angry-looking Derek.

'Is this the gentleman?' the lead officer, a six-foot-plus warrior in riot gear, said to Derek, who nodded in my general direction.

'What happened?'

'Nothing happened, sir. We walked into a very normal suburban house. The lady of the house offered us a cup of tea and a chocolate digestive biscuit.'

'But the house was empty. What about the map with the pins?'

'The house was fully furnished and we didn't see any map. Maybe your imagination got the better of you, sir.'

Derek's face was very red and the thick vein in his neck was pulsating.

'But what about Mrs Crawley?'

'What about her sir?'

'She's still missing,' I said, using my last trump card, but suddenly a car drove by and pulled into her driveway. The next minute Mrs Crawley got out, followed by her son. Talk about timing.

'Would that be Mrs Crawley?' said the policeman.

'Umm . . . yes,' I mumbled.

'Come on lads, a waste of bloody time,' said the policeman. Derek looked fit to burst.

'But I don't understand,' I said, looking at Emily for support, but none came. She looked livid.

I've been shafted. I'm alone. I don't understand. The woman of the house? Fully furnished? And where has Mrs Crawley been? I'm completely and utterly flabbergasted. I'm also terrified of what Derek has planned for me.

8.00 p.m.
Alone in the study. Smoking. Emily in Buckinghamshire. Dark and cold.

After Emily left I dashed over to Mrs Crawley's house to demand answers. Apparently she'd been to Eastbourne on holiday. I asked about the mess and she said it was her grandson. When they were leaving, he nipped back inside to find her mobile phone and had turned the place upside down looking for it. He hadn't found the phone and the house was left like a crime scene. She dotted the last of the i's and crossed all the final t's and made me feel even more like a complete and utter tit.

I also just realised that in all the commotion we missed watching Adam in the Boat Race. Emily left with her dad. She's staying the night in Bucks. Derek was so angry he couldn't say anything. The thick vein in his neck kept pulsating threateningly. I apologised a hundred times, but he didn't say anything. Emily told me she was very disappointed in me. It seems I have been abandoned.

FRIDAY, March 31st, 7.00 p.m.
Good Friday (is it?)

In the study. Emily watching TV. Eating beans on toast and drinking tea. Cold and blustery.

It's been a terrible week. Emily has barely spoken to me. I tried to call Derek and apologise again, but he wouldn't even talk to me. I fear I'm out of the family circle and off his list of possible golf partners. Rory was off school all week. He came down with a dreaded case of something that gave him severe constipation. Ironically, without him school was really shit. I marked an essay where the pupil had used the terms, 'cld', 'gr8t', and 'imho.' I failed him and said in my notes:

'Graham, FYI – How u write in your own time is entirely up 2 u, but if you want to have a glimmer of hope of passing any of your GCSE exams, cld u please use actual words and not text lingo. G8t! Mr Spencer.' I doubt he will fully appreciate the ironic undertones of my reply.

It seems the squirrel's gone into an even deeper depression. I called my parents but they were too busy to talk. Dad's trying to get membership at the golf club, while Mum's joined the local amateur dramatics society. It's a bit unfair really because she's been professionally dramatic for years. I'm feeling fatter than ever, my hair's receding at an even faster rate and I think I may have a heart attack very soon – I've had chest pains for the last two days. My life's officially rubbish. I'm on Facebook debating whether to send Jamie the following message.

Jamie, I'm sorry if I've been a bit up and down recently. It's tough because I would love to see you again, but I worry we might go too far. You're beautiful, gorgeous and sexy and I'm weak, pitiful and sexually frustrated – not a good combination. The photos of you only made it worse. They gave me all sorts of ideas. I'd like to be friends if that's possible. Just don't send me any more photos of your breasts otherwise I'll be forced to do something very naughty. Luv Harry XO

Reasons not to send the message:

1. It could encourage further sexual communication which could lead to an affair.
2. I'm married to Emily for better or worse, for richer or poorer and in sickness and in health.
3. Even though it isn't technically cheating, it certainly has the whiff of infidelity about it.
4. Rory told me not to do anything and I believe him.
5. I'm going to be a father in less than six months.
6. If Derek found out I think he might actually kill me.

Reasons to send the message:

1. Jamie has the greatest pair of breasts I've ever seen.

I push send. It's a close call, but the tits have it by a perfectly formed pink nipple.

april

SATURDAY, April 1st, 11.00 a.m.
April Fool's Day

In the kitchen. Alone. Eating a cheese and onion crisp sandwich. Emily spending the day with Stella in Kingston upon Thames.

In fourteen days Emily and I leave for Italy. We're going to visit some of the most romantic and beautiful places in the world, but at the moment I feel about as close to Emily as I feel to China. She's still mad at me vis-à-vis the whole next-door neighbours not being al-Qaeda shambles. She's barely talking to me, while I'm embarking on a possibly dangerous Facebook affair with Jamie. Emily's three months pregnant and we haven't done the beast with two backs and a funny-looking middle for what seems like an eternity. This isn't the best time to be going on the most romantic holiday of our lives. Still, we have two weeks until we leave. Maybe I can turn things around.

Off to see my sexually liberated grandfather and his flexible mistress, Audrey.

1.00 p.m.
Just back from visiting Granddad. As usual he gave me some tip-top advice.

'Granddad, I think I've been a bit of an idiot.'

'You're a man – it's in your DNA,' Granddad replied eruditely.

I explained everything. I told him all about Ali, Mrs Crawley, Derek and how Emily's still annoyed with me. I didn't mention Jamie. When I finished he looked at me with his sage-like face and said,

'Marriage is one big argument, Harry. Your grandmother and I were married for nearly forty years and she was in a mood for most of it.'

'And how did you cope with that? And don't say golf.'

'Golf, no, stupid sport. The only way to deal with women, Harry, is sex!'

'Sex?'

'Yes. If a woman's happy in the bedroom, no matter what she's annoyed about, if she's happy where it matters, you'll be fine.' Granddad finished with a warm smile. As usual he was right. How is playing golf going to help my marriage? I need to focus on my own balls and a very different sort of hole. 'If Emily's mad at you, Harry, just give her the shagging of her life. Trust me, nothing clears the air like a really great orgasm.'

'Righto, Granddad, will do.'

We spent some time talking about the wedding. As best man my duties are varied and apparently quite demanding. Audrey wants a dozen white doves and Granddad wants a stag weekend in Amsterdam. I explained that given the circumstances Amsterdam could be a bit tricky.

'During the war we manoeuvred almost two hundred thousand men across the channel to Normandy. I think we can get you, me and your dad to Amsterdam on easyJet, don't you Harry?'

I was walking down the hallway towards the reception to leave when I heard Granddad shout after me.

'Cunnilingus is the key, Harry, cunnilingus!' Just as he said that an old lady popped her head out of a door.

'Yes dear?' I looked at her for a moment. 'You called my name.'

'Oh, it was just my granddad.'

'Oh, I could have sworn I heard my name.'

'And what's your name?' I asked inquisitively.

'Connie Lingus,' she replied with a completely straight face.

4.00 p.m.

Just back from Waitrose. Emily will be home soon and I'm bringing out the romantic big guns. I'm making her a delicious dinner of beef Wellington, sautéed potatoes and wilted greens. For dessert, I have her favourite (pistachio gelato) and I rented the sexiest film of all time, *Unfaithful*. Our bedroom is full of candles, the massage oil is poised and everything is ready for a night of passion, lovemaking and romance.

6.00 p.m.

Emily's in the shower. Dinner was perfect. She was completely surprised. Next up it's the sexy film, and after that I'm going to give her a sensual massage. Then, lastly, I'm going to give Emily the best cunnilingus she's ever had.

1.00 a.m.

Just back from casualty. Lying in bed. Unable to move. My dignity in tatters. Emily downstairs.

Disaster! The evening was going as smoothly as a tub of fromage frais until I decided to follow Granddad's advice and pop downstairs and give Emily the orgasm of her life. She was all relaxed and oily after the massage and so I slowly worked my way between her legs and went to work. She started to groan, moan and writhe around above me. Her moans soon turned to screams as she got nearer to orgasm and that's when it happened. My back went. A sharp pain shot up my spine and I couldn't move. I was in complete and utter bloody agony.

'Don't stop, I'm almost there,' Emily begged from somewhere above me.

'Back,' I moaned in agonising pain. 'My back. I can't move.'

The next thirty minutes was like a Monty Python sketch. Emily eventually managed to prise herself away from me, but I was naked and on all fours. She had to get me upright, dressed, downstairs and into the car, while all I could do was weep in pain every time she moved me an inch. It would have been hilarious if it wasn't quite so bloody painful.

We eventually got to casualty at about eight o'clock, but I'm sure like every Saturday night it was jam-packed. There were drunks staggering around talking to themselves, children crying into their parents' shoulders, drunken teenagers with war wounds from a night out gone wrong and then there was me – a history teacher who'd put his back out while going down on his wife.

Emily was tired, probably frustrated and annoyed, but she was nothing other than wonderful. She is, after all, my wife and that's what we both signed up for. I love her more than ever. Eventually, after sitting painfully in my wheelchair for nearly four hours, a doctor saw me. I explained (without giving too much information) what had happened and he gave me an injection in my back, before sending me home with a big bag full of drugs and a prescription to rest. I explained that given my inability to actually move, rest wouldn't be much of a decision.

Emily is coming back with a glass of water and my drugs.

What a disastrous night. I was supposed to be bringing sexy back, not buggering up my back. I feel like an old fool.

MONDAY, April 3rd, 7.00 p.m.
Bank holiday. Easter Monday

Still in bed. Feeling a touch better. Nurse Emily making me dinner.

I watched a lot of television today. I watched both episodes of *Neighbours* and *Home and Away*. I watched a gardening show, two fashion shows, three cooking shows, the *Antiques Roadshow*, two old episodes of *EastEnders*, one episode of *Blackadder* and I think a show about either monks or skunks, I can't remember. I ate porridge for breakfast, two bananas and a block of cheese for lunch and I had a cup of tea and four biscuits this afternoon.

Steve, Fiona and their troop of Js came by this afternoon. Fiona looked quite pregnant and before they left Steve said, 'When you're all better, you and Emily will have to come over and watch the slide show from our last holiday to Cornwall. It will really get you in the mood for our little sojourn.'

I suddenly don't want to get better.

8.00 p.m.
Bed bath!

8.10 p.m.
Bed bath was unfortunately just a bed bath.

TUESDAY, April 4th, 10.00 a.m.

Downstairs on the sofa. Emily back at work after her long weekend. Sunny. Drinking tea.

Emily had to call Miss Simpson this morning and explain what had happened. I was dreading this, but Emily came back and said what a lovely woman she was. She obviously hadn't spoken to the same woman who constantly threatens to turn me into another dole queue statistic.

I finally felt well enough to come downstairs this morning. After a couple of days stashed away in the bedroom, it was nice to have a change of scenery. I also have my laptop.

Two messages from Jamie. Message number one.

Harry, I completely understand – I have great breasts! We can be friends but how about this? We will never meet for obvious reasons and so therefore, we can't actually do anything. You're sexually frustrated, I'm sexually frustrated and so why don't we help each other out! Luv Jamie XO

I finished reading and was left uncertain about what she was hinting at. However, after reading her next message it all became quite clear.

You're sitting at home looking at the photo of me and you're really horny. You start touching yourself but it isn't enough. You need me. You dial my number but I don't answer because I'm already in the room behind you and I'm naked. I grab the back of the chair and spin you around.

You're overwhelmed as you see me completely naked for
the first time. I get down on my knees . . .

I would go on, but I think the opening is fairly self-explana-
tory. She went on to explain, in graphic detail, all of the things
she wants to do to me and the multitude of things she wants
me to do to her. It was the sexiest thing I'd ever read and at
the end she said:

If you let me know your deepest, darkest desires, maybe I'll
send you another photo! Luv Jamie, XO

I was in a state of complete and utter bewilderment. I read her
message five times and each time I got more and more turned
on. As usual, I was left asking myself the same question over
and over again. What the fuck am I going to do? I don't want
to cheat on Emily. I want to be a good husband, a good father,
but there's something about Jamie that drives me wild.

2.00 p.m.
Dirty talk, sexting or anything of that nature has never been
something I'm particularly comfortable with. Emily and I have
never dabbled in the world of filthy chatter and not because
we're prudish or uptight, but because it isn't a part of the fabric
of our relationship. We once tried doing a bit of mucky talk in
the bedroom, but she could barely get past, 'Give it to me, big
boy,' before we were both on the floor in hysterics.

However, and here's the odd thing, with Jamie it feels
perfectly natural. Is this me? I live on a quiet, suburban street
in Wimbledon. I drive a ten-year-old Volkswagen Jetta. I shop
at Waitrose and enjoy a nice cup of tea. I watch the *Antiques
Roadshow* and voted Lib Dem at the last election, but I just

wrote, 'I want you to suck on my throbbing member!' I'm writing words like moist, throbbing, gush, sweaty and nibble with all the gusto and aplomb of a *Razzle* contributor. Despite being a staunch atheist, I feel the sudden urge to go to church.

4.00 p.m.
In the last two hours Jamie and I have swapped a dozen messages. Each one saucier and riskier than the last. However, at the end of her last sex fantasy she said.

As promised and because you're such a filthy boy here's
another photo. I hope you enjoy looking at this and
thinking about me. I'll just have to go home and play with
my toy. He's ten inches and I call him Dirty Harry! Luv Jamie
XO (OMG!!!)

Then she attached a photo. My heart was beating really hard in my chest while I waited for the bloody thing to download. However, when Internet Explorer had eventually caught up with my imagination, I wasn't disappointed. She was in her nurse's outfit and looking about as shaggable as is possible. I'm in serious trouble. It doesn't matter that I'm not doing anything physical with Jamie because my brain is involved and I want to do it. Facts are facts. I'm a cheater and completely and utterly ashamed of myself.

7.00 p.m.
I'm such a callous bastard. Emily came home early from work and bought me fish and chips. She's my Florence Nightingale and I'm her Dirty Den.

WEDNESDAY, April 5th, 9.00 a.m.

In the kitchen. Smoking a cigarette. Watching squirrel. He seems to have put on a bit of weight. Maybe he's started eating again. Able to walk like an old man. I still can't put my own socks on yet though. Sunny.

I need to get out of the house today otherwise I'll end up staying in and writing more filth to Jamie. So, desperate times and all that, I've decided to go to see Mrs Crawley.

11.00 a.m.

What a strange morning. Mrs Crawley's moving to Eastbourne. Apparently, her little jaunt was about more than just ice cream, windy walks on the promenade and saucy seaside postcards.

'That's very sad. The street isn't going to be the same without you,' I said while inside I was muttering words of joy. Her reign of terror is over!

'I leave in two weeks, Harry, and we need to uncover the truth about your new neighbours.'

'I think we were just wrong.'

'I've seen a lot of things in my life and I'm sure something suspicious is going on in that house. We can't let them get away with it.'

'But what can we do? The police came and went. We can't exactly call them again. Emily's still mad about that and her dad isn't speaking to me. I don't think we should dig up old graves. Let's just let sleeping dogs lie.'

'Oh, tosh. Stop throwing around worthless clichés and grow a backbone. We need to stop the Taliban otherwise they'll destroy us all!'

She was quite worked up.

'I don't know. My back really hurts and the doctor said I should rest.'

'Then if you won't do something about it, I will,' she said and that was the end of that.

We had a cup of tea and a single digestive biscuit each and then I left. I wonder what she's going to do.

2.00 p.m.
In the lounge. Lying down. Eating a pickled onion, cheese and bacon sandwich. Testicles the size of footballs.

I've spent the last hour swapping sex fantasies with Jamie. I've used a vibrator, been covered in oil, covered her in oil, been blindfolded, handcuffed, done it in Greenwich Park, done it in the back seat of her car, used love balls (still not 100 per cent sure what these are), had a lap dance, watched her strip and dress up as a schoolgirl and had incredible sex in the shower/bath. All of this, of course, took place online and in our heads. However, after a certain amount of time talking about having sex, but not actually having it, you have to stop. The physical pain of desire becomes too much and so we started talking about other things.

We talked about the good old days and laughed about all the things we did as teenagers. She told me what it's like to be a nurse and asked me about being a teacher. Then we started talking about our other relationships. I told her how happy I was with Emily, which was strange considering that only five minutes before she had me tied to a bedpost and covered in peanut butter.

I'm happy with Emily. I love Emily more than anything in the world, but that has nothing to do with Jamie. What I have with Jamie is completely separate in my mind. Jamie's sexy, she understands me and we have a history. She's beautiful, smart, funny and completely different from Emily. Jamie makes me feel liberated, young again and as if anything is possible, while Emily makes me feel secure, happy and grown up. With Jamie I don't have to worry about paying a mortgage, holding down a job with a tyrant for a boss or being a father. I'm free. I have no commitments, only desires. So now, whenever I talk to her, it's like I'm that me again. The old me. The young me. The pre-Emily-and-me me.

When we said goodbye, she said she couldn't wait to talk to me again. I felt the same, but I also felt like an absolute bastard. I want to make Jamie happy, but I can't. I want to be a good husband to Emily, but I'm not. I want everything, but at the moment, I'm risking ending up with nothing. How did this happen?

Am I a bad guy? I've always thought of myself as something of a new man. I consider myself sensitive with deep emotional layers and I always make sure Emily orgasms when we have sex. I've written poetry. I keep a diary. I help old ladies across the street and I'm always texting Emily to say how much I love her. Yet I'm embarking on the sort of debauched affair that typical bloody men with one track minds do every day of the week. The sort of men I loathe because they give the rest of us a bad name. When I hear about men cheating on their wives, I groan in displeasure and say how awful it is, how superficial they must be, but as it turns out, I'm just like them. The poetry, good intentions and promises mean nothing if you drop your trousers at the first pretty girl who comes along. It's disconcerting that I can reach my thirties with a very clear idea of who I am and then in a moment it can all come crashing down around me. Bugger.

THURSDAY, April 6th, 7.00 p.m.

In the lounge with Emily. Watching TV. Feeling much better. Able to put own socks on again!

I didn't fancy staying at home today and swapping more sex fantasies with Jamie so I went to the pub instead. I spent five lovely hours at The Alexandra, slowly making my way through seven pints, bangers and mash, ten cigarettes, the whole *Guardian* newspaper and a copy of the *Sun*. I watched a rerun of two Premiership games from the weekend and won and lost twenty quid on the fruit machine, before I hobbled home in time for dinner. A splendid day. I only wish Ben was there to share my new-found freedom with me. He sent another email today.

Harry you old slug, how's things? Katie and I are in Byron Bay. It's bloody lovely here. We swim, we dance, we drink and we shag like bunnies . . . it's paradise. How's life in the real world? Say hello to Emily from us. Speak soon. I may have some news. Ben & Katie x

News = bad news. He's probably not coming home, which is definitely not good news for me. I've been thinking about Jamie a lot. I can't seem to stop. I've been doing everything I can to keep myself busy, but she keeps popping into my head every five minutes.

8.00 p.m.
'Emily, I need to have sex now!'
  'Okay.'
  'That's it, I just had to ask?'
  'Yeah.'
  'Blimey, let's go.'

I dragged her upstairs and we were naked in two minutes. The sex was a marathon of gratification. We did things we haven't done for ages. Emily screamed in pleasure and I felt great, like a huge weight had been relieved from my testicles (it had). The only problem is I was thinking about Jamie the whole time. I'm a complete and utter wanker.

FRIDAY, April 7th, 10.00 a.m.

In the shed. Emily at work. Sunny. Squirrel outside and looking even fatter. Ali outside in his garden.

That was quite unexpected. I was taking a brief stroll in the garden this morning when I heard Ali calling to me over the fence. My first thought was to run. My second was that even though my back was feeling much better, I probably couldn't outrun Ali. My third thought was to hide, but he'd already seen me. It was time to face the music.

'Hello there,' I said far too loudly.

'Mr Harry, how are you?'

'Fine, fine, not too bad, you know, surviving. And you?'

'Oh yes, very good, very good. My family has finally joined me from Bradford.'

'Bradford?'

'Yes, I moved down here from Bradford alone. My wife and children stayed behind while my brothers and I got everything together.'

'Your brothers?'

'Yes. Gurdev, Satnam, Jagjit and Amrick. They've been staying with me. We've been living like refugees, Mr Harry, it's quite comical. But now my wife and children are here and the house is presentable.'

'Gurdev, that sounds . . . ?'

'Indian, yes, yes.' I suddenly had a very strange feeling. I'd been a complete knob.

'And you're not Muslim, are you?'

'Muslim? No, no, why would you think that? We're Sikh.' Oh. Dear. Lord. I have been a complete twonk. The poor man is no more a terrorist than me. 'We don't wear a turban, which confuses people as to our Sikh identity, Mr Harry, but I can assure you that we're definitely not Muslims. If you need proof I would be happy to show you my penis!'

'Your penis?!'

'Muslims are circumcised as an article of their faith, but I would be happy to show you that mine is very much as God intended,' Ali said and then started unbuckling his belt.

'No, no, you're fine. I believe you. I just, the name Ali sounded a bit, you know.'

'It's a nickname. I wore a turban to a fancy dress party once and the kids called me Ali Baba. It stuck. My real name is Alok.'

'Oh.'

'I meant to ask you, Harry, if you knew anything about the police visit we had recently? They also seemed to be under the impression that we were perhaps members of the Taliban.'

'No idea, sorry.' I'm a lying, racist bigot.

'Anyway, Mr Harry, no more talk of Muslims. I would like to invite you and your wife over tonight. We're celebrating my son's fifteenth birthday and having a bit of a house-warming party, if you would fancy it?'

'Oh, yes, of course, it sounds wonderful.'

'Fantastic, fantastic. We'll see you around seven?'

'Yes, seven,' I said and we both ambled off towards our respective gardens. I came to the shed to smoke and think about all the bad things I'd done.

11.00 p.m.

I can't remember the last time I had so much fun. The Sikhs really know how to throw a good party. The food was plentiful and incredible, but the jewel in the crown of the evening was when Mrs Crawley turned up. It was just past eight o'clock and the party was in full swing. Emily and I were having a marvellous time. The house was in complete contrast to the empty house I'd sneaked into before. Ali's wife Gajinder was lovely, as were the rest of his family. Most of the street was there, all except Mrs Crawley, who made an amazing entrance as Ali was bringing out the birthday cake.

'Terrorists!' she shouted, standing in the kitchen doorway, a crazed look on her wizened face.

Everyone in the room turned and looked at her. Someone turned the music off. It was deadly quiet.

'Excuse me?' said Ali.

'Terrorists, all of you!' continued Mrs Crawley. I wanted to say something but I was in shock.

'This is a birthday party for my son,' said Ali. He was handling the situation with quite a large amount of decorum. 'I'd appreciate it if you'd leave.'

'I'll leave when I'm ready,' said Mrs Crawley. 'I know what's going on here and it certainly isn't a birthday party.' To be fair, Ali was holding a birthday cake, which should have been the first clue. Then Mrs Crawley noticed me standing in the room. 'Harry, they got you too. This is worse than I feared. And Emily, oh my Lord. Terrorists. Muslim terrorists. I'll see you're all put away!'

'We are not Muslims; we're Sikhs,' said Ali.

'A likely story,' said Mrs Crawley. You had to admire her stubbornness.

'If you need proof, I would be more than happy to oblige,'

said Ali. Oh no. Surely he wouldn't do it in front of his entire family.

'And how are you going to do that?'

He was. The next minute Ali had his penis out and, fair play, he was definitely not a Muslim. Mrs Crawley screamed as Ali came towards her.

'Penis! Penis!' she screamed.

'Look at the foreskin,' Ali shouted after her as she ran away. We all followed them out onto the street where Ali continued after her. 'Look at the foreskin. How could this be a Muslim penis?'

'Terrorist! Penis! Terrorist! Penis! Terrorist! Penis!' shouted Mrs Crawley.

It lasted for about five minutes before Ali finally gave up. Mrs Crawley ran into her house, but we could still hear her screams long after she'd closed her front door.

SATURDAY, April 8th, 1.00 p.m.

In the lounge. Emily watching a film. Still raining.

It's parents' evenings all week and so I have to fill out pupil reports. I should have started this last week while I was incapacitated instead of participating in sexual game play with Jamie. Now I only have the weekend to write over a hundred bloody reports. This happens every year and every year I say I definitely won't wait until the last minute again. When will I learn? But more importantly, what have my pupils learnt? Here's a brief sample of the best ones so far:

'Peter would do a lot better if he actually showed up for class on a regular basis . . . or at all.'

'Carolyn is a popular pupil. She's always fun to have

around and always obliges with answers during class. She should do well provided she learns the correct answers.'

'Bryan is very quiet, which is probably why I didn't notice he was gone for a month during the first term. This has put him quite a bit behind the other pupils.'

'Mollie seems more interested in being popular than growing intellectually. Perhaps a career in politics.'

2.00 p.m.
'I'm bored,' Emily said, playfully punching me on the arm.

'If you're tired of London, you're tired of life.'

'I think I'm just tired of you.'

'Oh, very funny. Let's do something then.'

'Like what?'

'I don't know. What do you fancy doing?'

'Not sure. It's raining.'

'We can still go out somewhere.'

'But there's nowhere to go.'

'We live in London. There's a million places to go.'

'Like where?'

'I don't know, Em, but there's always tons of foreigners milling around every time we go anywhere. There must be something that attracts them.'

'Name one.'

'I don't know . . . the National Gallery?'

'Fine, let's go there.'

And so we did.

We spent our afternoon roaming the grand halls of the National Gallery in awe. We saw work by the Impressionists, the Post-Impressionists, the Pre-Raphaelites (although no-mention of the original Raphaelites), the Minimalists (just the one), the Post-Minimalists (very similar to the original Minimalists in my humble opinion), the Futurists and the

Fauvists. We saw a John Constable, a Van Gogh and a Claude Monet – it was like walking through a giant biscuit tin. It was quite an experience and the first time either of us had been inside the National Gallery (except to use the toilets).

My favourite part of the afternoon was just before we left. Emily and I were standing looking at an Impressionist painting, when an arty couple came and stood next to us. After a moment one of them started waffling on about the brilliant interplay of light and dark, the lyrical brush strokes, the fact it was painted 'en plein air' (in a terrible French accent) and how the composition was so avant-garde. Just before we walked away I said to Emily,

'Every time I see his work I just want to have a big old wank!'

The arty couple looked at me in horror while Emily burst out laughing. It was magical.

MONDAY, April 10th, 1.00 p.m.

First day back at school. I saw Miss Simpson in the staff room this morning and she gave me a very long and contemptuous stare. Rory was pleased to see me. He said that school without me was like the work of Marcel Duchamp, rubbish, and then he laughed. I didn't really get the joke but I laughed anyway.

TUESDAY, April 11th, 5.00 p.m.

In a pub near school with Rory. Second day of parents' evening.

'Are you still messing around with that Facebook girl?' Rory said over lasagne, chips and onion rings.

'Sort of.'

'What does that mean?'

'Well, yes, but . . .'

'Harry, there are no buts where infidelity's concerned.'

'But it's complicated.'

'Oh, is it. Please explain?'

'Well, you see it's like this,' I started, but I couldn't even attempt to explain how and why it was complicated. It just was.

'Shall I help you out?'

'If you like.'

'This girl is gorgeous. She's sexy, tells you how wonderful you are and that she wants to do things to you you've only ever seen in porn films. Meanwhile, your currently pregnant wife's gaining weight, not looking her best and the last time you had sex was sometime during the last millennium. You're having a mid-life crisis, even though you don't think you are and this coquettish little minx makes you feel young again.

'You really want to screw this girl, even though you know you shouldn't, but that little voice at the back of your head keeps telling you you'll regret it forever if you don't.

'You look at Emily and see security and happiness, but when you look at this internet angel, you just want to fuck her brains out. This is about as complicated as an American sitcom, i.e. not complicated at all. How was that?'

'Not bad, although you forgot about the bit where I really want to have sex with her. She has a dildo called Dirty Harry and she sent me a photo of herself with a cucumber, Rory, a bloody cucumber!'

'And you want you to be the cucumber.'

'In a manner of speaking, yes, but I also don't want to cheat on Emily.'

'And that's the choice you have to make, but if you want my advice, run away as fast as you can and don't look back. Cucumber or no cucumber, cheating is cheating and it will ruin everything.'

'Thanks, Rory,' I said and we finished our meals before we headed back to school to take on the parents.

10.00 p.m.

Another stellar night of parents defending their brainless, inept kids, while I attempted to explain that just because little Gordon eats his Brussels sprouts, it doesn't mean he's going to pass a single GCSE.

The night, however, was made bearable by our annual game of spot the MILF. The original idea was conceived by Alan Hughes (twenty-eight, single, Welsh and by far the filthiest man I've ever known). Parents' evening is held in the great hall (not actually that great) and every teacher has a desk and the parents wait in turn to speak to us. Alan Hughes, Rory and me then spend the evening all trying to spot the best-looking mothers. Points are awarded for best dressed, youngest-looking mum, best-looking mature, best pair of breasts, best bum, shortest skirt, most-visible breasts and for most make-up. We can also score additional points for getting a phone number and for the longest conversation.

So far Alan has won every year, mainly due to his no-fear banter, rugged good looks, penchant for very tight shorts and inability to see anything wrong with going up to a parent and saying things like:

'Your son has no athletic ability whatsoever, Mrs Miller, which is incredible considering his mum has the body of an angel.'

The highlights of this year so far:

Alan claiming the points for best mature and most-visible breasts on the same woman. We conceded because she was a stunner and any sudden movements would definitely have resulted in at least one breast popping out. For a moment, we considered setting off the fire alarm, but decided against it (Rory's the health and safety officer).

Rory talking to a girl for fifteen minutes before he realised she wasn't a parent but a pupil. 'It's so hard when they're out of uniform,' he said in his defence. Luckily, he didn't say anything incriminating to her.

I got the points for shortest skirt and most make-up and wished I hadn't (needless to say both were grotesque).

I was even propositioned by a single parent this year while Alan arranged to go home with one.

'Night lads. Give me an hour with this one and I'll be up to me nuts in guts,' were his parting words. The Welsh really are a filthy lot.

WEDNESDAY, April 12th, 9.00 p.m.

In the study. Emily watching TV in bed. Some awful American reality thing. Worst most awful desperate house-wives from Delaware, who live tawdry desperate lives and somehow got on TV. End of parents' night.

It's finally over. Three nights of parent/teacher hell, interspersed with spot the MILF, is over for another year. Alan Hughes won again. We told him because he's won three years on the trot he can keep the trophy (Rory made one in pottery class).

Jamie sent me two more messages today. I need to stop this before our trip to Italy. Rory's right. No matter how badly I want to have carnal knowledge of Jamie, I can't. And so I wrote her the following message.

Jamie, there's no doubt we have something special. It isn't just that you're sexy, want to cover me in oil, and unlike every other girl in the whole world, you admit to masturbating and have a friend called Dirty Harry! Of course, these drive me wild, but it's so much more than that. When I'm talking to you I feel alive. You make me feel like anything is possible.

I wonder what would have happened if we hadn't broken up after sixth form. Would we have stayed together, got married and be living happily ever after? I don't know, but what I do know is we can't keep writing to each other. As much as I enjoy it and as much as I love your photos, we can't be together and the longer we keep writing, the harder it's going to get.

I feel terrible for you. I want you to be happy. I wish it was me who could make you happy but it isn't. I'm sorry, but I think it has to be this way. It was fun. You're beautiful, sexy and wonderful and I'll never forget these moments we shared. Take care, Luv Harry XO

I pressed send, closed my laptop and joined Emily in bed.

THURSDAY, April 13th, 7.00 p.m.

Reply from Jamie.

I understand. It's been fun. Luv Jamie XO

I have to admit I was left feeling a bit deflated. After my rather heartfelt goodbye, I was hoping for something a bit more emotional, possibly depressed and certainly longer than a single line. We shared our deepest, darkest sexual desires and she sent me photographs of herself in positions usually only seen inside the covers of adult magazines, yet all she had to say was that she understood. Disappointed doesn't do it justice. It's over. Time to move on. Italy beckons!

FRIDAY, April 14th, 6.00 p.m.

In the kitchen. Eating a sausage roll. Emily upstairs packing. Just back from Dave's.

I went to get my holiday haircut and everything was back to normal. I walked in and there was Dave, sitting in his chair, reading the newspaper while Take That blared out from the speakers.

'Harry, welcome.'

'Dave, really happy to see you.'

'You too.'

'Is Troy around?'

Dave's face suddenly dropped into a frown.

'We had to let him go. Too many complaints.'

'He seemed keen though.'

'Too keen. He wanted to remove as much hair as possible on everyone.'

'Do you know what he's doing now?'

'He got an apprenticeship with a landscape gardener. It

should suit him down to the ground. He gets to cut grass all day.'

Then Dave went about his business with his usual professionalism. He gave me a great haircut and when I left, I gave him a two-quid tip and Dave thanked me a million times, 'Thank you, bye, thanks, take care, cheers, thanks again, bye then, see you later, ta, cheers, bye, thanks, cheerio . . .'

I could still hear him as I walked out onto the street. Brilliant. Life really is back to normal.

SATURDAY, April 15th, 8.00 a.m.
Day one of our Italian adventure

Cafe on the High Street. Emily's only having toast, while I'm having the heart attack special – double bacon, double sausage, double egg, hash browns, fried bread, mushrooms, tomatoes, black pudding, white pudding, beans, chips and a cup of tea.

'That's why you're going to die before me,' Emily said, looking down at my plate.

'Correction. This is why I'm going to die happily before you.'

'All of that grease and fat is disgusting.'

'Sorry, Emily, but I'm going to have to correct you again. It's the grease and fat which makes it delicious.'

'But you'll feel sick afterwards and want to lie down and complain you feel a bit dodgy.'

'And that's exactly what happened after the last time I did any exercise. At least I get to enjoy this first.'

'Sometimes I wonder why I married you.'

'Because I have an enormous penis?' Emily looked at

me in disgust while the lady at the next table gave me a wink and I could tell what she was thinking, 'Don't worry about her sunshine. I know you're an absolute legend between the sheets!'

Derek's picking us up at nine o'clock to take us to the airport. I wanted to get a taxi, but apparently he insisted. I haven't seen him since the Ali debacle. I wonder if he's still mad at me.

11.00 a.m.
Gatwick airport. He's still mad at me. The drive here was awkward, but the airport goodbye was even more uncomfortable. Derek and Emily gave each other a long hug and afterwards I went for the handshake but Derek completely ignored me.

'Oh, Daddy, don't be such a grouch, give Harry a handshake,' Emily pleaded.

Derek reluctantly agreed, but then went ahead and almost squeezed my hand off. I was relieved to get inside and past security.

11.45 a.m.
We board in fifteen minutes. Next stop Venice!

11.50 a.m.
The plane's been delayed by an hour. I'm also feeling a bit sick from my monster breakfast, but I can't tell Emily because she'll say she told me so and, to be fair, she did.

1.05 p.m.
Boarded (finally). Next stop Venice!

2.15 p.m.

Still on the runway. Emily's reading her baby book, *What to Expect When You're Expecting*. She keeps telling me interesting pregnancy facts.

'Did you know that during the third month my uterus is a little bigger than a grapefruit?'

'And at four months it will be the size of a melon.'

'And that during the fourth month the baby will develop fingerprints. Isn't that crazy?'

'They can also suck their own thumb. Imagine that.'

It isn't that I'm not excited about our baby and what's happening inside her womb, but I always get super nervous when I fly. My hands get all sweaty and I keep imagining the plane turning into a fireball during take-off (thanks *Final Destination*). So, as much as I want to talk about our baby and the size of Emily's uterus, all I can think about is our impending death.

Maybe I should read my own book, *The Bloke's Survival Kit for Being a Dad*. I'm currently on chapter ten, 'It's coming home, the baby's coming home'. Apparently, this is when us 'blokes' come into our element because the women have carried the baby for the last nine months, but now it's our time to shine, or as the book rather eloquently puts it, 'You've spent the last year playing for the reserves, you've been on the bench, but it's the cup final, you're one–nil down and you're on. It's Alan Shearer time!'

Inspiring stuff indeed.

8.00 p.m. (local time) Venice.

We finally made it. The plane didn't crash and we didn't die! We checked in to our hotel, the appropriately named Hotel Canal, which is (as you've probably guessed) right on the Grand Canal. Emily's taking a shower and then we're going out for dinner. Our first Italian dinner! I'm starving. It feels like a lifetime since my monster breakfast and they only served a very small packet of nuts on the plane.

SUNDAY, April 16th, 11.00 a.m.
Il secondo giorno

Ciao. Venice. At a real Italian cafe. Drinking real Italian espresso. Smoking real Italian cigarettes. Under real Italian sun. OK, that's going to get really annoying. Just assume everything's real and Italian from here on out. Emily's reading her tourist guide. Bloody happy.

It's a beautiful day. We're in Venice and I'm with Emily. What could possibly ruin this perfect day?

7.15 p.m.
Answer: A small yappy dog named Fofo.

We were strolling along the beautiful, ancient streets of Venice, heading towards St Mark's Square, when we encountered a wizened old woman with her yappy little dog. I took an instant dislike to them both. She looked like she hadn't smiled since 1954 and the dog looked like a canine version of Hitler. We stopped for a moment to look at our map and when we turned around, I stepped into a freshly laid yappy Fofo shit. It was enormous, sticky and all over my shoes. I swear the little fucker was laughing at me.

We were in the middle of Venice and my shoes were literally covered in Fofo crap and the flies were starting to swarm. Emily was having a good laugh at my expense and I was getting annoyed. Luckily, I managed to find a stick and remove most of the turd from my shoes, but for the rest of the day the smell of Fofo haunted me wherever we went. The little shit had ruined what would otherwise have been a dream day. It's not over yet though.

11.00 p.m.
In our hotel room. Naked. Waiting. Excited.

We had a lovely meal at a fantastic restaurant next to the canal. It was very romantic. I had my first sample of real Italian pizza and it was phenomenal. That's the last time I go to DialAPizza and order their meat feast with extra bacon and jalapeno chillies. We also had a really productive conversation.

'I'm sorry if things have been a bit weird recently,' Emily said.

'What do you mean?'

'I don't know, but I feel like we haven't been that close.'

'Maybe because I annoyed your dad.'

'No, it isn't that.'

'Or because I thought are neighbours were terrorists.'

'Nope.'

'Or because I wasn't that supportive about the baby.'

'No.'

'Or because you thought I was trying to rape your grandmother?'

'No.'

'Are you still annoyed about that time I dyed your hair blond and it came out looking a bit ginger? I explained before we started that I wasn't a professional colourist and you said you had faith in me.'

'I don't think it's any of that. I think it's been because of me.' This was a turn up for the books. I certainly wasn't expecting any sort of admission of guilt from her. Mainly because she hadn't done anything wrong. 'I think I've neglected you, Harry, and I'm sorry. Being pregnant is not an excuse, but I've been tired and not feeling well and I think I've let you down.'

I felt as guilty as a Catholic teenager buying his first pack of condoms.

'It isn't your fault, Em, you've been fine, honestly. If anything, it's been me.'

'But if I hadn't been neglecting you in the first place . . . Look, it doesn't matter now because I'm feeling better and I want to make it up to you,' she said with a mischievous grin.

'How?'

'I'm not wearing any underwear,' she said, crossing and uncrossing her legs opposite me. Blimey! 'And I've had a special sort of shave!' Double blimey!

'We should probably go back to the hotel.'

'Not yet,' she replied, rubbing her foot up and down my leg.

That was an hour ago. Since then I've been to sexual hell and back. I'm fit to burst. All over Venice we fornicated like a couple of randy teenagers.

The hotel room's dark, except for a few candles dotted around and Emily's in the bathroom. Oh, here she comes.

11.50 p.m.
Forty-five minutes of the best foreplay and sex we've ever had and the best bit, I didn't think about Jamie once. Off to sleep. Tired, delirious and dreaming about the tirade of pleasure Emily just showered upon my knob. Hooray!

MONDAY, April 17th, 3.00 p.m.
Day three of our Italian escapade

Venice. At a cafe. Smoking. Sipping on a cappuccino. Emily taking a nap. Italian girls frolicking in a nearby fountain while cool, sun-drenched guys ride mopeds around like fifties film stars.

I've been thinking about Jamie. I'm still a bit miffed about her goodbye message. After everything we shared that's how she chose to say goodbye? But then I started thinking that I shouldn't even care. Jamie and I are nothing. She's an ex-girlfriend who I had a bit of fun with. I hardly know her anymore. We haven't even spoken. So why does it bother me so much?

After a second cappuccino and a few more cigarettes, I realised why. It's because a part of me still wants her. I know it's ridiculous, but it's like when you're a kid and you see a brand new BMX in the shop window. Your parents say you can't have it (mine did) because you already have a perfectly good bike at home (but could I do wheelies on my racing bike, Dad?). Therein the analogy dies, but you get the idea. I had a perfectly good racing bike, but I wanted to pull the occasional wheelie and do a bunny-hop from time to time. You see that's the problem with bikes, you need more than one. Sometimes you really need a racer for those long journeys and sometimes only a BMX will do for the occasional bit of fun. I think the same probably applies to women.

TUESDAY, April 18th, 11.00 a.m.
Day four of our *piccolo soggiorno*

On the train to Florence. Eating a cheese and ham croissant. Emily reading her baby book. The countryside's so beautiful it's like taking a train ride through the renaissance.

8.00 p.m.
In our hotel. As we only planned on having one day in Florence, we did a whistle-stop tour of the best bits. We're off for a meal before an early night and then our train to Rome in the morning. *Buona notte.*

WEDNESDAY, April 19th, 1.00 p.m.
Giorno cinque

Rome. At our hotel. We're staying at a delightful little hotel called Hotel Villa del Parco, which is in a lovely little suburb of Rome away from the hustle and bustle of the city centre.

7.00 p.m.
We met another couple at the hotel. Andy and Ann from Sheffield (the double-A). They seem very nice. We're about to go out for dinner together. They've been here for a few days already and they offered to take us to a local Italian restaurant. It should be fun.

11.00 p.m.
It turned out Andy and Ann are swingers!

The evening started well. The double-A took us across the street to this little Italian ristorante. You could tell it was authentic because the menu was written in Italian and it was filled with Italians. Kids were running around, grandparents were sitting and talking and every conversation looked like the world's biggest argument.

As it was such a lovely evening, we decided to sit outside and watch the world go by. The food was superb and the double-A were great company. We drank lots of red wine and talked about everything and nothing. Andy was a teacher and so we had that in common and Ann and Emily both watched the same crap shows on television. However, the evening turned strange at about nine o'clock.

'I'm going to nip back and get my jacket,' said Ann. 'Harry, would you mind walking with me?'

Obviously this was a bit of a strange request. She could have asked Andy or she could have gone alone. However, we were all a bit tipsy and so I went.

Ann and I got back to her hotel room and she went inside to get her jacket. I was happy waiting outside, but she had other ideas.

'Why don't you come in?'

Again, a bit odd, but I went in anyway and this is when things got a bit racy. Ann disappeared into the bathroom and I loitered around the room when suddenly she reappeared ... NAKED! I was gobsmacked. I didn't know what to do. Did Andy know about this? Was he trying it on with Emily while I was away? What the fuck was happening?

Ann started coming towards me. She was quite attractive and had a great body, but I wasn't remotely interested in anything other than escape. However, just as I was planning my exit route, the door opened and in walked Andy and Emily! This was getting weirder by the second.

'What the fuck's going on?' said Emily, looking at Ann and then looking at me.

I think my face probably looked about as shocked and horrified as hers. Was Andy going to hit me?

Answer: No.

Instead he said in a very calm voice,

'It's alright, Emily.'

'Will someone please tell me what the fuck's going on?' Emily said again.

'We're all adults here,' said Ann provocatively. 'Why don't we have a little fun?'

At that point I think Emily and I both twigged what was happening. We had been swinged!

'I think we're going to leave,' I said walking towards Emily, but then things took an unexpected turn.

'Maybe we could stay for a minute,' said Emily.

'What?!' I replied.

The double-A looked on with expectant pleasure.

'It could be fun,' Emily said.

Had she gone barmy? What was she thinking? Did she want us to swing with the double-A? Andy was unbuttoning his shirt already. What was going to happen? Would he watch while I screwed his wife? Would I watch while he screwed my wife or would we all get naked and see what happened? Would I have to do anything with Andy? Did he have a bigger penis than me? I looked at Emily and my obvious look of distress caused her face to change. She started smiling.

'Sorry guys, only joking. Come on, Harry, this is really fucking weird.'

Then we both ran out of there as fast as we could and back to our room, falling onto the bed in hysterics.

'That was bloody cruel,' I said.

'What?'

'For a moment I thought you wanted to do the double-A.'

'You should've seen the look on your face, it was priceless.'

'Have you ever, you know, thought about doing something like that?'

'What? Sharing my years of hard work and training with another woman? You've got to be joking.'

'What do you mean, years of hard work and training?'

'When I first met you, you weren't exactly a professional in the sack, Harry. It's taken me time to tweak you and get you to do things properly. Don't look so sad.'

'At least I could find your clitoris when we first met.'

'Of course you could, love, of course you could.'

FRIDAY, April 21st, 8.00 p.m.
Day seven of our Italian romp

At a pizzeria near the Colosseum. Tired. Emily eating pizza. Last night in Rome.

After the double-A debacle, we spent the rest of our time in Rome doing the sights instead of our randy northern neighbours. We went to the Vatican (v. impressive), the Pantheon (v. v. impressive), the Trevi fountain (nice), the Forum, the Villa Borghese and, of course, the Colosseum. The whole place was incredible. We ate, drank and wandered around the streets like ordinary Romans.

We're both sad to be leaving, but we had such an incredible time and definitely reignited the passion in our relationship. We had sex like we haven't had since we first started dating. It was passionate, fun and, most importantly, I think it brought us closer together. It really feels like Emily and I are back on track again and the thing with Jamie was just a blip.

A silly, stupid, irrational blip, but a blip nonetheless. The Italian job . . . done! Arrivederci.

SATURDAY, April 22nd, 1.00 p.m.

On the plane. On the way home. Emily asleep on my shoulder. Everything's going to be alright. I think I'm probably too old for a BMX anyway.

TUESDAY, April 25th, 10.00 a.m.

In the shed. Eating a Scotch egg. Emily at work. Little squirrels running around the garden!

The squirrel must have been pregnant! It wasn't lovesick at all, but having babies.

Since Italy, Emily and I have been like a couple of silly teenagers. It feels like we found each other again, if that makes any sense. No more messages from Jamie. It's sunny. I still have five more days until I go back to school. Life's good. Off to visit Granddad.

3.00 p.m.

'Pork pies, Scotch eggs, little sandwiches, cheese and pineapple on sticks, maybe a salad, that sort of thing,' Granddad said when I asked him what food he's doing for the wedding. 'And, of course, Audrey's favourite.'

'What's that?'

'Jellied eels. She loves the bloody things.'

They've set a date for the wedding (Saturday, June 18th). They're going to get married at the home and it's caused quite a stir. Granddad's managed to convince them to let him hold the wedding in the garden. He's even managed to get the catering staff to put on a spread but he needs his best man to coordinate everything.

'Mrs Robinson in 3G, her son's a disc jockey and he's going to provide the music for free.'

'Righto.'

'And Audrey's Catholic, so we found a priest who'll come out, free of charge.'

'Of course.'

'And Norman Wilson reckons he can get his hands on a few doves.'

'Legally?'

'I don't ask questions, Harry. If he says he can get me doves, he can get me doves.'

'Fair enough. And what about your suit?'

'I need your help with that.'

'What do you need?'

'You're going to have to take me into town. Paul, who works here, his mate Benny Johnson, well his sister, Margaret, works in one of those wedding shops. He said she'd give me a deal. I just need you to take me in.'

'Of course, no problem. Just let me know when.'

'Will do. Oh and one last thing.'

'What's that, Granddad?'

'Did you give Emily the cunnilingus?'

'I did, Granddad.'

'And did it work?'

'Perfectly.'

'That's my boy,' he said, slapping me heartily on the back.

WEDNESDAY, April 26th, 4.00 p.m.

In the shed. Smoking. Drinking a cocktail (Ectoplasm!).
Sunny. Relaxed.

I've decided, against my better judgement, to give golf a bash.
Everyone raves about how relaxing and wonderful it is and
so on Saturday I'm going to trudge around eighteen holes
with Rory. Maybe golf will change my life.

THURSDAY, April 27th, 2.30 a.m.

Ben's engaged! I just got off the phone with him.

'Ben, its two o'clock in the bloody morning.'

'Sorry, mate, but I wanted you to be the first to hear the good
news.' I was still half-asleep and Emily was starting to stir.

'What's that?'

'I'm getting married!'

'That's terrific.'

'Thanks mate.'

'Although it would've been even more terrific if you'd got
engaged at a more suitable hour.'

'Alright, fair enough. Anyway, I've got more good news
and you're going to love this.'

'I'd better.' At that point Emily woke up and asked what
was going on. 'It's just Ben, he's engaged.'

'Oh, right, give him my congratulations,' she said and went
straight back to sleep.

'Emily says congrats. So, what's the better news?'

'We're getting married in England in September and
you're going to be my best man! Well, actually, joint best man
with Adam. What do you say?'

'Oh, mate that is good news. I can't wait and of course I'll be your joint best man.'

'I'm going to need your help with a few things as we're going to be over here until August, but I'm sure you can handle it.'

'No problem.'

Between Granddad and Ben, I'm going to have to create some business cards: Harry Spencer, wedding planner!

I couldn't get back to sleep after talking to Ben and so I had a cigarette by the back door. It's been a strange few months, what with one thing and another, but things are starting to get back on track again. Granddad's getting married, Ben's getting married, the squirrel had babies, Emily and I are happy again and I'm going to be a dad in about four months. I'm a lucky man indeed.

11.00 a.m.
In the study. Emily at work. Four days until I go back to school. A message from Jamie.

I really need to talk to you. Please call me and I'll
explain everything. Luv Jamie XO

Call her? Explain everything? Really needs to talk? What's going on? Fuck!

2.00 p.m.
I've spent the last three hours debating whether I should call Jamie or not. Despite all of our mucky messages, we haven't actually spoken yet and so this is taking things to the next level. I've decided to give her a call. What harm can come from a simple phone call?

2.45 p.m.

OMG! She's married! Everything she told me was a lie. Well, not everything, but the part about being single. She's been living in Greenwich for the last ten years. She's married to a policeman called Paul. She explained how her life has become so mundane and they don't have sex anymore and when I got in touch, she wanted to have some fun again.

At first I was angry, but then I felt sorry for her. She's clearly miserable and saw an affair with me as the only way out. I'm in shock. She asked to meet me for a drink. I said yes. We're meeting for lunch tomorrow at a pub in Greenwich. I realise this is probably a terrible idea, but she just wants to talk. I hope Emily doesn't ask what I'm doing tomorrow because I'll have to lie and I'm the world's worst liar. I always go bright red and start doing my best Hugh Grant bumbling Englishman routine, 'Well ... umm ... err ... argh ... yes ... you see ... umm ...'

11.00 p.m.

In bed. Emily fast asleep and snoring quite loudly. Emily asked what I was doing on my last day off before school. I lied and said nothing. I felt guilty, but I couldn't tell her the truth. Luckily, it was quite dark and so she couldn't see my bright-red face. It's OK. I'll meet Jamie tomorrow and then never again. It's a one-time deal. Just a drink, a chat and that's it.

FRIDAY, April 28th, 10.00 a.m.

In bedroom. In turmoil. In underwear.

I can't decide what to wear. I want to look good, but not too good. I want Jamie to still fancy me, but not too much. I want to smell good, but not too good and I want it to go well, but not . . . well you get it. I'm leaving in fifteen minutes and I'm standing in my underwear (not a good look).

3.00 p.m.
Back from Greenwich. Talk about difficult.

I arrived at the pub and because it was such a nice day, I got a table in the garden and started chain-smoking. Eventually, she arrived looking absolutely stunning. Unlike me (who couldn't decide what to wear), she'd obviously made the decision to look drop-dead gorgeous. She was wearing an above-the-knee skirt and a top which not only made her breasts look phenomenal, but as if they might pop out at any moment. I was in trouble. Every male head in the place turned as she walked in and then they looked at me with the same expression, 'You lucky, lucky bastard.' If only they knew.

'You look wonderful,' I said as she gave me a hug. A long, incredible, hug. I could feel her breasts pushing against me and so I had to sit down quickly to hide the sudden bulge in my trousers.

'You too,' she replied, sitting down across from me.

It was strange seeing her in the flesh, knowing I'd been masturbating to naked pictures of her and knowing she knew that. We talked for a while about the old days and what we've been up to since the last time we saw each other. The conversation flowed easily, almost like we'd never been apart. That's the thing with Jamie; it's always been like that. We have chemistry. Eventually, however, the conversation started getting a bit more delicate and difficult. Reminiscing was fun, but at some point we had to start talking about the things that mattered.

'I'm so sorry I lied to you, Harry.'

'I understand. It's fine.'

'I didn't want to, but I thought maybe if you thought I was single you might crumble and have an affair with me. I know it's so sad.'

'It isn't sad, it's . . .'

'It is, really sad, desperate, tragic, but it's not too late you know,' she said, leaning forward so I could see most of her breasts.

They were unbelievable. The bulge in my trousers had returned. I didn't know what to say. It was easier to say no when she was just an image on the screen, but now it was impossible. How could I say no to Jamie?

My Jamie.

My first love.

'But I love my wife . . .'

'I know and I still love Paul, but that message from you was like a light at the end of the tunnel. I'm not living the life I should be and I don't think you are either. Don't you ever wonder what would have happened if we'd stayed together?'

'Of course, all the time.'

'We would have been so happy.'

'I know and it kills me, Jamie. It kills me, but we both made choices.'

'Choices which can be undone . . . I hope. It isn't too late for us, Harry. We can still be happy together. We need each other. We need something more. Something a bit naughty and you know how naughty I am.' I did. 'Imagine all of the things we could do right now. God, I want you so much. My place is just around the corner . . .' She left it tantalisingly in the air.

I was in a state of shock. Had she lured me there just to have sex with her? The thing was I wanted to say yes. I suppose a part of me had hoped this would happen. I had dreamt about this moment for the last God-knows-how-many years. I had to say yes. However, I knew if I did this, my life would be different because it wouldn't just be the once. We could pretend it was just a one-off, but the sexting, the emails, the meetings would continue and before we knew it, we would be embroiled in an affair. My life would be fragmented. However, despite this, I still wanted to say yes. So, I did the only thing I could think of. I went and got another round.

'What's it going to be?' she said when I was sitting down again. 'And in case you're undecided, I'm not wearing any panties.'

This was my moment of truth. To fuck or not to fuck. To be a bastard or to be a good husband. I had no idea and she wasn't wearing any panties. Just hearing her say the word panties drove me wild with desire and lust. Looking across at her, I began to melt. I had to say yes. She was too gorgeous, too beautiful and our connection was too strong. It wasn't our fault. You can't help who you fall in love with. She was so full of life, love and laughter and she deserved to be happy. I needed time. I needed advice. I needed Rory.

'I need to make a quick phone call,' I said. I got up, walked back inside and dialled his number.

'Rory, I'm in a spot of bother.'

'Is it to do with your Facebook fling?'

'We're at the pub together, having a drink and she wants me to do things.'

'What sort of things?'

'Does it matter?'

'I suppose not.'

'What should I do?'

'I think the answer's pretty obvious, Harry. Get the hell out of there with your integrity and trousers intact.'

'I know, but it's so tempting. She's so sexy and I can't stop imagining her naked.'

'Here's the thing. It's just sex. She's gorgeous, yes, the sex will probably be great, but I guarantee when you finish, you'll feel terrible. You'll feel sick to your stomach and that feeling won't go away for a very long time. No matter how mind-blowing the sex, is it worth all of the pain?'

He had a point. I would feel awful. This was the rest of my life. The rest of Emily's life. The rest of our baby's life. The delicate balance of everything was teetering on a very sharp point.

'But it isn't just sex. I think we might be, you know.'

'Don't say it.'

'Falling.'

'Don't think it.'

'In.'

'I don't want to hear it.'

'Love.'

'For fuck's sake, Harry.'

'I know. If it was just sex, of course, I could say no, but it's more than that. Much more.'

'Then I can't help you. You're going to have to figure this one out on your own.'

'I know, thanks, mate.'

'No worries. Oh and while you're on the phone, do you and Emily fancy coming over for dinner next week? I thought it might be nice if the wives finally meet. We could have dinner, a few beers. Miranda does the most amazing pasta dish. It's literally to die for . . .'

'Not really the best time, mate.'

'Oh, right, well, just let me know.'

'Will do.'

I hung up and still didn't know what to do. Jamie was

sitting outside waiting for an answer. Was I going to cheat? Was I going to be That Guy? Could I look her in the face and say no? Could I look Emily in the face knowing what I'd done? It was impossible. Whatever I did, there would be regrets. Whatever I didn't do, there would be regrets.

Standing at the bar, I took one last look at Jamie waiting for me in the garden and made a decision. I was going to do a runner. It was the only way. If I stayed, something was definitely going to happen. I couldn't resist Jamie: she was just too beautiful and I wanted her too much.

I texted Jamie from the train station and apologised. I felt awful, but what else could I do? I had looked infidelity in the face and survived with trousers and dignity intact (just).

SATURDAY, April 29th, 6.00 p.m.

Home. Tired. In pain. Plasters on every finger. Emily watching telly. I despise golf.

Rory and I played golf today and to say I'm not a natural golfer would be an understatement. I lost thirty-seven balls and went around the course in one hundred and forty-two shots (seventy-two over par). I made holes in the fairways, hit someone with a ball and spent most of the time in the sand. Rory, bless him, was the world's most patient man, but even he was getting a touch disillusioned.

The day started off in wonderful fashion. We had a top-notch breakfast at the golf club before we set off to the first tee. It was a glorious morning, the sun was shining and I felt good. I mean, seriously, how difficult could it be? I took a few practice swings and everything seemed to be working. Rory went first and hit a beautiful drive that landed plumb in the middle of the fairway about two hundred or so yards in front of us.

'Lovely shot,' I said in my borrowed golf shoes and cap. I looked the part, at least.

'Remember, keep your head down, look at the ball and relax. Just a nice easy swing. Don't worry about hitting it hard. Just hit it. Nice and easy. It's all in the hips. Head down.'

'Gotcha. Shouldn't be a problem,' I said, limbering up.

I settled myself, looked long and hard at the ball. I eased into a flexible, easy swing before I completely missed the ball.

'Keep your head down,' said Rory behind me.

'Gotcha.'

I settled myself again. I took another swing and completely missed the ball again.

'Head,' said Rory behind me.

'Gotcha.'

I knew then it was going to be a long day. On the fifth attempt, I actually hit the ball. It went about ten yards (downhill).

'I hit it.'

'Yes you did. Only three hundred and forty yards to the flag now,' said Rory.

It didn't get a lot better. By the ninth hole I had blisters on all of my fingers.

'Should it be this painful?' I asked Rory while he eyed his second birdie of the day.

'Not usually.'

My hands were bleeding. By the eighteenth hole I was ready for a few beers.

'That's the last time I play golf,' I said to Rory in the clubhouse.

'Probably best,' said Rory.

I don't know what everyone sees in it. Dad says it's

relaxing and helps him unwind, but from what I can see it's hard, stressful, painful and about as relaxing as being forced into a car wash without a car. The allure of golf is vastly over-rated. Harry + Golf = Hell.

may

MONDAY, May 1st, 5.00 p.m.
Bank holiday

In the study. Eating an apple. Emily taking a nap on the sofa. Composing a message to Jamie.

Dear Jamie, I'm truly sorry for leaving so abruptly the other day. The truth is I was too tempted and I was worried I was going to do something I might regret. I should have told you in person, but I didn't know if I could say no to you. I'm weak. Sorry. Luv Harry XO

Is this a good idea? Probably not. Maybe I should leave it alone and do nothing, but I feel bad and Jamie deserves better than that. She's obviously very unhappy and so after a moment of dallying over the send button, I push it.

8.00 p.m.
Over dinner tonight Emily said casually, 'We have an appointment next Tuesday with that pregnancy therapist Steve and Fiona recommended.'

'Excuse me?'

This was the first time I'd heard anything about a pregnancy therapist.

'The one Steve and Fiona saw. I told you all about her. They said she was marvellous.'

'And why do we need to see a pregnancy therapist?'

'I thought it would be fun.'

'Fun?'

'It might be. Steve and Fiona both said . . .'

'Steve and bloody Fiona. You are aware we aren't Steve and Fiona.'

'Jesus, Harry, why do you have to be so negative about every little thing?'

'I'm not being negative, Em. I just don't see why we have to see a therapist when everything's perfectly fine.'

'Because it might help us. I think we both probably have concerns about being parents and it will be good to share those concerns in a relaxed, friendly environment.'

'And which pamphlet did you read that from?'

'This one,' she said, handing me a leaflet. 'Deidre St Cloud – Licensed therapist.'

'You want me to go and tell someone called Deidre St Cloud my deepest, darkest fears?'

'Exactly. The appointment's at five o'clock. Don't be late.'

Bloody Steve and Fiona. The last thing I want to do is open up about my childhood, repressed fears of homosexuality and oedipal fantasies to a woman I don't even know, with a ridiculous name. For the record, my childhood was fine, I'm not gay and I don't want to shag my mother. That should save us about an hour.

TUESDAY, May 2nd, 6.00 p.m.

A message from Jamie.

Dearest weak Harry, it's alright, I understand. The funny thing is I'm not usually like this. If you knew the regular me you would laugh to yourself. That's the trouble, Harry, I'm bored. My life is dull and you're the only excitement I have. When I saw you the other day I wanted you so badly. I wanted to go back to mine and have wild, animal sex. I'm sorry if I'm making your life difficult. I don't mean to and I understand if you don't want to keep in touch. It's been fun, but I suppose all good things must come to an end, right . . . ?

8.00 p.m.
I replied.

Thanks Jamie. I know this is difficult. When I was with you the other day I really wanted to say yes. I wanted to go back to yours and have wild, animal sex too. It would have been great, but we can't because it wouldn't be just the once. We would want to do it again and again and then what? Sorry. I wish things could be different, but you're married and I'm married. We'll just have to control ourselves. Luv Harry XO

THURSDAY, May 4th, 10.00 p.m.

In bed. A tad tipsy. Emily snoring like a champion.

We had dinner with Rory and his wife, Miranda (IT Manager), tonight at their Tooting flat. We arrived just before seven and Rory took our coats. Miranda was cooking in the kitchen while Rory gave us the abridged tour.

'This is the lounge, kitchen's over there.'

'Hi guys,' Miranda said through a cloud of steam.

'Here's the toilet, our bedroom's through there and that's the tour. Wine?'

'Please,' I said while Emily patted her tummy.

'Oh, right, we have soft drinks too,' said Rory.

A short while later and Rory and I were heading outside for a cigarette when Miranda said, 'While you're out there, Harry, can you convince him that having kids isn't the end of the world?'

I had a sudden sense of déjà vu. I didn't want to be like Steve. Was I already? Rory and I went outside and sparked up. I didn't want to ask but something inside of me just had to know.

'So, mate, honestly, why don't you want to have kids?'

'Oh, you're going to do this.'

'Humour me?'

'I'm just not ready. Whenever I think about being a dad, I feel sick to my stomach.'

'That's how I felt too.'

'And now?'

'Now I'm excited. The hardest part is deciding to do it. Once it's done, you just sort of get used to the idea.'

'But that's the thing, Harry, you didn't have to decide, I do.'

'Fair point, but I can tell you this. It isn't as scary as you think.'

'I think it's really bloody scary.'

'It's less scary than that.'

'Thanks. I'll think about it.'

'Miranda will be chuffed.'

'We'll see. You do realise you've become the epitome of the very thing we used to laugh at and mock.'

'I do.'

'Good, I just wanted to check you were fine with being that guy.'

'You know what, I think I am.'

And it's funny. When I think back to the conversation I had with Steve in January about having kids, I really wasn't ready. I thought he was a knob and that all parents were the most boring, annoying people in the world, but now I'm one of them. I have the t-shirt, the cap and the baby is in the mail.

The rest of the evening was fun, lively and we had a really great time. Unlike Steve and Fiona, they didn't only want to talk about kids and unlike Ken and Kara, they didn't act like they were seventeen. Rory and Miranda were just like us. Rory and I drank far too much wine for a school night, while Emily and Miranda got on like a house on fire. Maybe we've found our perfect hangout couple. It's hard as you get older because your single friends drift away into singledom, while other married couples change and you don't have as much in common anymore. When we left we all said we should definitely do it again soon and I'm pretty sure we all meant it. I know I did.

SATURDAY, May 6th, 1.00 p.m.

At IKEA. Emily determined to spend a fortune. Overcast. Eating a Swedish biscuit.

How can she spend four hours shopping? We got here at nine o'clock this morning. We had the cheap as chips breakfast (actually it was cheaper than chips), but since then Emily's been doing her best to maximize our credit card potential, i.e. she's bought most of the shop. Admittedly, most of it is for the baby, but still four hours is a long time to spend anywhere and I like IKEA. I enjoy the little faux-rooms and I like trying out the beds, but after four hours even I'm bored bloody stiff.

She's currently looking at kitchen items. She thinks we

need all new knives, forks and plates. I'm staying out of it. Never argue with a pregnant woman. I long to be at home, drinking a cocktail and smoking a cigarette in the shed.

For the record, Swedish biscuits taste just like English ones.

1.15 p.m.
Emily's mad at me. She asked what I thought about two sets of identical plates.

'They look exactly the same,' I replied wisely to show I was definitely paying attention. This was obviously some sort of test.

'But they're completely different, Harry.'

'But I thought— Oh, never mind. Fine then, that one.'

'For fuck's sake, Harry, if you don't care just tell me.'

'I do care.'

'No you don't. You don't care about anything. I could buy paper plates and you wouldn't give a toss.'

'It would save on washing up.' Another example of my poor comic timing.

'I don't know why I bother.'

Then she stormed off and started looking at rugs. I'm sitting by light bulbs. Why do trips to IKEA always end up in arguments? The last time we came we had a disagreement about a towel rack and now it's plates. It's no wonder Sweden has such a high suicide rate.

SUNDAY, May 7th, 9.00 a.m.

Email from Ben.

G'Day you little ripper! It's been a busy few weeks. I hope all's well in the house of Spencer. Katie and I have been to Surfers

Paradise, Frasier Island, Airlie Beach, been on a three-day boat cruise of the Whitsunday Islands, spent five magical days on beautiful Magnetic Island, went scuba diving on the Great Barrier Reef, did a tandem parachute jump and hiked rainforests in Cape Tribulation. It's been immense. I'll call soon so we can talk about the wedding. Miss you mate. Ben and Katie over and out x

Very bloody jealous. Ben is living la vida loca, while I'm having silly arguments in IKEA over cutlery.

MONDAY, May 8th, 10.00 p.m.

In bed. Emily fast asleep. Drinking hot chocolate.

Granddad rang me tonight. He doesn't call me that often and so I was slightly concerned.

'Hello, Harry.'

'Everything alright, Granddad?' I heard giggling in the background. 'Who's that?'

'It's Audrey.'

'Oh, right. Are you OK?'

'Never better, Harry, never better. I just wanted to say,' he said and then stopped and started giggling.

'Are you drunk, Granddad?'

'No, never, no, no, not drunk, Harry.'

'Then what's the matter? Why did you call?'

'Because I wanted to say I love you, Harry.'

'I love you too, Granddad.'

'Audrey wants a word,' said Granddad and then I heard him handing the phone to Audrey. In the background I heard some whistling, then some rustling and then I thought I heard what sounded like a duck.

'Harry?'

'Hello, Audrey.'

'Your grandfather's a wonderful man.'

'I know.'

'He's kind, generous and so very giving.'

'He is.' Audrey sounded drunk too.

'He also has a very large penis!'

'That's nice.'

'Oh, it is nice, Harry, very nice. I'm going to put him back on the phone now. Nice speaking with you.'

'Yes, you too, Audrey. Take care.'

'Ah, Harry, it's me again.'

'What's going on, Granddad? Have you been drinking?'

'Certainly not, although I do have a favour to ask.'

'What's that?'

'Would you mind stopping by with some snacks? Audrey said she would really like a pork pie and I would like a bag of chips from George's. Don't go to Neil's Plaice on the High Street. Their chips are no good, Harry. Too greasy.'

They were asking for food. They sounded drunk. They were giggling for no reason. They were stoned!

'Granddad, are you and Audrey high?'

'As a kite, Harry, and it's wonderful, except we're really, really hungry. What's the word on the food?'

'Granddad, it's almost ten o'clock on a school night.'

'The night's young, Harry.'

'Not for me – I'm off to bed. Please make sure you drink plenty of water before bed. I'll call you in the morning. Love you.'

'Never stop believing!' Granddad shouted and then he was gone.

TUESDAY, May 9th, 9.00 a.m.

What do you get if you add me, Rory, thirty-two teenage kids, a coach and a coach driver who looks like Ronnie Corbett together? Answer: A school trip to Hampton Court Palace. Rory wasn't supposed to come, but Eddie Collins (other history teacher) is off sick (roaring alcoholic, probably lying in a pool of his own vomit) and so Rory volunteered. This is perfect because once we dump the kids off, I know a nice little pub around the corner.

12.15 p.m. (in the pub)

Rory asked about Jamie and I told him everything. I even told him about the sexting. He told me sexting was just a Welcome Break on the motorway to infidelity. Maybe he's right. I need to stop.

3.00 p.m.

We could be in trouble. Rory and I were ten minutes late getting back, which would have been fine if two of my pupils hadn't insisted on setting off the fire alarms and having the whole place evacuated. Rory and I were walking back to Hampton Court just as hundreds of people were filtering out. Some of my pupils were sitting on the ground waiting for us, some were fighting and two were missing.

'What the hell's going on?' I asked.

'Matt McDonald and Paul Hardy, sir. They set off the fire alarm and we all got kicked out, innit.'

'And where are Sean Graves and Sally Onslow?'

'Doing it, sir.'

'Doing what?'

'You know, sex, sir. They went that way,' the pupil pointed off towards the Thames.

'Right, you all stay here. Mr Wilkinson and I will go and find them. Phillips, you're in charge.'

Rory and I headed off towards the river and we soon stumbled across Sean and Sally going at it under a tree. Luckily, Sean wasn't very skilled in the art of removing bras otherwise things could have been much worse. We finally rounded everyone up and we were let back into Hampton Court.

Tonight's our first therapy session with Deidre St Cloud.

I'm dreading it.

9.00 p.m.
Oh. Dear. Lord. It was worse than I feared. Emily, of course, thought it was bloody brilliant. Deidre St Cloud's a nutter. She is late thirties/early forties and looks like she spent the last twenty years at a hippie retreat in North Wales. I half expected her to roll up a joint, get out a guitar and start playing Bob Dylan songs. It was like being at a really bad university party.

She wanted us to talk about our deepest, darkest feelings and fears and about what it meant to be parents. She asked about our relationships with our own parents and we had to workshop typical parent/child situations. It was awful. Emily's annoyed because she said I didn't take it seriously. I mean, how could I take this seriously?

Deidre: Harry, I want you to imagine you're the baby, yeah. What would you like to say to Emily?

Me: Excuse me?

Deidre: I know it's a bit strange, yeah, but just go with it, yeah. Imagine you're the baby, yeah. Emily's holding you, yeah. She's taking care of you, nurturing you, yeah. What would you like to say to her? And Harry, I want you to look at Emily, yeah. OK, now go.'

I turned to Emily. What was I supposed to say? I didn't know what she wanted from me.

'Thanks.'

'And?'

'Good job.'

'For Christ's sake, Harry, I've been carrying you for nine months and that's all you have to say?' Emily said, annoyed.

'Come on, Harry, really open up, yeah,' enthused Deidre.

'Great womb,' I said, which only made Emily even angrier.

'You see what I have to deal with?' she said to Deidre, who just nodded annoyingly.

'Harry, what are you afraid of?'

'I don't understand.'

'What's behind the humour? Is it a defence mechanism? Do you have commitment issues? Tell me about your relationship with your mother?'

I bloody knew it. It always came back to fucking Freud.

'I'm sorry to disappoint you, Deidre, but I don't want to fuck my mother.'

'No one's saying you do, but we can talk about that if you'd like.'

'Look, I'm sorry, Deidre, but I don't think this is for me, yeah,' I said, getting up. Emily looked at me in disgust.

'When you're ready to talk, I'll be here, yeah,' Deidre said in the same conceited tone.

Emily and I barely talked on the way home. I tried to apologise, but she said she was too tired to fight. I said I didn't want to fight but this only made her angrier. We got home and she went straight to bed. This is the trouble with therapy, it makes people angry.

Unfortunately, we have another appointment next week.

WEDNESDAY, May 10th, 9.00 p.m.

At home. Emily asleep. Eating a mini sausage roll and watching a repeat of *Gavin & Stacey* in bed.

I was forced to pop over to Steve and Fiona's after work today. I had to go and pick up some baby clothes, books, toys and other paraphernalia Emily deemed too important to wait. Hence, at five-thirty, instead of relaxing at home watching *Neighbours*, I was sitting in Steve and Fiona's lounge watching telly with the oldest J, Jane.

I asked her what she was watching. It was a kid's programme I'd never seen before, which wasn't that surprising considering the last time I watched children's TV was some time around the early nineties. The programme had no resemblance to the shows I watched as a child and frankly it was quite disturbing.

My memory of watching shows like *Rainbow*, *Button Moon*, *Dogtanian and the Three Muskahounds* and *Blue Peter* was that they were wonderful, educational, innocent and somehow better. The show Jane was watching was awful. It was too loud, too much was going on, the content seemed inappropriately adult and I couldn't stand the idea of my baby watching this rubbish. Jane seemed to be enjoying it though.

I started thinking about my own baby and, for some illogical reason, I want them to have the same idealistic childhood I did. I don't want them to have a mobile phone by the age of five, play videos games and to watch this American rubbish on the telly. I want them to play football or ride their bike in the park after school. I want them to watch the same classic shows I loved so much.

Children nowadays spend their entire lives glued to small

screens, texting their mates or playing computer games for hours on end. Most of them never pick up a book or play in the park. They go to the park but only to smoke, smash bottles, graffiti things or snog each other, but none of them are actually playing.

Is it a sad indictment of our times or a sad indictment of me? Am I just a sad old git living in the past? Probably, but what's wrong with that? The past was better. Jane is only seven, but already she's wearing earrings, has on the latest fashion and has posters of boy bands on her wall. Seven years old and she's already wiser in the ways of modern culture than me. I have no idea who half the people on telly are nowadays and it takes me half an hour to type a simple text (fat fingers), but I don't care because it isn't my world.

Unfortunately, I know the little life growing inside of Emily's belly is going to change all of that. I fear that instead of them embracing the life I crave, I will be forced to embrace the life they want.

'Here you go,' said Fiona, dumping two big bags of stuff on the floor.

'Thanks.'

'No problem, it's just sitting up there and we have so much stuff already.'

'Can I ask you a question?'

'Sure.'

'How do you cope with her watching that?' I pointed to the telly.

'Oh, yeah, not exactly *The Wombles* is it? It's life now. You can argue until you're red in the face, but the reality is they're going to watch it regardless. We do our best to make sure what she watches is age appropriate.'

'This is suitable?'

'Compared to some of the other rubbish, yes.'

'Blimey.'

'Things have changed a lot since we were kids, Harry. I had this idea our kids would be just like us but they're not. They're wiser, older, more aware and sadly by the age of seven already lost to the great marketing machine from across the pond.'

'That's sad.'

'That's life.'

It seems I have a lot to learn about being a parent.

THURSDAY, May 11th, 10.00 p.m.

In bed. Eating a packet of Twiglets. Emily asleep.

Why is life so bloody complicated? Life should be like football. It should be fast, fun, entertaining and surprisingly easy to play. Instead it's like cricket. It seems easy enough until you actually start doing it and then it just gets more and more complex. Even to this day I still don't fully understand the follow-on rule in test cricket.

Why am I talking absolute bollocks you may ask? Jamie sent me a message asking if we could meet up again. She says she needs to see me and wants to meet at her house on Saturday. Why is she doing this to me? What am I going to do? The obvious answer would be to say no, definitely not. However, and here's the follow-on rule, I want to go. I don't fully understand why, it makes no sense and my life would be much easier if I didn't, but I just need to know. I need to know what it would be like to be with her again. I think if we did it just once that would be enough. After all the sexting, the mucky messages and filthy photos, this would put everything to bed (literally). I need more time to think about it.

And so, with thoughts of shagging Jamie and the intricacies of cricket, I'm off to bed.

FRIDAY, May 12th, 6.00 p.m.

Me: Could I cheat on Emily?

Brain: You shouldn't.

Me: That isn't what I asked.

Brain: I realise that.

Me: Well?

Brain: I think you could.

Me: I don't want to, but it's too tempting. Jamie's too tempting and it's just sex.

Brain: Right, just sex.

Me: What does that mean?

Brain: Isn't that what all bastard men say to excuse their general weakness? It's pitiful.

Me: Thanks.

Brain: What do you want me to say? Go on, shag her senseless, it's fine, Emily won't mind.

Me: Of course not.

Brain: If you sleep with Jamie, everything will be different . . . for the both of us.

Me: I know, but I can't say no. I don't want to hurt Emily. I love her so much.

Brain: But not enough to turn down a quick romp in the sack with Jamie.

Me: Apparently. I feel awful. Why am I so weak?

Brain: Because you have that thing down there. Brain number two. If you listened to me you would be alright, but oh no.

Me: OK, I get it.

Brain: Just remember that Emily's your wife. You agreed to be together in sickness and in health, until death do you part.

Me: I know.

Brain: Not until sex do you part.

Me: Thanks, brain, I realise that, but I don't see any other way out of this.

Brain: I could give you one.

Me: I'm sure you could, but this isn't about you. If I was just a brain my whole life would be different, but I have a heart.

Brain: And a penis.

Me: Yes and a penis. But that's the thing, if my life was left up to you, I wouldn't have married Emily in the first place. We wouldn't even be having this discussion.

Brain: Well, yes, but.

Me: No buts. If it was up to you, I'd still be single, living in a sexless state of boredom, playing Tetris night and day.

Brain: It's a great game.

Me: It is, but it isn't life. Life's about emotion, passion, love, relationships. Everything you don't consider important. I don't know why I asked for your advice in the first place.

Brain: Neither do I.

Me: Fine, well, goodbye.

Brain: Bye.

I've decided to meet Jamie tomorrow. I know it's wrong. I know I shouldn't and will probably regret it forever, but I can't help myself. I have to do this. I need to know.

SATURDAY, May 13th, 9.00 a.m.

In the bathroom. Getting ready to possibly have wild, animal sex with Jamie. Emily downstairs. Feeling quite nervous and very guilty.

The day of deceit, dishonesty and deception is finally here. I feel sick to my stomach. Why am I doing this? I told Emily I had to pop into school for a few hours. I was expecting her to ask why, but she nodded and said fine. I was sweating buckets. I thought she would see straight through me but she didn't. I think I might throw up. I'm not equipped to live the life of a philanderer. I've showered, trimmed excessive hair from various regions of my body, put on my best underwear and applied a little bit of Hugo Boss magic.

10.00 a.m.

I almost blew it. I was in the bathroom putting the finishing touches to my little ensemble, when Emily walked in.

'You're getting a bit dressed up for school.'

'Oh, you know, just fancied making an effort.'

'Should I be worried?'

Fuck. She suspected something. It was written all over my face. Of course it was. I'm a terrible liar. The world's worst. The game was up. I had to tell her. I'M GOING TO SHAG MY EX-GIRLFRIEND, OK!

'Unless you're worried about me and Rory,' I said limply, hoping and praying she wouldn't see straight through me.

'He is an art teacher.'

'I'll tell him that.'

I laughed like the cold-hearted evil bastard I am.

11.00 a.m. (Greenwich)

I suddenly have a pang of last-minute jitters. What if this is terrible? What if I can't perform or it's just bloody awful? It's one thing to write paragraph after paragraph of smut, but actually doing it is a lot different. It's like watching porn and having sex; the reality is a million miles from the fantasy. I'm not a stud. I can't have sex while standing up (tried and failed). I don't have a large, hairless penis and a great body (average, hairy, blindingly white and out of shape) and doing it from behind always ends up with Emily getting bored and asking, 'What the hell are you doing back there?'

Why did I think I could do this when quite clearly I can't? However, another part of me is thinking the exact opposite. What if it's incredible? What if it's the best sex I've ever had? What if with Jamie I am a porn star stud? I guess there's only one way to find out. I need to walk across the street and knock on her door. I take a deep breath and begin the march of madness. I'm actually going to do it. I'm going to cheat on Emily.

4.30 p.m.

In the hospital. Emily asleep. I'm a wreck.

The worst thing happened. I was about to walk across the street to have sex with Jamie when Emily rang. She was in pain. She was bleeding. She was crying hysterically. She needed me. She'd called an ambulance. I had to meet her at hospital. She was sorry. I was suddenly stone cold with fear. Could we lose our baby? Had we already? What was I doing? I was about to commit adultery and my wife was lying on the floor at home, possibly having a miscarriage and I wasn't there. I wasn't there. I hated myself. I cried for a moment and then started running.

I rushed to the hospital, ran down corridors and into her

room. She was crying, I was crying and everything went white and I couldn't hear. All she could say was, 'I thought I'd lost our baby, Harry. I'm so sorry. I thought I'd lost our baby.'

I held her and didn't ever want to let go. The doctor was talking to us but I didn't hear a word. I was too busy thinking about what an idiot I'd been. How could I have been such a fool? I could have lost everything today but I hadn't. I'm the luckiest man in the world and I'm never going to take this for granted again. Jamie is done. I want to be a good husband. A good human being and, above all, a good father.

'Your baby's fine,' the doctor said when I finally came back to reality. 'We ran some tests but they're fine. This sort of thing happens from time to time, but nothing to worry about.'

I've never felt such relief in all of my life. I watched Emily sleeping for hours and thought about how beautiful and wonderful she is and what a stupid, immature idiot I have been.

9.00 p.m.
I texted Jamie and explained everything. She said she was sorry. She said she understood if I wanted to cool things off for a while, but I told her it was over. I can't be That Guy anymore and if the truth be told, I'm not sure I ever was.

SUNDAY, May 14th, 1.00 p.m.

Back at home. Emily's parents visiting. Making tea.

I had a really good chat with Derek today. He apologised for being angry with me and I said sorry for making him look like a prat in front of the police. We're friends again and he even invited me to play golf with him soon. I didn't mention about my golfing disaster with Rory, but still, I'm back in the family circle again.

I also had a great chat with Emily this morning. I explained I was sorry for being a terrible husband, for not taking the therapy seriously, for not being there for her and for being immature and stupid. I told her I was going to grow up, stop masking my insecurities with humour and that I was going to be the best husband and father she could ever wish for. Perhaps the conversation began because of guilt, but I meant every single word. It's time to change. Time to grow up. Time to become a man.

It sounds so trite, but I suppose these feelings and phrases become clichés because they're true. If life really is just a series of moments, then this is one of those big, defining ones. Martin Luther King had a dream. Winston Churchill wanted to fight them on the beaches. I just need to stop dicking about and grow up. Simple.

TUESDAY, May 16th, 7.00 p.m.

In the lounge. Emily watching *Mistresses*. Eating ravioli on toast.

It was our second session with Deidre St Cloud tonight and it was marginally better than the first. Perhaps because I was taking it seriously or maybe because she didn't ask such ridiculous questions (or mention my mother).

We talked about being parents, our fears, hopes and dreams and I even 'opened up' according to Deidre and took, 'big emotional steps'. It still felt like a big bunch of hippy bullshit, but at least we got through it and Emily was happy.

We have one more session next week before we graduate.

Deidre said that when our emotional journey was over, our physical one could begin and we could toss aside the shackles of repression that stop us from developing a true family oneness. Is this why Steve and Fiona are so bloody annoying? There was one point when I had to use every ounce of restraint I had when Deidre said (and I'm not making this up), 'Harry, yeah, you have to think of you and Emily as one giant breast, yeah. The baby needs to suck on the nipple of that love, yeah.'

Maybe I had taken 'big emotional steps' because I didn't burst out laughing or say anything sarcastic.

WEDNESDAY, May 17th, 10.00 a.m.

Miss Simpson called me into her office this morning. I walked in and could immediately tell from the look on her wrinkled face that it wasn't good news.

'I just had a very interesting conversation with a man from Hampton Court.'

'Oh yes.' I tried to play it cool and nonchalant but I knew what was coming.

'And when were you going to tell me about the incident?'

'By the incident, you mean . . .'

'The fire alarm, Mr Spencer, the fire alarm. Was there more than one incident?'

'No, no, just the one.'

'Please explain why I wasn't informed of this?'

'Well, Rory, I mean Mr Wilkinson, and I handled it and we didn't think you needed to be involved.'

As soon as I said this, I wanted to take it straight back but it was too late. She pounced on me like a lion attacking a baby gazelle.

'Oh, I'm sorry Mr Spencer, but am I to understand you think I'm not needed and that you're somehow qualified to run the school without me?'

'Of course not, what I meant was . . .'

'Well, that's what it sounded like. Let me be the first to tell you, Mr Spencer, that I'm in charge of this school and I'll be the one dishing out punishment. As I'm sure you're aware, we have to foot the bill for the fire alarm so I'll be conducting a full investigation of events. No stone will be left unturned. Is there anything you want to share with me now while you still have the chance?'

'I don't think so. Mr Wilkinson and I were there the whole time. Unfortunately, while we were engrossed in the tour, two of our pupils decided it would be fun to set off the fire alarm. Both were given two weeks' detention and a severe talking to.'

'Right, well, both will be suspended forthwith for two weeks. Please send in Mr Wilkinson and let it be known that if I find any blame whatsoever on your doorstep, Mr Spencer, there will be repercussions. Do I make myself clear? Repercussions!'

'As always, yes.'

'Then get out of my sight.'

I'm in deep shit.

I told Rory to tell her we never left Hampton Court. I can trust him, but Miss Simpson's a scary and manipulative old bag. She'll probably torture him until he speaks. I had better start looking for a new job.

On a lighter note, tomorrow we find out the sex of our baby. It will grow up penniless and in a shed once I lose my job, but at least it can suck on the nipple of our love when it gets a bit peckish.

THURSDAY, May 18th, 6.30 p.m.

At home with Emily. Cuddling on the sofa and rubbing her belly.

It's a boy! Tom William George Spencer. It's crazy when you find out the sex because suddenly you feel so much closer to them. It isn't just a baby anymore but a little boy. We can start decorating his room and buying him clothes. I can talk to him and call him Tom. I'm so happy. Emily's so happy. All that nonsense with Jamie feels like a lifetime ago. What was I thinking? How could I jeopardise all of this for a quick shag? Of course, it was about more than just sex. It was about clinging onto the past and trying to be something I'm not. Either way, I'm glad it's over and I can focus on Emily and little Tom now.

SATURDAY, May 20th, 4.30 p.m.

Just back from another eye-opening visit with Granddad. Emily in Kingston upon Thames. Raining. Weatherman said possible chance of rain in the north-east. He obviously didn't do well at geography as we live in the south you fool!

'I need to go into town and get my suit,' Granddad said when I arrived. He was already dressed and ready to go. 'I spoke with the girl yesterday. She's expecting us.'

I love Granddad dearly, but I was dreading taking him into town. Granddad gets distracted very easily and it takes him a million years to do anything. A simple trip to pick up his suit could take all day.

'New car?' said Granddad as we got into the same Volkswagen Jetta I've had for the last ten years.

'No, Granddad, same one.'

'German.'

'Yes.'

'Good cars. Last a lifetime.' And so it began. 'That's changed. I see that's closed down. That pub's different. Look at the state of her. It's not like it used to be. Is that old Paul Jessup? No it can't be, he died five years ago,' Granddad said as we drove through town. Then the conversation went from the mundane to the ridiculous. 'Audrey's got this book, Harry.'

'Oh yeah.'

'A sex book!' Granddad exclaimed. I was so shocked I almost crashed the car. 'It's got filthy pictures and things I've never even heard about.'

What could I say to that?

'That's nice, Granddad.'

'We're on page thirty-two at the moment.'

'And what's that?'

'We get to do it outdoors!'

Luckily, we were almost at the shop, so I quickly changed the subject before he carried on and gave me the lurid details. I asked how the wedding preparations were going. Granddad said that Norman Wilson had come through with four doves and possibly a fifth, and his Scottish mate, Willie McDougal, was going to play the bagpipes.

We went in and got measured for our suits and like every-thing else it had a bit of a hush-hush, under-the-table feel about it. At one point the girl said, 'We have to be quick, my boss will be back soon,' which didn't make me feel comfort-able that what we were doing was strictly by the book. We got measured and our suits will be delivered to the home on the morning of the wedding.

On the drive back, I asked him how he always got

everything on the cheap, but in typical Granddad style he just looked at me and smiled, 'I could tell you stories that would blow your mind, Harry.' And I got the feeling he probably could.

TUESDAY, May 23rd, 8.00 p.m.

In bed. Naked. Waiting for Emily.

Deidre St Cloud is a genius. Those are words I never thought I'd be writing in my diary. She may look like a reject from the sixties and ask us to do things which seem to be stark raving bonkers, but after three sessions I think I've changed. I don't think I've quite taken the 'emotional bull by the metaphorical horns' as she claims, but I do feel closer to our baby and more prepared to be a father. However, the reason she's a genius isn't because of her psychoanalytical expertise, but because tonight she spoke about the need to keep me happy sexually during the pregnancy. She rather eruditely told Emily, 'Harry's a giant penis, yeah. He needs constant stimulation, yeah. Love him and make him happy, yeah. A happy, joyful, fully appreciated penis is crucial to every relationship and being pregnant is not an excuse, yeah. He has needs you and I will never fully comprehend, yeah. Embrace the penis and don't be afraid to take it orally, yeah.'

Bloody genius. Here comes Emily.

8.30 p.m.
Emily wasn't afraid to take it orally!

WEDNESDAY, May 24th, 1.00 p.m.

At school. Rory and I are holding firm with our story about Hampton Court. Miss Simpson keeps popping into my room and watching me. She sits at the back of the class taking notes which is very off-putting for my pupils.

'Why's Miss Simpson in class, sir?' said Liam Hobbs (class idiot).

'No reason. Just pretend she isn't there and concentrate.'

'But, sir, sir, she's sitting right behind me. Are you in trouble, sir?'

'No, Hobbs, no one's in trouble.'

'Then why's she taking notes, sir?'

'Just look at me and listen.'

'But I can hear her breathing, sir.'

The morning was a nightmare. As much as I'm dreading going on holiday with Steve and Fiona, it can't be any worse than this.

FRIDAY, May 26th, 5.00 p.m.

In the shed. Smoking. Drinking a cocktail (Slippery Nipple!). Squirrels running around the garden. Emily packing.

I made it! That was one of the longest weeks of my life. Miss Simpson's determined to find proof I lied about Hampton Court. It appears she wants me gone. What did I do to deserve this? At least I have a week off now and I get to spend seven days with Emily, Steve, Fiona and their troop of Js in a small cottage in Cornwall. This should be interesting.

SATURDAY, May 27th, 7.00 a.m.

In the lounge. Looking out of the window. In a blind panic. Emily still asleep.

I got a text from Jamie this morning.

Paul knows everything. He found the emails and photos. I had to tell him. He said he's going to find you and tell your wife everything. So sorry.

I don't know what to do. I thought it was over. I've been frantically trying to work out if he could even find me. I never gave Jamie my address, but her husband's a policeman and she had my phone number. Could he find my address from that? I don't know what to do. We leave in two hours, but what if he turns up before then?

8.30 a.m.
Still no sign of Paul. Emily eating breakfast. This is awful. I am a sickly fish bobbing about in the sea of fate and Paul is a shark just waiting to gobble me up.

9.05 a.m.
Steve, Fiona and their group of Js were here exactly on time. It looks like I'm going to escape the clutches of Paul. At least it will give me a week to figure out what to do next. Time to load up the car and get going. Deep breaths, Harry.

4.00 p.m.
Newquay, Cornwall. Smoking a cigarette. Steve, Fiona, the Js and Emily shopping for food. Sunny.

That was horrible. Steve and Fiona arrived and we started loading up the car. I was popping back to the house to check everything when Paul turned up. I looked at him and he looked at me. Steve, Fiona and Emily were all watching from the car as this man came walking down our driveway towards me. I was shaking in fear. What was he going to do?

'Harry Spencer?'

'Paul?'

'Right.'

We were at a sort of standoff. He looked very angry and I'm sure he had all sorts of ideas about what he wanted to do to me. However, now he was here, he didn't really seem to know what to do. We stood there for a moment in silence before Emily shouted from the van, 'Is everything alright?'

'Is it?' said Paul.

'Fine, yes, no problem, he just needs directions,' I shouted to Emily, who smiled at me and continued her conversation with Fiona. 'Look, Paul, I'm really sorry,' I started gabbling away. 'It was stupid, misguided and we didn't want to hurt anyone. We didn't actually do anything. It was all just talk, stupid, I know, but it was silly and we're about to go on holiday. I don't know what you want, but maybe we can talk when we get back. We could have a drink. Jamie loves you, Paul, she loves you . . .'

'Shut up. I don't care that you didn't do anything. I don't care about you or what you want. All I want is for you to tell your wife what you did. She has the right to know. I can't stand lies.'

'But it will destroy us.'

'Oh, I'm sorry and what the fuck do you think it's done to me and Jamie, eh?'

'Of course, I'm sorry. It was . . .'

'I know what it was. You have one week, Harry. If you don't

tell her, then I will. One week,' he said before he turned around and walked away.

Either I tell Emily about Jamie or he will. What am I going to do? I have a week. I knew this holiday was going to be awful, but I had no idea it was going to be this bad. Fuck.

SUNDAY, May 28th, 2.00 p.m.

At the beach. Overcast and windy. Eating an ice cream. Steve and Fiona off somewhere historic together.

I'm watching Emily play with the three Js and I'm almost in tears. Why did I have to cheat on her? She didn't deserve this. At the moment she has no idea her whole world is about to come crashing down around her. Everything she believes in and trusts is going to disappear. I love her so much and all I want is for her to be happy. I didn't want an affair. It was stupid. What is going to happen to us? What is going to happen to our baby? I've been such a bloody fool.

I keep thinking about telling her and I get a sick feeling in my stomach and I know I can't do it. Then I start thinking that maybe I can talk to Paul again. He was probably just angry. Maybe I can convince him to keep quiet. One thing I do know is that I can't tell Emily at the moment. Maybe I'm weak, but I can't take the risk. What's hard to stomach is that the fate of my marriage lies in the hands of a complete stranger.

june

WEDNESDAY, June 1st, 10.00 a.m.

At a café with Emily. Steve, Fiona and the Js off on a hike. Eating a full English breakfast. Emily nibbling on toast. Damp.

Being on holiday with Steve and Fiona is a bit like being on holiday with The Wiggles. The drive here was song after song about eating, brushing your teeth, bananas in pyjamas, marching ants, baby bumble bees and driving in the car. I'm sure if Steve hadn't been driving, he would have busted out his guitar and started strumming along. At one point, Fiona reached into her handbag and produced a pair of maracas! Since then it's been nonstop. Even the kids seem a little annoyed by their constant happiness and penchant for breaking into song at any moment.

I'm trying not to think about Paul and what will happen when we get back. This could be the last few days Emily and I spend together as happy as this. I wish we didn't have to leave. Maybe we could elope. Is it still eloping when you're already married?

THURSDAY, June 2nd, 11.00 a.m.

At the house. Everyone else at the beach. Sunny. Nervous. Eating a packet of chocolate digestives.

I lied to Emily and said I didn't feel well so I could have some time alone. I'm going to call Jamie and see if she can talk to Paul. I can't stand just waiting to see what happens. I need to do something. Carpe diem!

11.30 a.m.
I just got off the phone with Jamie. We were until very recently sharing our dirtiest fantasies with each other, but now we're like complete and utter strangers. The conversation was strained, uncomfortable and we didn't know what to say to each other. It seems Paul has moved out and they've broken up. I felt awful, but I had to ask if she could do anything to stop Paul from telling Emily. She was my last chance saloon.

'He's really hurt, Harry. There's no telling what he might do.'

This didn't alleviate my worry. So much for seizing the day. I feel worse now than ever and to make matters worse, Steve and Fiona are putting on a puppet show tonight. Steve wrote it and Fiona made the little costumes! Oh. Dear. Lord.

10.00 p.m.
The puppet show lasted for over an hour! The youngest J fell asleep. I nipped out for a cigarette and came back to find out they had waited for me. I couldn't work out the plot. It seemed to be a mixture of traditional nursery rhymes but set in Wimbledon and featuring all of their Js. Steve played eight characters and each one had their own voice, but he kept getting them mixed up. Fiona had to keep standing up because her back was hurting and so she was playing the characters but we could all see her. At one point Steve played guitar for seven minutes and sang a song which I think may have been slightly racist. All in all, a truly terrible evening.

FRIDAY, June 3rd, 9.00 a.m.

Smoking. Thinking. Hoping. Terrified.

Our last day in Cornwall and my last day to tell Emily about Jamie before we go home. Obviously I don't want her to find out from Paul but I can't face telling her myself. I'm at a total loss.

9.00 p.m.
Incredible! We felt the baby kick for the first time today. We were lying down this afternoon in the spooning position. I had my hand on Emily's belly and suddenly there he was. At first we weren't completely sure, but then he did it again and it was magical. He kicked a few times and each time we both just smiled at each other. Our little baby. Our son.

It made the whole thing more real and it made me think even more about the possibility of losing Emily. This poor, defenceless little child is still in the womb, just starting to discover himself, while his selfish, good-for-nothing father is about to destroy everything. It should have been one of the most wonderful moments of my life, but because of my own stupidity, it was one of the saddest. We both cried, but while Emily's were tears of pure joy, mine were laced with sorrow and regret.

SATURDAY, June 4th, 3.00 p.m.

In the study. Emily upstairs asleep. In a constant state of anxiety. Sunny.

11.00 p.m.
In bed. Watching Emily sleep. Is Paul going to show up and ruin my life?

SUNDAY, June 5th, 11.00 p.m.

At Ben's flat. Heartbroken. Emily at home. My life in tatters.

I'm standing on the balcony of Ben's flat looking down at the murky water of the Thames. It finally happened. I was in our bedroom when I heard the doorbell. I rushed towards the stairs, but before I could make it, I heard the front door open and then Paul's voice.

'Mrs Spencer?'

I immediately knew the game was up. I was frozen at the top of the stairs. I should have run down and stopped him but I couldn't move. I heard everything. 'I'm sorry to have to tell you this, but your husband's been having an affair with my wife.'

'Don't be ridiculous. Who are you?' Emily was incredulous. She didn't believe him. Of course she didn't. She trusted me. I was her Harry. 'Harry, where are you, come down here?'

I had to do it. I had to face them.

I went downstairs and there he was.

Emily looked pale.

'This man says you're having an affair with his wife. Tell me this is rubbish. Tell me none of this is true. Tell me.'

She was looking at me. Her face was pleading for an answer. What could I say? I could have lied. I could have tried to cover it up, but I knew it was time to come clean.

'I'm sorry, Em. I'm so sorry.'

Emily looked at me in horror before she burst into tears.

Paul looked at me and said, 'And now we're even.'

For a moment, I thought about punching him, but I quickly decided against it. I'd been the one fooling around with his wife and he had every reason to hate me. He was also much bigger than me and a policeman and so I just watched as he turned around and walked away.

The next few hours are a blur. I tried to explain everything to Emily. She cried a lot. I cried a lot. I told her how much I loved her. I tried to cuddle her, to hold her, but she wouldn't let me near her. I told her nothing had actually happened and that it was just a stupid, silly mistake. She seemed to be settling down until something happened. I don't know why, but she stopped and looked at me.

'Where were you that day?'

'What day?'

'The day I thought we'd lost our baby. The day I was rushed to hospital. Where were you?'

Again, perhaps, I should have lied. Maybe I shouldn't have told her the truth but I didn't want to keep lying anymore and so I told her.

'Get out!' she screamed. 'Get out! Get out! Get out!'

She was throwing her arms at me. She was crying hysterically. I didn't know what to do and so I grabbed a bag of clothes and left.

MONDAY, June 6th, 8.00 a.m.

Ben's flat. Smoking. Sunny. Emily at home (I assume).

It was strange waking up alone in Ben's bed. Better than waking up in Ben's bed with Ben I would imagine, but still, it was odd. For a moment, I didn't know where I was. I reached across and felt for Emily before the sudden memory of yesterday's events played over and over in my mind like the horror story it was. Every word and moment like another dagger in my stupid, callous heart.

Have I lost Emily forever? I need to see her. I need to stay positive. Yesterday she was probably just in shock. Maybe after a night's sleep things will be different. Time to carpe diem. This is the second time I've written that in less than a week, but so far I've done a lot of seizing with very little end product. Fingers crossed.

11.00 a.m.
Wimbledon. Sipping tea in the kitchen. Emily upstairs. Squirrels running around the garden. Drizzling.

It was slightly surreal coming home and letting myself in. Despite it only being one night, I felt like a complete stranger in my own home. I didn't know what to expect. Would Emily be home? Would she even talk to me? The house was deadly quiet, but as I walked through I heard her in the kitchen. I walked in slowly.

'Tea?' she said. Her tone was flat and cold. Her face looked pale and puffy. She'd obviously been crying. Probably all night knowing Emily, and who could blame her.

'Please,' I said, sitting down at the table. Emily made us both tea and then she sat down opposite me. 'I'm so sorry, Em.' I looked at her, but she had the same stoic, detached expression.

'I've been up all night, Harry, trying to figure out why you would do this. I just don't understand. Were you that unhappy? Am I a bad wife? Did I not satisfy you in bed? Why, Harry?'

It was a good question, but unfortunately I didn't have a good answer. Everything I could think of sounded shit. I was afraid of growing old. I wanted to reclaim my youth. My life felt like it was suddenly so set in stone and Jamie was my escape. I was having an early mid-life crisis. I couldn't help myself. All so fucking clichéd. The truth is I'm a man and a gorgeous, sexy woman wanted me and the temptation was just too much. I'm another sad, stereotypical bastard of a husband who cheated on his perfect wife. Rory was right, it is simple. I just wish it wasn't.

'I don't know, Em, but I love you. You're a fantastic wife, a great lover and I'm so happy with you. It was stupid, reckless, thoughtless . . .'

'Then why, Harry? Why did you feel the need to go to this other woman? I need to know.'

'Because I'm stupid. Because I'm a man. I don't know. I don't. It was a mistake, a terrible mistake. I love you, Em. I want to spend the rest of my life with you.'

'But you want to fuck her?'

'But I didn't. We didn't do anything.'

'But you would have.'

'Maybe, I don't know, but we didn't. It was all just talk. It was fun to pretend, but at the end of the day, I didn't do anything because I love you.'

'But don't you see, Harry, it doesn't matter. You broke the trust. You lied to me and so it doesn't matter whether you actually did anything or not.'

'Of course it does. How can it not matter? How can sleeping with her and not sleeping with her be the same?'

'Because it just is.'

Even in that tumultuous situation, I couldn't help but think how illogical she was being. How can screwing Jamie and not screwing Jamie be the same? It took every ounce of restraint I had not to sleep with her and now I find out it didn't even matter.

'So what now?'

'I don't know, Harry, but I think it's best if you don't stay here.'

'You're kicking me out?'

'Not kicking but I need time to think. Can you stay at Ben's for a while?'

'I suppose, but I don't see how being apart is going to help.'

'Because right now all I want to do is punch you.'

'Fair enough,' I said, getting up. 'I'll get some things together.'

That was thirty minutes ago and now I'm all packed and ready to go. I don't want to go. I want to talk about it and get it figured out but what can I do? I'm the one that fucked up and so I have to do what Emily wants. They say time heals all wounds. I hope they're right.

TUESDAY, June 7th, 1.00 p.m.

At school. Having lunch with Rory.

I told Rory everything.

'Shit. Fuck. Bugger. Blimey.'

'Exactly.'

'Let's go out for a drink tonight. My treat.'

'Thanks mate, but I'm not really in the mood.'

'What are you going to do?'

'Hope and pray she takes me back.'

'She will.'

'But what if she doesn't?'

'Don't think like that. Emily loves you. Right now she's

angry; she isn't thinking clearly. Give her time. It isn't like you actually did anything with Jamie.'

'That's not what Emily thinks. She said it doesn't matter whether I did anything or not.'

'Of course it matters. It's completely different. Like I said, she's angry and not thinking clearly. She'll come around.'

'I hope you're right, mate.'

I can't imagine a world where he isn't.

5.00 p.m.
Ben's flat. Listening to Snow Patrol. I tried calling Emily but she didn't pick up and so I left her a long, rambling message. Drinking wine, smoking and looking out across London. Right now millions of people are having the time of their lives: going out, starting relationships, losing their virginity, starting new jobs, going on holiday, falling in love and getting married, while I'm alone. A singularly depressing thought. I wonder what Emily is doing right now.

7.00 p.m.
I just got off the phone with Jamie. We're going for a drink tomorrow night. Probably a bad idea.

WEDNESDAY, June 8th, 4.00 p.m.

I spoke to Granddad. He wanted to know where we're going for his stag party. In all the Jamie/Emily commotion, I forgot all about it. I asked what he wanted to do and he said paintballing.

'It's all the rage, Harry.'

'I'm not sure paintballing is a good idea, Granddad. How about a pint at the local?'

'Will there be strippers?'

'In the Fox and Hound's lounge bar on a Saturday afternoon? Probably not.'

'Could we get strippers?'

'I'll look into it.'

'And what about tattoos? I was thinking about getting a tattoo.'

'We'll see, Granddad.'

'And did you tell everyone when it is?'

'By everyone, you mean?'

'Your father. You, obviously.'

'And who else?'

'I suppose that's it. A few of the old codgers from the home will be coming.'

'We'll come by and pick you up on Saturday.'

'And there'll be strippers?'

'We'll see, Granddad.'

'See you on Saturday, Harry. it's going to be wild.'

7.00 p.m.
Off to meet Jamie.

11.00 p.m.
That didn't go exactly as I thought it might. We met at a small pub in New Cross. I walked in and Jamie was sitting by herself. She hadn't made as much of an effort as the last time but she still looked gorgeous. I got us both a drink and sat down opposite her. At first the conversation was a bit awkward, but we soon settled down into a steady rhythm and I started thinking how easy it would be to be with her. She's beautiful, funny, intelligent and we get along so well, but of course, the answer to that question is simple. I love Emily. Jamie, however, had different news about her and Paul.

'We've split up and I'm moving back to Scotland. It was going to happen eventually, but I think this whole thing just saved us both a few more years of misery. This is why I wanted to meet tonight, Harry.' For a moment, I thought she was going to ask me to go with her and my skin tickled nervously. However, it wasn't that at all. 'I realise now that what we had or nearly had was just an escape for the both of us. We were attracted to each other. We both probably wanted to remember what it felt like to be seventeen again, but the thing is, Harry, you love Emily. Paul and I were already done, but you and Emily have a shot at happiness and I want to put things right.'

'And how are you going to do that?'

'Let me talk to her. I can explain everything and make her see how much you love her.'

'I don't know, Jamie, I'm not sure that's the best idea.'

'How are things between you at the moment?'

'Terrible.'

'So how can I make it any worse?'

She had a point and so I agreed. She is going to pop around and see Emily tomorrow. I got in another round so we could talk. We both had things to get off our chest.

'You know it wasn't just about the sex,' Jamie said.

'I know.'

'I mean, the sex would've been incredible.'

'I know.'

'I honestly think we could have been great together. I know we can't, but I guess I was hoping that maybe, I don't know.'

'It's OK. I understand.'

When Jamie and I said goodbye, I felt a strange mixture of sadness, relief and heartbreak. We hugged and for a moment I thought about how strange life is. Jamie could have been my wife, my lover, but now she is going to be nothing. I don't believe there's just one special person out there for us. The One. I know I could be happy with Jamie. She's wonderful and if we hadn't broken up after sixth form, or if we had met again before I married Emily, who knows what might have been. But as I watched her walk away, I knew I wouldn't ever see her again and I felt sad because a part of me didn't want to lose her forever. A part of me wanted to live that life with Jamie. I also knew I was letting go of a lot more than just Jamie.

Jamie will always be my what-if girl. I don't believe in destiny and all that rubbish. People always harp on about how things happen for a reason but that's just bollocks. Life's random, it doesn't make sense, there isn't an all-powerful God and we do have the free will to fuck everything up. Jamie's wonderful, but I'm married to Emily. It could have been either one. It could have been neither. The only thing that matters is I chose Emily. The rest is just regrets, desires and what-ifs.

FRIDAY, June 10th, 8.00 p.m.

Ben's flat. Eating a kebab. Drinking a beer. Thinking about Emily. Listening to a party across the hall and feeling very mawkish and self-indulgently soppy.

I had a very strained conversation with Emily on the phone today.

'Did you know she was coming to see me?'

'She asked if she could. She felt terrible and wanted to help make things right.'

'Well she didn't.'

'Sorry.'

'Harry, I don't need your fucking lover to come over for a cup of tea to know how much you love me. I know that. I'm not stupid. It isn't about love.'

'Sorry.'

'Because now all I can think about is how pretty she is and all the messages you swapped and that you almost had sex with her. I can't stop thinking about it.'

'But nothing happened. It's over, Em. Jamie's moving back to Scotland. I'm never going to see her again. It's over. Done.'

'But don't you see, Harry, it doesn't matter. It isn't what I think you're going to do that bothers me. It's what you've done. You broke my trust and I don't know if we'll ever get that back.'

'What are you saying?'

'I don't know, but right now I'm not ready to forgive you.'

'Then take more time. Take all the time you need. I love you and I'll wait for you.' I had to say this even though I didn't want to. She needed time and I had to give it to her. 'As long as it takes.'

'I can't promise anything.'

'I know,' I said before we started talking about more mundane things. I asked her how she was feeling with the baby. I told her about Granddad's stag party and asked if she was coming to his wedding next week. For a moment, it almost felt normal until she said, 'Of course I'll be there, but not for you, Harry, for him.'

We said goodbye and I felt worse than ever. How much longer can we go on like this?

SATURDAY, June 11th, 7.00 a.m.

At a cafe around the corner from Ben's flat. Granddad's stag day. Emily in Wimbledon.

It's sad how you can take the smallest things for granted until they're gone. I woke up this morning and realised I had no clean underwear. Then I ran out of toothpaste, there was no milk in the fridge and I had a headache but no headache medicine. All the things Emily did for me without blinking, which alone I didn't even think about until it was too late.

12.00 p.m.
Granddad's home waiting for Dad. Granddad looks very dapper in his suit and is very excited about his stag party. He, along with three other old geezers, Norman (the dove man), Albert (out of his mind) and Scottish Willie (permanently drunk), were already knocking back the whisky when I arrived. This should be a very interesting afternoon.

10.00 p.m.
At my parents' house. Mum and Dad asleep. Smoking by the back door.

It was. After my father turned up, we all headed into town to the Fox and Hound pub. The plan was simple. We were going to have a few pints, a nice lunch, perhaps a game of darts, before we headed back to the home for dinner. It was going to be a leisurely afternoon with a few octogenarians and my dad. However, from the moment my dad turned up and whispered in my ear, 'I've got a surprise for my old man,' I knew it was going to be one of those afternoons. Here are the abridged highlights:

1.00 p.m.: Started drinking. Norman disappeared and we found him trying to convince a girl to follow him to the toilets.

1.25 p.m.: Albert was last seen heading towards the door.

2.00 p.m.: Granddad challenged Willie to a drinking competition. Willie agreed and they both ordered tequila. I looked on with silent trepidation.

2.10 p.m.: Dad joined in with the drinking competition. Norman did card tricks for a group of girls.

2.15 p.m.: Landlord asked me to keep an eye on Norman after the girls complained about his magic trick. It appeared that his 'trick' was to make cards disappear down girls' tops with Norman trying to retrieve them by hand.

2.30 p.m.: Willie started singing old Scottish folk songs at the top of his voice.

2.35 p.m.: Willie was joined by a group of local Scots, who had a guitar and a harmonica.

2.45 p.m.: Willie was standing on a table playing the harmonica.

2.46 p.m.: Willie was on the floor playing the harmonica after falling off the table. He didn't miss a note.

3.00 p.m.: Still no sign of Albert. I was starting to get worried. Granddad said it was fine because Albert was always going missing but said he nearly always turned up again.

3.15 p.m.: Dad disappeared for five minutes and came back with a nurse (who looked suspiciously like a stripper).

3.20 p.m.: She was a stripper! Granddad was sitting in a chair in the middle of the room while the stripper removed her clothes to the T-Rex song 'Get It On'.

3.25 p.m.: Granddad had her bra over his head and her breasts in his face. Norman looked jealous. Granddad looked very, very happy. Willie was still singing songs with his new Scottish friends.

3.40 p.m.: Still no sign of Albert.

3.45 p.m.: The stripper finished her act. She was completely naked, except for a very small G-string, sitting astride Granddad. Norman asked the stripper if she enjoyed magic.

3.46 p.m.: Norman chanced his arm and grabbed a breast. The stripper slapped Norman.

4.00 p.m.: Granddad announced he wanted to go for an Indian. We all left the pub and headed across the road to an Indian restaurant. Still no sign of Albert.

4.25 p.m.: Asked to leave the restaurant after they claimed Willie had urinated in the corner. Willie admitted he had and so we left.

4.30 p.m.: Back to the pub. Willie was singing again. Granddad still drinking, Dad was drunk and couldn't drive home and Albert was still missing. Norman attempted to produce a rabbit from his trousers to a small crowd of girls.

4.45 p.m.: The rabbit turned out to be his penis.

4.50 p.m.: We're asked to leave the pub.

4.55 p.m.: Granddad wanted to go to a club. Willie wanted to go to Scotland. Dad wanted to go to the toilet. I wanted to go home. Albert was still missing.

5.00 p.m.: We decided to go home. We found Albert sitting in a park feeding the pigeons. Willie threw up in the car.

5.30 p.m.: We dropped Granddad, Albert, Norman and Willie back at the home. Granddad said it was the best stag party he'd ever had. Willie was in tears about his beloved Scotland, Norman was happy he'd finally touched a breast and Albert didn't seem to realise where he was.

SUNDAY, June 12th, 9.00 a.m.

In my parents' kitchen. Eating breakfast. Drizzling outside. Dad hung-over. Mum fussing.

'It's so nice to have both of my boys at the breakfast table. More bacon, Harry?'

'No thanks, Mum.' I'd already eaten four slices.

'How's Emily? Is she alright? How's the baby? Is everything alright?'

Mum has the annoying habit of asking every question twice. If only she knew what was actually happening between us she'd be hysterical. She'd be moving into our house and Dr Phil-ing us through it.

'She's fine. Everything's fine. How's the amateur dramatics?'

'Oh, Harry, it's wonderful. I feel like a new woman. I'm playing the part of Mercutio in *Romeo and Juliet*. Me, your mother, can you believe it?'

'Wasn't Mercutio a man?'

'Yes, yes, he was, but our director, Jeremy, says it doesn't matter. He thinks with my range I can pull it off.'

'He wants you to pull him off more like,' Dad chipped in.

'That's ridiculous, why would you say that? Jeremy's a lovely man. He's been married and divorced three times, Harry, but he's still looking.'

'At your tits,' said Dad glibly.

'That's disgraceful,' said Mum. 'I'm sorry, Harry, but your father's turning into a jealous, miserable old sod. It's all that golf. It's a wretched game.'

'I'd better get off. Emily will be wondering.'

I didn't want to be stuck in the middle of an argument between my parents about whether some randy lothario wanted to bang my mother.

'Take care. It's lovely to see you. Say hello to Emily and give her stomach a kiss from Grandma. Tell her I'm thinking about her. Tell her to call me if she needs anything. Drive safe. The Corbetts from number four said hello. We saw them at the pub quiz. Maureen's put on some weight. Norman hasn't changed. They said hello. Make sure you tell Emily. Love you. Big kiss.'

I have no idea who the Corbetts from number four are.

8.00 p.m.
I'm fairly sure I have bottom cancer. My bum's been really sore since yesterday. I didn't think anything of it until now. I was just finishing up on the toilet when I felt a small, hard lump at the opening of my rectum. It must be cancer. That's the last thing I need at the moment. I must make an appointment to see Dr Prakish.

TUESDAY, June 14th, 8.00 p.m.

At last a breakthrough! Emily rang tonight and said she wanted to talk. Admittedly, her suggestion is that we go and see Deidre St Cloud together, which I'm not thrilled about for obvious reasons (she's mental), but it's a start. It's tomorrow night at six.

Bottom's sore and lump is bigger. I did some quick research online and it could be any number of ailments, but apparently rectal cancer is one of the most common forms of cancer and one of the top killers. Great, deadly and embarrassing.

WEDNESDAY, June 15th, 9.00 p.m.

Ben's flat. Drinking, smoking and generally feeling awful. Emily in Wimbledon. Bum still painful.

Deidre St Cloud is an idiot. Her brilliant psychoanalytical skills have only made things worse. Emily explained what had happened and the wonderful Ms St Cloud decided the best course of action was for me to explain in graphic detail why I wanted the affair, what was so great about Jamie and what didn't I like about Emily. The three things I have avoided talking about at all costs. Now Emily won't talk to me at all. Here's the abridged version of the conversation we had with Deidre:

Deidre: So, Harry, yeah, why did you want to cheat on Emily?

Me: I never wanted to cheat on her, which is why nothing actually happened.

Deidre: But why did you seek solace in the arms of another woman?

Me: It was a mistake.

Deidre: It's never just a mistake, Harry. There's always a reason, yeah.

Me: I suppose I was attracted to her and we had a history.

Deidre: Yeah, got it. So you were attracted to her physically, yeah. What exactly did you find attractive about her?

Me: You want details? (Emily looked at me with a cold scowl. I definitely didn't want to give details.)

Deidre: It's important, yeah. What exactly did you like? Her breasts? Her legs? Her face? (I looked at Emily for some kind of support.)

Emily: Oh please, do share. (Fan-fucking-tastic. Thrown to the lions of psychology.)

Me: She was very attractive generally and like I said, we had a history.

Deidre: Did you see her breasts, Harry? (Fuck. How was I supposed to answer that?)

Me: Not exactly.

Emily: What do you mean, not exactly?

Me: I didn't see them in the flesh.

Deidre: So, some sort of photo or online?

Me: Yes. (I mumbled and Emily shot me a look. I had never fully explained the details of my messages with Jamie.)

Deidre: So this woman sent you pictures of her breasts, yeah, and anything else? Did you see her vagina?

Me: Sorry, but I don't see how that's relevant.

Deidre: It's relevant, Harry, yeah. Was it shaved?

Me: Well, yes, but . . .

Emily: For fuck's sake, Harry, what else did you see?

Me: It doesn't matter, Em, it was all just fantasy. She sent me a couple of photos, but that was it and I never saw anything live. (Although I was starting to wish I had because now it seemed like it didn't even matter.)

Emily: Do you still have them?

Deidre: Great question, Emily. Do you still have them, Harry?

Me: No I don't. I deleted them all.

Deidre: That's great, Harry, yeah, really super, yeah. Do you still want to have sex with her?

Me: No, of course not, it was just one of those things. It's over now. Finished.

Deidre: That's great, Harry, yeah, but the thing is, yeah, is that I don't believe you and more importantly, nor does Emily. (Emily nodded.)

Me: But . . .

Deidre: It's alright, Harry, yeah we'll get to that later. Right now I want to focus on Emily's flaws as a wife, yeah. What's she doing wrong? And don't worry, Emily, yeah, we'll be talking about Harry next week.'

This is where it all started to go badly wrong. What could I say? I tried to explain that it had nothing to do with Emily, but as always Deidre St Cloud explained how it had everything to do with Emily. But it didn't. What I had and felt for Jamie was completely separate. I didn't love Emily or fancy her any less than before. I felt like a different person around Jamie, but I couldn't tell Emily that.

Eventually, after thirty minutes of mumbling, stumbling and scrapping my way through more overly personal questions, Emily was fuming. She didn't understand me and she didn't understand what she'd done wrong. Deidre was sitting there looking her usual smug, self-important self, while our marriage disintegrated before her eyes. Then, as Emily and I left, she said how great the session had been and how she couldn't wait to see us again next week. We went in talking and left not talking. I ask you, how is that a good session?

THURSDAY, June 16th, 7.00 p.m.

When I was eight years old I confessed my love to Hannah Brown. It took me over a month to pluck up the courage to do it and only a second for her to laugh at me and walk away. I was heartbroken. When I was fourteen I was caught masturbating by my mum. I was experimenting in the shower, but unfortunately I'd forgotten to lock the door. She didn't speak to me for two days and forced Dad to have a chat with me about self-harming (her words not his). These are both highly embarrassing moments from my past, but neither of them was as embarrassing as my appointment with Dr Prakish today. It started inauspiciously.

'What seems to be the problem this time?' said Dr Prakish.

After my last visit, I seem to have been tagged as some kind of hypochondriac nutter.

'I have a . . . err . . . lump.'

'And where is this lump exactly?'

'On my . . . umm . . . rectum.'

I saw the expression on his face immediately change, probably because he knew what was coming.

'Let's take a look at it then.'

I had been dreading this all day. Unless you're gay, there aren't many times in your life you have to bend over and show another man your bottom. Dr Prakish pinged on the latex gloves and I dropped my trousers and underwear and bent over. It was awful. I would definitely have to change doctors after this. Dr Prakish started poking around my bottom before his hand settled on the lump. The cancerous lump. The deadly lump that was probably going to kill me in the most embarrassing fashion possible. I could already imagine the conversations at my funeral.

'So, what did he die of, exactly?'

'Bottom cancer. He had cancer of the anus.'

'Oh.' What can you say about bottom cancer? 'Must have been very uncomfortable.'

'Haemorrhoids, Mr Spencer, nothing serious,' said Dr Prakish. Haemorrhoids? Wasn't that something only old men and pregnant women got? 'You just need some medication and you'll be fine in no time.'

For the second time this year I went to see Dr Prakish because I thought I was dying, and for the second time it was just something minor. I should be relieved and I am, but when you're convinced you're dying and your doctor is so blasé about it, you almost want to have something terminal, just so you can prove you aren't a hypochondriac nutter. Aha, take that Dr Prakish, I'm dying of a terminal disease, who's the hypochondriac now?

FRIDAY, June 17th, 8.00 p.m.

Ben's flat. Eating beans on toast. Emily in Wimbledon. Raining. Bottom still tender.

Another tense phone conversation with Emily tonight. She's coming to Granddad's wedding tomorrow, but she went to great pains to reassure me she was only going for him and definitely NOT for me.

How is it possible I can feel so far away from someone I love so much?

The medicine for haemorrhoids needs to be inserted into my bottom. A very strange and uncomfortable experience. The lump is still there and it's still very sore. I tried looking at it using a small mirror but it all looked quite disgusting and so I gave up quickly. I would be a terrible homosexual.

SATURDAY, June 18th, 8.00 a.m.

Granddad's wedding day. The sun is shining across London. Sitting on the balcony. Reading the newspaper. Eating poached eggs on toast and drinking tea. A glorious morning.

I'm slightly nervous about today. I'm nervous to be the best man and to give a speech. I'm nervous to see Emily in front of my family as they have no idea what's going on. I'm nervous something will go wrong for Granddad and I'm nervous Granddad and Audrey won't wait until their wedding night to consummate the marriage.

4.00 p.m.

The wedding was wonderful. It almost didn't happen though. When I arrived this morning, Granddad and Willie were already on the whisky. 'A wee dram to get the day going,' said Willie. That was at ten o'clock! Then the suits didn't arrive until thirty minutes before the service. Granddad was sitting on his bed in his underwear (not a pretty sight), drinking coffee and trying to sober up, while Willie was still drinking. I knew then he wasn't going to be in any fit state to play the bagpipes. We did, however, manage to get Granddad to the wedding on time.

Unfortunately, four of the seven doves that Norman 'acquired' escaped, but otherwise everything went to plan. Audrey was given away by her son. I didn't lose the rings and the priest turned up.

Audrey looked lovely in her dress. Granddad was the happiest I'd ever seen him. Emily looked beautiful and my parents didn't seem to detect the obvious tension between us. Willie managed to play the bagpipes as the happy couple walked back down the aisle, albeit a bit off key, and the remaining three doves were set off as planned. All in all, a triumph. I'm in Granddad's room getting ready to give my speech. Nervous.

9.00 p.m.
The speech was great. It was funny, heartfelt and everyone cried. I think I even saw a tear in Emily's eye. Emily and I are doing our best to seem normal though we're anything but. We danced together, but it was strange. Luckily, my dad cut in and I danced with my mother, which was only slightly less awkward.

The band's playing at the moment and it's chaos out there. Some of the old people are already asleep, some are high from the combination of their medication and alcohol and some are quite clearly off their tits. Norman's running around trying to grope whatever he can. Albert was last seen heading towards the car park (still missing) and Willie is passed out with his bagpipes. Granddad and Audrey were last seen heading towards his room. Just your typical old-person wedding in a retirement home.

11.00 p.m.
In Wimbledon. In spare room. Emily asleep next door.

Emily said I could sleep in the spare room. She didn't want me drinking and driving. It feels strange to be in the same house because even though we're physically closer, we couldn't be any further apart. This is awful. I'm sexually frustrated, emotionally frustrated and frustrated in general. I can't go on like this. I go to bed thinking about Jamie. Not a successful wedding day for me.

SUNDAY, June 19th, 2.00 p.m.

Ben's flat. Still cloudy. Emily still in Wimbledon. Still confused. Smoking heavily.

Emily finally came downstairs at about nine-thirty this morning and it was about as tense as a World Cup final penalty shoot-out. We said good morning; I made her a cup of tea and we made some banal chit-chat. At about eleven, I said I was going to get off. I was hoping she might tell me to stay, have lunch, maybe talk, but instead she just said,
    'I'll see you on Wednesday for our session with Deidre.'
    'Yes. Right. Of course,' I mumbled back and that was that. We're farther apart than ever.

7.00 p.m.
Email from Ben.

G'Day, mate. Katie and I are back in Sydney again. How are things in Wimbledon? How's Emily? I miss my best drinking buddy. I spoke with Adam and parents and they're going great guns with the wedding. The only thing I want you to do is organise the stag party. I was thinking Prague, Barcelona or Amsterdam, any one is good. If you need help, give Adam a call. He has the list of people to invite. I expect a weekend of debauchery, drinking and high-jinks. Speak soon. Ben and Katie x

TUESDAY, June 21st, 12.00 p.m.

Rory walked into my room today looking worried.

'What's the matter?'

'She called me into her office this morning.'

'Who did?'

'Who do you think?'

'Oh.' He was talking about our lovely head, Miss Simpson.

'She's getting desperate, mate. She said she was close to finding out about Hampton Court and that if I told her everything, I would be exempt from punishment. Basically, she wants your balls and not in a good way.'

'There's a good way?'

'Probably not, but be on your toes. I didn't say anything but she knows something's up.'

'Thanks for the warning, but I have more important things to worry about at the moment.'

'Things still not working out with Emily?'

'If by that you mean, Does she still hate me? then the answer would be yes. I just don't know what to do.'

'Give her time – she'll come around.'

'I hope so.'

'She will. She's punishing you. If she didn't still love you and want you back, you would already know. Trust me, once she thinks you've suffered enough, she'll let you back into the marital bed.'

'I'd be happy to be under the same roof. I'm getting very lonely at Ben's flat.'

'The bachelor life isn't suiting you?'

'If I was actually a bachelor it would be fine but I'm not. I'm an estranged husband waiting for his wife to take him back. There's a big difference.'

'Maybe it's time you took the initiative.'

'What do you mean?'

'It's your house too, right? Move back in. Force her to see you every day and see what happens. It can't be any worse than it is at the moment.'

Rory was right. It's my house too and, yes, I was the one who'd had the affair, but what good is it doing being apart? We need to be together to sort this out. Whether Emily likes it or not, I'm going home!

6.00 p.m.

Home. I turned up an hour ago and Emily wasn't here. She's going to be in for a surprise.

8.00 p.m.

As it turned out, I was the one in for a surprise. Emily came home with another man! Malcolm, her lecherous, smooth-talking boss gave her a lift home because she was working late (so she said). I'm sure he knows all about our marital strife and is trying to take advantage.

'Oh, Harry, you're here,' said Emily.

Malcolm looked on sheepishly behind her.

'Yes, I am. Hello, Malcolm.'

'I was just giving her a lift home, Harry, nothing to worry about, eh,' said Malcolm.

'Right, well, thanks,' said Emily to Malcolm.

'Yes, yes, of course, no problem,' Malcolm said and then

he scuttled off towards his BMW, hand-woven Italian scarf between his legs.

'What are you doing here?' Emily said, walking through into the kitchen.

'I live here.'

'But you agreed to give me some space, Harry.'

'I changed my mind. I'm not asking you to forgive me right away . . .'

'Good, because I don't,' Emily said, rattling cupboards.

'But if we're going to get through this we need to be under the same roof, Em. I hate being apart from you, it's bloody miserable.'

'You know what else is miserable? Finding out your husband wants to sleep with someone else.'

'But I didn't because I love you.'

Emily stopped and looked at me.

'Harry, I don't know what you want from me. I'm not ready to forgive you. I'm not ready to live with you and I don't know when I will be.'

'I'm going to set up camp in the spare room,' I said and she didn't say no and so operation 'Win Emily Back' is go. It's going to be a long, hard campaign, but one I intend to win.

WEDNESDAY, June 22nd, 8.00 a.m.

Operation 'Win Emily Back' (day one). Bottom on the mend. Lump is almost gone.

I woke up early and made Emily a special breakfast. I squeezed orange juice. I made tea, crumpets, fruit, eggs, bacon, pancakes and two kinds of potatoes. I arranged cereal on the table and I fished out the toast rack we got for our wedding (used once) and made her white and brown toast with a sampling of butter and preserves. I laid everything out as Emily came waltzing down the stairs.

'Breakfast, my lady,' I said, waving my arms across the table like a magician.

'I'm not hungry and I'm late. I'll see you tonight,' she said and then waddled out.

I have a lot of breakfast to eat.

4.00 p.m.
Home early from school to make a romantic meal for two before our session with Deidre St Cloud.

5.30 p.m.
Still no sign of Emily and the spinach and ricotta cannelloni (made from scratch) is getting cold. The salad is wilting by the second and I think the dark chocolate soufflés are going to be a disaster. I already opened a bottle of champagne and I'm drinking that while I wait.

6.05 p.m.
Text from Emily. She's eating out with Stella in Kingston upon Thames and will meet me at our session. I have a lot of dinner to eat and I'm still fairly full from breakfast.

11.00 p.m.
In the spare room. Emily asleep on the other side of the wall. Tonight was awful. I knew it wasn't going to be good, but it was worse than I could have imagined. I think if we keep seeing Deidre St Cloud we have no chance of reconciliation. All she's doing is driving a wedge between us. Tonight she asked Emily to name some of my worst qualities. I knew I had a few, but Emily had obviously been making a list. A very long list.

'Harry is emotionally immature. He's afraid of growing up, of being responsible and having a proper life. He still longs to be a teenager, despite being in his thirties. He can sometimes be shallow, vacuous and petty. He jumps to conclusions without thinking things through properly. He can't have a real conversation about anything and when we try, he closes up and changes the subject. He's weak, spineless and afraid of confrontation. He often chooses his friends over me, although he has improved, it's mainly for show because I know he'd rather be at the pub drinking than at home with me. I also recently discovered that he's a liar . . .'

This was the bulk of her answer. She did go on, but I sort of fell into a coma. How is this possibly helping? Back at home, I tried to have a normal conversation but she said she wasn't ready to be conversational. What the fuck does that even mean? And to make matters worse, I feel sick from all the food I ate today. I'm not sure the dark chocolate soufflés were cooked properly. I may have food poisoning.

THURSDAY, June 23rd, 9.00 p.m.

In the shed. Smoking. Drinking a cocktail (Cuba Libre!). Raining. Emily asleep. Bottom healed. Hooray! Operation 'Win Emily Back' (day two).

Day two was worse than day one. Emily doesn't want to talk to me. I made us another romantic meal for two tonight (which at least she ate), but the conversation was depressingly awkward. It's like we don't even know each other anymore. Every time I tried to talk to her, it took us down the same worn, cobbled, old pathway to the same crappy, unhappy place. She can't get over the fact that I cheated on her. It's simple. I just don't know what to do about it.

FRIDAY, June 24th, 12.00 p.m.
Midsummer's Day

It finally happened this morning. Miss Simpson called Rory and me into her office.

'Gentleman, I have some bad news,' she said with a smile. 'I know you were at the pub while two pupils under your care set off the fire alarm at Hampton Court.' Fuck. 'And don't even try to lie your way out of this, Mr Spencer, because I have proof. The only thing I need to decide is whether I fire one of you or both of you.'

This was serious. It was obvious she only really wanted to fire me and no matter what she was going to fire me anyway. So, I did the honourable thing and took all the blame. I told her Rory didn't want to go to the pub, that it was all my idea and that he shouldn't be in any trouble. She gave Rory a slap on the wrist and let him go.

'I hate to fire good teachers, Mr Spencer,' she said before looking at me with a disdainful glare. 'But you aren't a good teacher and so I have no trouble letting you go. I'll have to go through the appropriate channels, so for the time being you can carry on in your classroom, but I would be prepared to leave very soon. Now get out of my sight.'

SATURDAY, June 25th, 3.00 p.m.

At the old people's home. Emily in Buckinghamshire. Sunny. Eating Scotch eggs, Scotch pancakes, Scotch pies, Scottish haggis and something called stovies. Drinking whisky.

Willie is cooking up a Scottish storm. He is wearing his kilt and singing old folk songs. Granddad and Audrey are more in love than ever. In a moment alone, he leaned across and whispered to me.

'We're up to page forty-eight of our sex book, Harry.'

'And what's that?'

'Toys!' Granddad said excitedly. 'It's wild, Harry.'

'I bet.'

We had to hide the whisky when one of the nurses came around. It seems that Granddad and Willie are a known quantity around the home and are often in trouble for violating rules. Just before I left, Granddad and I took a walk in the garden so we could smoke and he asked how things were going with Emily.

'I don't know what to do, Granddad. She can't get over the fact I betrayed her.'

'It's going to take time, Harry. You can fall in love in seconds, but trust's something that takes time and once it's lost, it can take a long time to get back again. The thing is, Harry, we're men. Men aren't designed to be monogamous. We're hunter–gatherers with penises. I think every man at some point wants to be with someone else. It's only natural. Some men fight it and some don't. It's every man's greatest battle.'

'I'm sure we'll work it out.'

'And if not then you'll be fine. If there's one thing I've learnt from Audrey, it's that it's never too late to fall in love. I loved your Nan, but honestly I've never been happier.'

'That's great, Granddad and thanks,' I said and gave him a hug.

MONDAY, June 27th, 11.00 a.m.

It's a miracle! Miss Simpson has been fired! I came into work this morning expecting the worst but instead I'm saved. We were called into an emergency staff meeting where we were told by our new head, Mr Jones (a burly and bald Welshman), that Miss Simpson has moved on and he was now in charge. Anyway, the point is she didn't have time to report any of the Hampton Court business and so my job's safe. This is the best news I've had for a very, very long time.

7.00 p.m.

I told Emily all about Mr Jones and she seemed happy. We had a reasonably normal conversation and she even laughed a couple of times. It was nice. Maybe my luck's finally on the turn. Maybe everything's going to be alright after all.

WEDNESDAY, June 29th

Granddad died today.

july

FRIDAY, July 1st, 6.00 p.m.

At home. Looking at photos of Granddad with Emily. Cloudy.

Dad rang on Wednesday evening and I could tell straight away that something terrible had happened.

'It's Granddad,' is all he had to say before I burst into tears.

He had a heart attack. He was eighty-two, but to me he always seemed so healthy and full of life. I hadn't ever considered he might die. My next thought was for Audrey. They'd only been married a week. She must be devastated. Emily and I went to see her yesterday. She was doing her best to keep it together, but you could tell she was heartbroken. We all are. Granddad was an incredible man.

His funeral's on Monday. Despite our recent problems, Emily's been nothing but supportive since we found out. She even took yesterday off work so we could spend it with my family. I don't know what I'd do without her.

SATURDAY, July 2nd, 6.00 p.m.

At parents' house with Emily, Audrey, Mum and Dad. Sleeping in the same bed as Emily tonight.

We came this morning to spend time with the family and remember Granddad. Emily and I were supposed to leave before dinner, but one thing led to another and I started drinking and the next thing I know, Mum offered us the spare room. I looked at Emily and she nodded her approval. We're going to be in the same bed again.

It's been a sombre day. We've been reminiscing about Granddad and making final preparations for the funeral. Dad and I popped to the pub earlier while the girls had a cup of tea and a natter. Dad isn't taking Granddad's death very well, which is to be expected I suppose.

Death's such a peculiar thing. It's ever present in our lives from watching the news, reading the newspaper, personal experience, but when it eventually happens, it never fails to take us completely by surprise.

At the moment, I actually envy the religious because at least they have something positive to hang on to. They believe in heaven and the afterlife and I hope they're right. I hope Granddad's up there now looking down at us and having a good old chuckle. I wish I believed in that but I don't. I think death is the final act, which is also why it's so sad. I love Granddad so much and the thought of never seeing him again makes me feel sick to my stomach.

SUNDAY, July 3rd, 8.00 a.m.

In the kitchen. Emily still asleep. Mum making everyone breakfast. Dad in the garden and Audrey still asleep.

Last night was very odd. It was like Emily and I had never seen each other naked before or had sex eight hundred and seven times (not that I'm counting). She got undressed under the duvet, while I felt like a teenage boy in bed with his first girlfriend. I didn't know what to do with my hands. Every accidental touch of a leg resulted in quiet apologies and the conversation would have been easier if we'd been speaking different languages. The end result was that she went to sleep first, while I lay there thinking about Granddad and wondering if my life was ever going to be normal again. I felt guilty for worrying about Emily when I should have been thinking about Granddad, but life doesn't stop because we need it to. I wish it did.

I woke up early this morning and came downstairs. Sleeping in the same bed may have been a breakthrough, but it doesn't feel like it at the moment. If anything, it reminded me how far we've drifted apart and how much time it's going to take to close the gap.

MONDAY, July 4th, 7.00 a.m.

Granddad's funeral.

8.00 p.m.

As funerals go that one must be up there. There were tears, laughter, stories and, at the end of the day, we all left knowing Granddad had had a decent send off.

I'm not a big fan of funerals. Not that anybody is, I'm sure, but not because they're sad, depressing and I'm forced to go to church and pretend to sing the hymns, but because how can you begin to say goodbye to someone in a single day? It seems a bit futile, trivial and nowhere near enough to reflect upon an entire life, but I suppose it's the only way. Granddad hated funerals too. He also never went to church because he said it was too stuffy.

'There may be a God, Harry,' he once told me. 'But I'm sure this is not how he wanted us to worship him.' I couldn't have put it better myself.

The small church was packed to the rafters. People from his retirement home, family, friends and people that were probably just checking he was actually gone. The vicar, a meek-looking man with a big voice, took us through the usual funeral service before Dad got up and read a passage from the Bible.

'Granddad would have hated that,' I whispered to Mum, which made her giggle and sniff up a tear.

Emily was sitting next to me and held my hand the whole time. I did alright with the tears until it was my turn to read. I could feel my legs begin to shake and a few tears rippling around my eyes. I cleared my throat and began.

'Granddad hated funerals. Sorry Granddad. I would like to thank so many of you for coming today. I don't know every-one, but you knew Granddad and decided he'd touched you enough, so thank you. He would have been proud of the turnout.

'As I'm sure you're all aware, Granddad was a unique man. At times he was hot-headed, desperately awkward and, well, quite rude, but he was also so full of passion that you couldn't help but love him.

'I spent most of my childhood believing he was a deco-rated war hero. That he was solely responsible for introducing John Lennon to Paul McCartney. That he often met the Queen for afternoon tea and had invented the car. As it turned out, he hadn't done any of these things, but it didn't matter. I loved Granddad not because he had landed on the beaches during D-Day, was responsible for The Beatles or because he knew the Queen, but because he enlightened my life with his stories, wit and passion.

'As an adult, he still continued to inspire me. Only last week he was married again to his lovely wife, Audrey. I was best man and in typical Granddad style, he didn't make it the easiest job in the world. At first he wanted his stag party in Amsterdam. I managed to quash that idea, so instead he suggested we go paintballing. The actual stag party was still an interesting day. Needless to say, after we were thrown out of the pub for being too raucous, Granddad still wanted to go on to a club. I was ready for bed, but eighty-two-year-old Granddad wanted to continue on.

'This sums up Granddad. His passion for life was unquenchable and if both he and I are wrong and there is a heaven, then I'm sure he's up there right now wreaking havoc. Granddad, wherever you are, I love you. Rest in peace.'

I managed to keep the tears in check until I got back to my seat, but then I cried like a baby for the rest of the service. After we laid Granddad to rest, we had the mandatory wake at a local pub. Granddad would definitely have approved of that. Willie brought along his guitar and we all got drunk and had a really good sing-a-long. We had a good old-fashioned knees-up, just like the good old days Granddad used to go on about so often. All in all, it was a fitting tribute to a wonderful man.

WEDNESDAY, July 6th, 10.00 p.m.

By the back door smoking. Emily asleep. Cloudy.

Today I finally plucked up the courage to confront Emily. We were about to head off for our session with Deidre St Cloud when I stopped her in the hallway. Maybe it was Granddad's death, but suddenly I felt this surge of energy and passion rise up inside of me. I was tired of sleeping in separate beds.

I was tired of being a stranger to my own wife and I was definitely bloody tired of Deidre St Cloud. Life was too short.

'Stop,' I said, grabbing her by the arm. She turned around and looked at me. 'Let's not go.'

'But it's important, Harry.'

'It's fucking useless, Em. She isn't helping. We're in separate beds. We don't touch. We don't kiss, hug or do anything that a married couple should be doing. I'm tired of pretending. I'm tired of living like this. I fucked up. I made a huge mistake, but at some point you need to forgive me. You need to commit to us. Do you want this to work?' I wasn't shouting but I could feel the blood coursing through my body. I felt truly alive for the first time in months.

'Of course I do, Harry, but it isn't as easy as just saying I forgive you and that's it. It's going to take time.'

'I understand, but I'm afraid we're going to get stuck like this.'

'Like what?'

'Like this. Like strangers. I hate it, Em,' I said and I don't know what came over me but I grabbed her, pulled us together and kissed her. It was our first kiss since she'd found out about Jamie. For a moment she responded. Our lips were joined and it felt like our first kiss all over again. It felt new and special, until she pulled away.

'No, Harry, you can't make everything better with a kiss,' she said and ran upstairs and into our (her) bedroom.

Thirty minutes later she came out and we talked. She said she understood. She said she wanted everything to be good again and that I could move back into our bedroom. It had worked. We didn't end up going to our session with Deidre St Cloud. It goes to show that if you seize the day enough times, eventually you'll reap the rewards. A major breakthrough (I hope).

SATURDAY, July 9th, 9.00 a.m.

The birds are singing, the sun is shining and I have a hard-on the size of the Eiffel Tower. OK, so I'm blowing my own trumpet a bit too loudly, but you get the idea. Sleeping in the same bed as Emily and not having sex (barely touching actually), is causing all sorts of problems downstairs. My balls are the size of melons again and my morning glory is becoming a minor disability. I need a cold shower, possibly followed by a brisk walk to get rid of my pent-up sexual energy.

Part of the problem is that Emily hasn't forgiven me yet. I respect her decision and I know it's going to take time. The other part of the problem is, because of her size, she sleeps with about twenty pillows wrapped around her body. So even if I wanted to, I couldn't get within two feet of her without upsetting the gentle balance of her pillow mountain. It's like sleeping next to a pile of dominoes.

I understand her hesitation, but I have needs, wants, desires and a very demanding penis. I need to have some sort of sexual release soon. It was OK when I was sleeping alone, but now I'm so close to Emily physically but so far away sexually, it's driving me to the brink of my pain threshold. I can't go on like this.

SUNDAY, July 10th, 11.00 a.m.

In the study. Eating a bacon, fried egg and black pudding sandwich. Sunny. Emily in the lounge.

We're going to our first birthing class this week at the hospital. I'm nervous because I don't know what to expect. Will we have to watch an actual birth? Will we have to sit around breathing heavily? Will there be a test? What if I fail? Will I be banned from attending the birth of my own child?

MONDAY, July 11th, 6.00 p.m.

In the kitchen. Listening to the Stereophonics. Making a romantic meal for two. Emily on her way home from work.

I can't remember the last time Emily and I had sex (Italy?). All I know is that it's been a long time. I realise that essentially it's my own fault, so in theory it's up to me to fix it. So, in an attempt to put the flame back in the marital bed and have some hot sex with Emily, I have concocted the world's sexiest meal. Basically, once Emily's eaten a few bites, she'll probably grab me by the testicles and drag me upstairs and into bed. Actually, she'll probably be too aroused and we'll just have to do it on the dinner table.

I Googled sexy food and surprisingly found quite a few recipes. This is a science and as Mr Hecklesford (Science) always says, 'You can't argue with science.' I hope he's right.

7.00 p.m.

Emily was delightfully surprised. I laid the table with flowers, candles and I even used our best china. She loved the food, although she has no idea the effect it's soon going to have on her. Dessert should definitely seal the deal!

8.00 p.m.

Smoking. Drinking wine. Emily asleep.

It seemed sexy food had the opposite effect on Emily. After dessert, she went to bed and not with me but alone to sleep. It seems science isn't always right. I'm downstairs alone, horny and with the washing-up. Least sexy night of all time.

TUESDAY, July 12th, 5.00 p.m.

'Harry, why do you always buy bananas?'

'Because I like them.'

'If you like them so much, why do you always end up throwing them out?'

'I don't always.'

'You do. Every week you buy four bananas and every week you throw three of them away.'

'I don't like it when they go all black and mushy.'

'Then why don't you buy one banana instead of four.'

'Because they come like that. I would feel cheap tearing off just one banana. Here you go person behind the till at Waitrose, here's one, singular banana.'

'So you'd rather pay more money for bananas you know you aren't going to eat.'

'I might eat them.'

'But you never do.'

'Well this time I will.'

'I'd like to see that.'

'Oh you will.'

I must make sure I eat all four bananas this week. I ate the first one right in front of Emily, just to show her how committed I am to the bananas.

WEDNESDAY, July 13th, 5.00 p.m.

At home. Eating chicken curry. Tonight's our first birthing class at the hospital. Nervous.

The class is at seven and lasts for two hours! Emily's really excited about it, but I have to say I'm a tad sceptical. It seems to me that Emily just has to push really hard, while I have to hold her hand and say really encouraging and supportive things like, 'You can do it, baby!'

Am I wrong about this? Have television and film been lying to me all these years? I suppose we'll find out tonight.

10.00 p.m.
In the study. Emily asleep. Eating a cheese and pickle sandwich.

That was quite an eye-opener, but not in the way I would have imagined. It was also slightly surreal, completely useless and very, very odd. Let me start at the beginning.

We arrived at the hospital and made our way to the small room that would be our birthing class home for the next three Wednesdays. We were early, but another couple was already there. We introduced ourselves, but it was quite clear from the off that Brenda and Bryan were both fucking mental. She was huge and wearing her pyjamas, while Bryan looked as though he had just rolled out of bed after a four-day drug binge. And they were apparently going to be parents!

'Twins,' said Brenda, pointing at her enormous belly.

'We still can't believe it,' said Bryan, as if he still didn't.

Next up was Karen and Abigail (token lesbian couple!) and Gurinder and Balvinder (token Indian couple). Then lastly, our instructor, Pauline Shepherd, came strolling in and right away I knew this was going to be a disaster. Pauline made Deidre St Cloud look reasonably sensible. Pauline had long dreads, a nose piercing, multiple tattoos, a long, flowery hippy dress, no shoes and she must have been at least twenty stone (at least she wasn't a vegetarian). I'm not one to judge people on first impressions (Ali aside, my record's fairly unblemished), but I would have been surprised if she wasn't stark raving bonkers.

Ten minutes later, when we were all sitting in a circle beating on bongos, I knew my initial instincts were spot on. This was how we were going to get to know one another. Apparently, according to Pauline, music breaks down the barriers of convention. We all had to go around and sing a song about ourselves. How fucking embarrassing. However, apart from me, everyone else seemed to really embrace it. Big Brenda sang a disturbing song about her childhood (she was almost certainly a prostitute for a number of years), while her husband (the equally scary Bryan) did a surprisingly upbeat rap about being terminally unemployed. The lesbians did a great joint song about being lesbians, although I think I may have read more into it than there was. The Indian couple wove a very dramatic (and long) tale about love, death, possibly incest and it ended with an elaborate wedding scene. Then it was my turn.

I've never been gifted musically and I despise performing in public. I started tapping the bongo and let the words flow out of me. It didn't go well. I was outperformed by everyone, including unemployed Bryan. Not a great start, but it's hard to find words to rhyme with Harry, Wimbledon and teacher. All I could think of was Barry (I don't even know anyone called Barry, so this didn't help), Dumbledore (which doesn't even rhyme with Wimbledon but it sounds similar) and preacher. Needless to say, it was awful. I ended up singing a song about a preacher called Barry, intertwined with a loose Harry Potter theme.

The rest of the night went on in much the same vein. We did lots of things with tambourines, rhythmic breathing and a pregnancy yoga session. Pauline brought along a cassette of whale noises, which we listened to for about fifteen minutes. It was like being in a bloody aquarium. The only thing we didn't do was talk about actually giving birth, which, correct me if I'm wrong, was the whole point.

On the way out, I was expecting Emily to say what a load of old bollocks it was and we wouldn't be going again. However, she didn't. In fact, she thought it was brilliant!

'Oh, what fun,' she said on the way to the car. 'Fun yet informative. Just what we needed.'

'Yeah, brilliant.'

I was already on thin ice and if I ever wanted to have sex again, I couldn't cause a fuss, but seriously, we didn't even see one picture of a vagina.

THURSDAY, July 14th, 10.00 p.m.

In the study. Eating a bowl of frosted flakes. Emily asleep. Frustrated.

It all came to a head tonight. Emily and I were getting into bed when she asked if I could rub some lotion on her. Since her belly went from a size eight to a size sixteen, she's begun to itch ferociously. Her skin is drying out and so she needs to apply buckets of lotion each day. She has lotion to moisturise, post-moisturise and prevent stretch marks and another one that seals in the moisture. She usually does this to herself but because she's getting more rotund by the day, she needed my help. I started by rubbing some on her belly, back and shoulders, but then she turned to me and said,

'And a bit around my boobs.'

'Excuse me?'

'Just some around my boobs, is that OK?'

Was that OK? She expected me to just rub moisturiser on her breasts and stop there? Did she know me? Did she know the last time we had sex? Do I? This was too much. Unless she was ready to forgive, forget and make love not war, I couldn't just rub some around her boobs. I'm not a lotion rubbing machine. I'm a man!

'Is this going to lead . . . ?'

'Going to lead to what?'

'You know,' I said, hinting with a nod of my head towards her groin area.

'Oh, for fuck's sake, Harry,' Emily said, grabbing the tube of cream from me. 'Is that all you can bloody think about?'

'At the moment, yes. We haven't had sex in months and I have needs, Emily, needs!'

'And I'm growing a fucking baby inside of me, Harry. So I hope you'll excuse me if I'm not feeling like a porn star at the moment.'

She turned her light off, rolled over (slowly) and went to sleep.

FRIDAY, July 15th, 4.00 p.m.
St Swithin's Day

At school. Only one week of school left until the summer holidays. Dark and cloudy.

It's said that if it rains on St Swithin's Day, it will rain for forty days.

> *St Swithin's Day if thou dost rain*
> *For forty days it will remain*
> *St Swithin's Day if thou be fair*
> *For forty days 'twill rain nae mare*

The BBC weatherman must be a nervous wreck. He predicted it would be dry all day. It's suddenly very dark and gloomy overhead.

There comes a time in every man's life when he just needs to go out and get really pissed. That time is tonight. Emily's having a girls' night in with Stella in Kingston upon Thames. They're having a Patrick Swayze marathon (minus his best film, *Roadhouse*. I ask you, how is it a marathon without *Roadhouse*?). I'm going out on the town with Rory and Alan Hughes.

SATURDAY, July 16th, 2.00 p.m.

On the sofa. Eating chicken soup (for my soul). Emily not showing any signs of sympathy.

NEVER AGAIN! I think I might be dying.

It all started this morning. Well, technically, it started last night, but I have no memory of last night and so it began this morning on a strange sofa. It's always weird when you wake up with absolutely no idea where you are, how you got there and who the person standing over you is.

'Harry, wake up,' the pretty young girl said.

My first thought was the obvious one. Am I naked? I

looked down and luckily I was fully dressed. My next thought was, had I had sex with the pretty young girl standing over me? If I was fully clothed the answer had to be no, because who has drunken sex and then puts all of their clothes (including shoes) back on again? Obvious question number three: If I hadn't had sex with her, who the hell was she and where was I?

'Yes?'

'It's time to leave.'

She was younger than me. Probably early twenties. She obviously knew me. I just wish I knew her. I did, however, remember the one cardinal rule about awkward morning-after moments. Never let them know you have no idea who they are.

'Right, yes, of course,' I said, sitting up on the sofa. It appeared I was probably in whatshername's lounge. It was time to find out the lie of the land with some probing, yet sensitive questions. 'Good night last night.'

'Yeah, it was. Although I'm surprised you can remember anything. You were hammered.'

'I was. It's a big foggy, but it's starting to come back to me.' It really wasn't.

'Your mate's still in bed with Caroline.' My mate? It must be Alan, the dirty Welsh bugger. It was starting to make sense now. 'And the other one's still in bed with Mandy.' The other one? Shit. Fuck. Bugger. What had Rory done?

'And me and you?'

'I listened for hours about how much you love your wife, how excited you are to be a dad, before I cleaned up your puke from the bathroom floor.'

'Sorry and thanks.'

'You're welcome and in case you're wondering my name's Liz.'

'It's nice to meet you.'

I shook her hand and felt for the first time the rumbling inside my head. I knew then it was going to be a long day. I had to find Rory and get out of there.

Liz left the room to get ready and so I sneaked into the first bedroom I could find, hoping to find Rory, but all I saw was Alan's naked bottom staring back at me. What sort of man has a tattoo of the Welsh flag on their bum? I closed the door quickly. Alan could fend for himself. The next door was along the hallway and so I slowly opened it. Hopefully Rory would be fully dressed. Unfortunately, both people were underneath the duvet. I was going to have to take a peek. I walked quietly over to the bed and reached down. I slowly pulled back the duvet and this is when they saw me and I saw them. They screamed first and then I screamed. It wasn't Rory. It was a girl (who looked vaguely familiar) and a man I'd never seen before (with an exceedingly large appendage. Just looking at the thing I felt an acute sense of inadequacy).

'You're not Rory!' I screamed.

'Who the fuck are you?' screamed the man. They were both completely naked.

'Alright, Harry,' said the girl.

I was confused and so I made my apologies and left quickly.

Good old Rory had gone home as planned. I called him on my walk of shame. He was fine, while I was going to be in big, big trouble. Emily had left me a text asking where I was and so I knew I was going home to the Spanish inquisition. Luckily, Rory said he'd cover for me and so I told Emily I'd slept on his sofa.

Since getting home, my situation has gradually declined. I took a shower, had coffee, had a light breakfast, took more than the recommended dose of aspirin, but I still feel like I'm on the verge of death. Being hung-over is no fun in your thirties. What I need now is a relaxing weekend with nothing to do but mope around on the sofa watching the telly, while Emily brings me tea and toast.

P.S. It didn't rain yesterday. I'm sure much to the relief of the BBC weatherman.

SUNDAY, July 17th, 6.00 a.m.

At hospital with Steve, Fiona and Emily. Very tired. Very annoyed.

Steve called at four o'clock this morning to let us know they were going into labour. Why? Apparently, Fiona wanted her closest friends to be there. So? It seems we're their closest friends. Fuck!

My weekend of doing nothing lasted for only one day. Now we're sitting at the hospital with Steve and Fiona, waiting for J number four to arrive. Luckily, all of the other Js are with Fiona's parents. I'm already onto my third cup of coffee.

11.00 a.m.

Why did they call us so early? Why couldn't we just come at the very end? Why was Emily enjoying this so much? Why was Fiona (and Steve for that matter) happy for me to be in the room when they checked to see how dilated she was? Why didn't I close my eyes? Why was she suddenly happy for me to see her tits? Did I have to stay for the actual birth?

11.15 a.m.
Yes. I told Steve I felt a bit weird about seeing his wife's tits and bits, but Steve wouldn't take no for an answer.

'It's such a beautiful, wonderful, profound thing, Harry.'

'And you really don't mind me seeing your wife's vagina?'

'But that's the thing, old boy, when they're having a baby, it isn't a vagina. You won't even think of it as a vagina.'

All I can think about now is seeing Fiona's vagina. Is she hairless? Is she too hairy? What shape will it be? Will she have a strange, over-sized clitoris?

12.00 p.m.
I'm bloody starving but no one else has even mentioned food. I don't want to ruin the moment, but while Fiona needs to empty her stomach, I need to fill mine. I'm sure everyone's hungry. I'll just tell them I'm going to get food.

12.05 p.m.
Apparently, no one else is hungry and I can't leave because the baby might come at any moment. I'm not trying to be difficult, but we've already been here for seven hours and nothing much has changed. I very much doubt if I pop out for fifteen minutes, the baby will pop out too.

1.00 p.m.
What a massive fucking surprise. Still no baby and I'm dying of starvation. I could have gone, come back and eaten by now. This is ridiculous. I need to eat.

2.45 p.m.
I popped out to get some food. Everyone else said they weren't hungry and so I didn't get them anything. Of course, I came back with a burger and chips and they all stared at me

like I'd just invented fire. In the end, Emily stole half of my chips and I gave Steve most of my burger because he looked like he was going to faint. I'm still hungry and Fiona hasn't opened her vagina any bigger than the last time they checked. Longest day ever.

8.00 p.m.

At home (finally). Baby number four eventually arrived at four o'clock (the irony). It was traumatic to say the least. When she started to push, I was standing to the side trying my best to keep out of the way and not look at her vagina. However, when things started getting more intense, Emily dragged me over to have a look. It was a fucking mess. That's all I'm going to say.

'Isn't it beautiful?' said Emily. I didn't know what to say.

'She doesn't have an abnormally large clitoris,' I said. Even in that most dramatic of situations, everyone in the room stopped and looked at me. 'Very normal.'

'Push, baby, push,' said Steve getting proceedings back on track again, before he started singing a song which sounded like, 'Row row row your boat,' but he cleverly changed the words to, 'Push push push the baby out of your birthing canal.' Slightly disturbing, especially when he started doing the motions as well.

I think the thing about childbirth is that if it isn't your own, you don't want to see it. I had no interest in Fiona's vagina or the baby that was soon to miraculously appear from it. There was lots of blood, guts, screams (Steve) and grunting (Steve). When it's Emily and me, it will be completely different, but watching Steve and Fiona go through it made me feel nauseous.

When it was all said and done, it was incredible to see the little baby and to hear her cry for the first time, but that's the last time I want to watch a birth I'm not to blame for.

'Everyone, meet Jasmine,' said Steve, holding up the baby like you might the FA Cup trophy. That's four fucking Js!

TUESDAY, July 19th, 12.00 p.m.

At school. Sunny.

I love the last week of school because there's a party atmosphere in the halls and classrooms. Tomorrow's sports day and Rory and I are playing in the staff v students football match. This should be interesting as I haven't played in years. I used to be quite good back in the day, but since then I've gained about two stone, a dodgy knee, glasses and the ability to only run about four feet before I start to wheeze, cough and faint.

WEDNESDAY, July 20th, 4.00 p.m.

As you get older, you start to realise all of the things you're not and won't ever be. I remember being a teenager and thinking that with enough hard work and commitment there wasn't anything I couldn't do. It was a nice idea, but as the years have rolled on, it's become quite clear I was wrong.

I know now I won't ever be able to play the guitar like Johnny Marr. I won't ever be that good-looking, be as tall as I'd like, tell jokes without forgetting the punch line, drive a fancy sports car, be well travelled, have long hair again or be drunk for two days straight without taking a week to recover. Today, I added another one to the list. I won't ever be able to play football again.

The staff v pupil game was a disaster. I started at right

fullback and began brightly. My first touch was a lovely lay-off, followed by a delicious back-heel. Then I made a terrible mistake. I got carried away. For a second, I thought I was Brazilian and decided to run all the way up the wing. I got there. The ball was played out to me. I took it with one touch, beat two players with my trademark shimmy before I took aim and let fly. I was fifteen again. It was going to curl into the top corner. It was going to be glorious. It was going to be the goal of the season. It went well wide, high and handsome and then the next moment, play was going on again. Someone was shouting at me to get back in position, but I couldn't. My body felt like it was on fire. I couldn't breathe, I couldn't run and my heart was exploding inside of me. My moment of glory had cost me dearly. I was a plonker.

The next seventy-five minutes were an absolute night-mare. I was run ragged by kids half my age. They won 17–1. Rory scored our only goal, a great free kick from the edge of the box. At the final whistle I fell to the ground a broken man. That was two hours ago. I may need a wheelchair to get home. I have definitely pulled my groin, hamstrings, calves and my back's in agony. Even my fingers hurt. The only good thing is I didn't have a heart attack and die on the pitch. The bad thing is that tonight is our second birthing class at the hospital.

5.00 p.m.
Bugger. I came home and Emily was standing in the kitchen holding three black, mushy bananas over the bin. I had forgotten all about the bloody bananas.

'No more bananas,' she said, dropping the bananas in the bin.

'Fine.'

Another small battle lost.

10.00 p.m.
In the lounge. Can't move. Can't sleep. Emily asleep upstairs.

Tonight was even worse than last week. I was also in complete agony which didn't really help, especially during the pregnancy massage section. Tonight we learnt about the sort of drugs you could take if needed (why wouldn't you?), alternative ways to cope with pain (drugs?) and massage techniques to help with the pain (refer to my earlier answers regarding drugs). It seems Pauline is definitely against drugs. We did, at least, see some sketches of wombs and vaginas. Next week the big finale, the actual birth. This is where we will get to breath, grunt and scream. I can't wait.

THURSDAY, July 21st, 8.00 p.m.

In the study. Eating a Scotch egg and drinking a beer. Emily watching TV in bed. Pain slightly better, but that's probably the large amount of drugs I've taken.

Email from Ben.

How's the stag party coming along? Let me know what ideas you have. Give Adam a call. He wants to meet for a drink and talk. All well here. Making pies. Making love. Making friends. Making plans. Speak soon big fella. Love Benski x

I suppose I'd better start making plans for the stag party.

FRIDAY, July 22nd, 7.00 a.m.

In the kitchen. Drinking tea. Emily eating cereal. Last day of school. Most of the pain seems to have gone, except in my groin, which is still very tight.

'Don't forget to meet me at the doctor's tonight,' Emily said.
    'I won't.'
    'The appointment's at five o'clock.'
    'No problem. I'll be there with bells on.'
    'You'd better be.'
    'Can we have sex tonight?'
    'No.'
    'Just thought I'd ask.'
    Emily gave me a kiss and left for work. On the last day at school we're done by two o'clock and then we usually head off to the pub for a few end-of-year pints. Six weeks of freedom. Although in roughly four weeks, Emily and I will be welcoming a little person into our lives. No more quiet, relaxing summer holidays for me. I'm going to enjoy the next four weeks. I have nothing to do except clean out the shed, drink cocktails and take long walks to the pub and back. Other than that, I'll be doing bugger all.

8.00 a.m.

On the drive to work today, I found myself thinking about Granddad. It still feels so ridiculous. I guess that's the trouble with death, it's so final. It's like being naked. There's nothing left to hide behind. I almost started crying at the traffic lights by Iceland, but I managed to pull myself together by the time I reached Superdrug.

9.00 p.m.
Another disaster. School finished and we all went to the pub. I was busy talking with Rory while Alan Hughes was doing his best to chat up Miss Beaumont (sexy first-year French teacher). However, before I knew it, it was five o'clock and I was late for our doctor's appointment. I dashed there, but I was still almost thirty minutes late. Emily was livid and we've barely spoken since.

She's upstairs asleep. Sometimes I wonder about us. She's always mad about something and I'm always giving her reasons to be mad. Will we ever be happy? Maybe we just aren't meant to be together.

SATURDAY, July 23rd, 4.00 p.m.

In the Home Counties visiting parents. Emily visiting Steve, Fiona and the Js (I couldn't handle it). Overcast (BBC weatherman mentioned very tentatively that a heatwave is on the way). Groin basically back to normal.

I found myself alone with Mum this afternoon and I asked her how Dad was doing.

'You know your father.'

'That isn't really an answer.'

'It's all the answer I have. He doesn't talk about your granddad. He goes to work, plays golf and we go to the pub quiz every Thursday night. I asked if he wanted to talk, but he just grunted and walked away. He's never been a great communicator.'

'I know, but I thought with Granddad dying, it might change things.'

'Nothing will change your father,' she said, which made me start thinking about myself.

Can I change? Is it possible for any of us to change? I want to change. I want to be a better husband. I don't want a 'man-tention span'. I want to be a better person, but I don't know if it's possible. Dad will never change. His father just died and that didn't change him, but maybe that's the point. Everyone is always harping on about change and improving, but why? Get thinner, make more money, buy a bigger house, a faster car, but does it make us any happier? Would Emily and I be happier if we were richer? Probably not. Maybe we're how we are for a reason and perhaps we have to accept that and be ourselves, instead of always striving to be the person we think we should be.

TUESDAY, July 26th, 9.00 a.m.

In the shed. Smoking. Sunny. Emily at work. Squirrels running around. No sign of heatwave (BBC weatherman hasn't mentioned it again. I think he realised his mistake).

There are many things in life that can make you feel bad about yourself. Standing next to a particularly tall man on the tube and realising that the six-foot dream died years ago. Walking past a gym and seeing all of the fit people working out, while you spark up a cigarette and feel that old twinge in your chest. Watching *University Challenge* and realising you aren't quite as intelligent as you thought. However, none of these is remotely as bad as spending fifteen minutes in the company of Ben's brother, Adam. I'm meeting him for lunch in Covent Garden to discuss the stag party and I'm dreading it. Don't get me wrong, I love Adam dearly, but five minutes alone with him and I'm going to start realising how inept, ugly, stupid, short and unfit I am.

5.00 p.m.
Home. A bit tiddly. Attempting to make dinner (homemade lasagne). Emily due home soon.

I met Adam at Walkabout in Covent Garden. I haven't seen him for a while, and even I'd forgotten how ridiculously good-looking, tall and athletic he is. He has Jude Law's good looks, the body of an athlete, the height of a Scandinavian model, plus the voice of Hugh Grant, the intelligence of Stephen Fry and the wit of, well, Stephen Fry. He is also charming, self-effacing and every other quality that makes him just about perfect.

Adam got in a couple of drinks and talked about the stag party. Ben wanted somewhere foreign, but the problem with that is the stag party is going to be towards the end of August and Emily is due in mid-August. Could I go away for a weekend, perhaps only weeks after having a baby? Emily would go ballistic and what if she is a week or two late? I couldn't miss the birth of my first child for a weekend of drug- and drink-fuelled debauchery in Amsterdam. Could I? Err . . . no. Don't be an idiot, Harry.

'Emily isn't going to like it,' said Adam.

'She's going to hate it. Hate me. And when she's done with me, she's going to come after you.'

'Shit. How about we stay in the country. We could do one of those action days in the country. Paintballing, clay pigeon shooting, that type of thing. Then we could pop back into London for drinks and a club, before we put Ben on the last train to Aberdeen.'

'Sounds perfect, apart from the bit about Aberdeen.'

'Too far?'

'Just a touch. Maybe Bristol. Give him a fighting chance.'

'Fair enough.'

And so we decided that instead of a weekend away, we would have one incredible day at home. Ben wouldn't mind and it might help my already rocky state of affairs with Emily.

For the rest of the afternoon we talked about our lives. Well, Adam talked about his, because he actually has one, while I mentioned a few details about mine.

Adam is twenty-two, on the cusp of greatness, is single, about to graduate from Cambridge University, has competed in the Boat Race, is about to go travelling for a year with his two best buddies (Rupert and Steve), before returning to train as a doctor. Adam has the world at his feet, while all I have at my feet is the nagging feeling that my life is slowly becoming more and more shit and an overgrown toenail. Bugger.

WEDNESDAY, July 27th, 10.00 p.m.

In bed. Eating a Snickers. Emily asleep.

Tonight was our last birthing class and it really went off. Pauline had us simulating the actual birth. Now, far be it from me (a lowly history teacher) to question Pauline's methods, but I don't see how us acting out how we think the birth is going to go is much help. We paid for these classes because we wanted someone to tell us.

Big Brenda and mental Bryan got straight into it. She was screaming, grunting and flailing her arms around. It was like watching a bad school nativity play. I couldn't stop looking at the lesbians because their version of events was actually quite sensual and involved kissing, massaging and at one point, Abigail (non-pregnant lesbian) took her top off so she was just in her bra! I didn't know what this had to do with the birthing process but it was quite erotic. Emily got very annoyed and told me to stop staring. The Indian couple took a long time to get going. They had brought along some books, candles, small statues and they spent about fifteen minutes chanting and praying, before they went very silent and lay there looking very serene. It didn't look very realistic. Seeing Steve and Fiona recently gave us a good idea of what it would be like and so we gave it our best shot. However, I couldn't get into it. It felt stupid and I didn't see the point.

'Come on, Harry, this is your first child,' Pauline was shouting across the room.

'Come on, Harry,' said the lesbian without a top on. I smiled at her, but this just made Emily hit me. It was useless. I was useless. Emily got the hump and refused to carry on.

The rest of the night carried on in much the same vein. Emily got more annoyed, while everyone else seemed to be enjoying it. Why couldn't I? What is wrong with me? At the end of night, Pauline gave us all our graduation certificates and everyone (except Emily and me) cheered. Bryan and Brenda gave us their phone number and told us to keep in touch (no thanks). Pauline gave us all a really long, uncomfortable hug at the end and wished us well on our 'magical journey'. Emily and I barely spoke on the way home (again).

FRIDAY, July 29th, 11.00 a.m.

In the kitchen smoking. Emily having a lie down. A month since Granddad died.

I tried to have a conversation with Emily over breakfast, but it didn't go as planned. I had hoped to lay my cards on the table. I wanted to be open, honest, regretful and optimistic and I hoped we could put everything behind us and move on. Baby Spencer's due in a few weeks and I don't want to go into that with things the way they are. It was time (once again) to seize the day and make everything alright. Unfortunately, the day wasn't so much seized, but lost.

'Emily, I'm sorry,' I said.

'For what?'

'For everything.'

'You aren't sorry,' Emily said. 'You're just sorry I'm still annoyed with you. It's pathetic.'

'It isn't pathetic, Em. I am sorry. I'm sorry about Jamie. I'm sorry about me, about being late for our appointment the other day, about always putting you second and being thoughtless. I'm sorry I don't see the point in birthing classes and therapy. I'm sorry.'

'And yet you still keep doing the same shit over and over again. It isn't about being sorry anymore, Harry, it's about actually changing. Actions speak louder than words and right now your words don't mean that much.'

'So what does that mean?'

I wanted to know how long she was going to be mad at me for. I needed a time frame. A few weeks? A month? A year? But Emily was too smart to actually give me a figure.

'When you've shown me you can change, that you're sorry and not because you feel guilty or because you want to have sex with me, but because you're actually sorry, then maybe we can move on.'

I understood what she was saying, but I had no idea what she meant. Shit.

3.00 p.m.

Attempting to tidy shed. Emily inside. Hot. It seems the heatwave is finally here. The BBC weatherman predicted it would be cloudy. Once again, he second-guessed himself and blew it.

We're over halfway through the year. Our baby is due in two weeks. The shed (like my life) is still a mess. What the fuck happened? The whole point of keeping a diary is so I can analyse my life, see where I'm going wrong and work out the complicated knots of my existence. However, reading back over the year, it seems my life has become more complicated, more full of knots and I have no idea how to undo any of them.

Emily's still angry with me. I've lost the one person who I could talk to about it. My relationship with Jamie ended her marriage, almost ended mine, made me realise that love, like life, isn't always black and white. I'm about to become a father, but don't feel anywhere near ready and I haven't had sex in months. Something needs to change. I have two weeks to turn things around before Tom comes. Two weeks to save my marriage. Two weeks to turn my C minus of a life into an A star!

august

SUNDAY, August 1st, 2.00 a.m.

In the study. Unable to sleep.

How do you show someone you're sorry? I was lying in bed thinking about it. Emily wants me to show her I've changed and that I'm sorry, but how? I told her I was sorry, but apparently it isn't enough.

I keep thinking about the fact I'm going to be a father in a couple of weeks. Our lives are going to be changed forever, but our marriage is still on the rocks. It isn't how I thought it would be. The birth of your first child should be one of the most incredible moments of your life, but all I can think about is how Emily is mad at me. I need some advice. I need to go and see Granddad.

11.00 a.m.

Just back from visiting Granddad. I took some fresh flowers and laid them on his gravestone and we had a good chat. I told him all about Emily and asked him what I should do about it. It's going to sound silly. OK, it is silly, but after I asked him, the wind whipped up for a moment and blew across my face and I swear I felt something. It felt warm, almost as if Granddad was there with me. It's ridiculous. Granddad would agree, but for some reason I felt a lot calmer than when I arrived.

I bought Emily some flowers, but she didn't seem that bothered by them. Apparently, it's going to take a lot more than a bunch of flowers to win her back.

MONDAY, August 2nd, 10.00 a.m.

In the shed. Emily in Buckinghamshire for a couple of days. Heatwave in full swing (BBC weatherman suddenly seems to be taking full credit for the heatwave).

Emily announced this morning that she is going to spend the next couple of days at her parents' house in Buckinghamshire. It's her first day of maternity leave and I was going to see if she wanted to do something together, but what she really needs is a few days of complete and utter rest. Apparently, she can't get that at home with me. So much for giving me the chance to prove myself. I'm cleaning out the shed between cocktails. Windsurf board, skateboard, calligraphy set, tandem bike and radio-controlled aeroplane all going on eBay. A bittersweet day.

4.00 p.m.
Email from Ben.

G'Day you big lolloping fruity pop. How are things in lovely Wimbledon? Katie and I are coming home in a week! We brought it forward because I didn't want to miss the birth of my best mate's first. I spoke to Adam and he told me all about the stag party. All sounds good. I can't wait. We arrive August 8th, Heathrow at 2 p.m. Adam's coming to pick us up with the parentals. See you soon. Love to Emily. Ben and Katie x

I can't wait to see Ben again. My drinking buddy, best mate and confidant is back just in time. Maybe he can help save my marriage.

TUESDAY, August 3rd, 1.00 p.m.

In the garden. Emily still in Buckinghamshire. Stinking hot. Ali in his garden with the family (BBC weatherman taking all the plaudits. He's a big fraud!)

Sitting in the garden, smoking, drinking (bottles of beer in a bucket of ice = genius), listening to Blur on my iPod and reminiscing about my good old teenage years. A glorious day. It's a shame my wife isn't here to share it with me.

2.00 p.m.
Ali very kindly invited me over to his house for dinner. Off to break naan with the neighbours.

9.00 p.m.
Home alone, although not in a cute comedy featuring a young Macaulay Culkin way, but in a sad, grown-up, estranged from pregnant wife way.

I had an amazing time with Ali and his family. It turns out that Ali and his wife have an arranged marriage and they're very happy. We westerners often scoff at the idea of an arranged marriage, but Ali has a wonderful, close-knit, beautiful family, while on the other hand, I have a crumbling marriage and a probably-soon-to-be-bastard child.

WEDNESDAY, August 4th, 1.00 p.m.

Alone at The Alexandra. Emily still in Bucks.

Emily was supposed to come home today, but she decided to stay another day. I'm at the pub alone. I just saw two of my pupils try and get served. Luckily, they were turned away.

I can't wait for Ben to get back. I wonder what Rory is doing?

3.00 p.m.
At the pub with Rory.

THURSDAY, August 5th, 10.00 a.m.

'I leave for a couple of days and this is what I come home to?'

'Sorry, Emily,' said Rory.

'It isn't your fault, Rory,' said Emily. 'It's him.' She pointed at me.

'I think I'd better go,' said Rory.

'That might be a good idea,' said Emily.

Rory said goodbye and left me alone with a large, fuming Emily. I was in the lounge on the floor in a sleeping bag. I don't know why because Rory had fallen asleep on the sofa while we were playing Playstation. There were a few cans of lager around the place and a bit of leftover kebab on the armchair, but it wasn't that bad.

'I actually thought if I gave you a couple of days alone you might change. That you might see some sense and grow up, but instead you do this. Same old Harry. Nothing ever changes. I don't know why I bother.'

'Be fair, Em. I didn't expect you back so early. I was going to tidy up.'

'But that isn't the point, Harry.'

I was trying to think what the point was, but while I was thinking about it, Emily left the room and trudged upstairs.

That was thirty minutes ago. It seems that whatever I do, I'm destined to be in the doghouse.

SUNDAY, August 8th, 10.00 a.m.

Home. Still bloody hot. Emily reading in the lounge. Ben's coming home today!

'Look at this,' I said to Emily over breakfast. I showed her the newspaper article I was reading. Emily was squeezed in across from me at the breakfast table. Only a week until the little nipper is with us and Emily is the size of a house. She looks very uncomfortable. 'A man suffered third degree burns on his penis when his trousers caught on fire due to a faulty mobile phone. Ouch. Poor bastard.'

'Look at this,' said Emily, showing me her page. 'Five reasons why men cheat.' Fuckety fuck. 'Let's see which one you fit into shall we.'

'Do we have to do this?'

'We don't have to but it might be fun.'

I had to sit through all five reasons, while Emily gave me disgusted looks as she read out each one in turn. I didn't fully agree with any of them and I don't think I fit snugly into any. The five reasons were.

1. Boredom. I wasn't bored with my life and if I was, it would be much easier to get a new hobby than a new lover.

2. Genes. Apparently, men just can't help it. I couldn't argue or defend this one, but it's a lame excuse if you ask me. Sorry, Em, but it wasn't me, it was my genes.

3. Ego boost. I'll admit that yes, it did feel good that Jamie wanted me so much, but it wasn't why it started. It

may have played a part in why it continued, but I don't think I'm that shallow.

4. Not getting enough sex at home. Again, perhaps partly to blame, but I don't think it's that easy. Plus, Jamie and I didn't even have sex, so it wasn't like I was going to her for a daily shag.

5. Low self-esteem. I don't have low self-esteem and even if I did, it had nothing to do with Jamie.

'So, Harry, which is it?'

'None of the above.'

'Then what was it?'

This was a good question and a question I wasn't going to answer. I'm not going to put what Jamie and I had into a cosy little box and say, yes, there you go, that's what it was. I don't like that. It doesn't belong in a single box and it certainly couldn't be defined by a crap article in *The Sunday Times*.

'It doesn't matter because it's over. All I want to talk about is us and moving on.'

'And you don't think it's important we discuss what happened?'

'No, I don't. I think you want to talk about it because you haven't forgiven me yet, but what's the point in digging it all up again? The only way we're going to be happy again is when you start to forgive me and the only way that's going to happen is if you let go.'

'You want me to let it go? Just like that.'

'It's the only way.'

'But I don't know if I can. What then? What if I can't let go, Harry?'

'Then that's it.'

Emily and I looked at each other and then she started to cry. I knew then we were in big trouble.

6.00 p.m.
Off to see my old mate Ben.

MONDAY, August 9th, 11.00 a.m.

In the kitchen. Emily lying on the sofa. Still bloody hot (BBC weatherman predicting this will last another week!).

I went for a drink with Ben and it got a bit emotional to say the least. I got to his flat and said hello to Katie. They both looked exhausted, but Ben said he'd pop out for a quick drink. We went to the local across the road from Ben's flat and that's when it started. I poured. I didn't even know I had so much emotion in me. The floodgates opened when Ben said how sorry he was about Granddad and before I knew it I was telling him everything about Jamie and Emily, and tears were streaming down my face. It wasn't the sort of pub to be openly crying in, but I couldn't help it. I was a weepy, mawkish mess.

'Mate,' said Ben, giving me a sturdy tap on the shoulder. 'I'll get the whisky.'

Ben went and returned shortly with a couple of shots. We said cheers and then downed them in one. It's funny how a good shot of whisky can suddenly put things in perspective. My head cleared and the tears subsided.

'I'm sorry, mate,' I said.

'You've been through a lot. It's alright, but you really need to get things figured out with Emily.'

'I know. I just don't know how.'

'It's not going to be easy and you've only got a week until the baby.'

'A week to save my marriage.'

'The thing is though, mate, she loves you. She wouldn't have taken you back at all if she didn't. It's a start.'

'I know, but what good's love if she doesn't trust me and won't forgive me.'

'Fair point. So, honestly, are you completely over Jamie?'

The best thing about talking it over with Ben is that he's just my mate. He isn't going to judge me, hate me or think I'm a complete bastard and even if he did, he wouldn't tell me.

'I think I'll always have feelings for her. She was my first and we have a special bond. There's something about her I can't put into words, but I love Emily and I want to be with her. She's my wife.'

'Then go and get her tiger.'

'I'm sorry, mate. Tonight was supposed to be about you coming home and getting married in a few weeks. I'll sort this mess out.'

'If you need me though.'

'I know where you are. I lived there remember?'

It was wonderful to see Ben again and great to get a lot of things off my chest. It isn't that he can necessarily help, but he's my best mate and I know he understands. In fact, he probably understands me better than anyone else alive.

We spent the next few hours playing pool, drinking, smoking and Ben told me all about Australia and how much he loved Katie. It was great to see him so happy. It was great to be together again.

I got home late and Emily was asleep in her usual position, surrounded by her barrier of pillows. I watched her sleep for a while. I wanted to hug her and kiss her but I couldn't. Mainly because of the pillows, but also because we don't have that at the moment. We haven't hugged and kissed for a while. She's my wife and I love her. I love the baby that's growing inside of her.

I'd been an absolute bloody fool, but she had to forgive me because what's the alternative? Trial separation? Actual separation? Marriage counselling? Divorce? Could we do that to each other? To our baby?

TUESDAY, August 10th, 1.00 p.m.

In the shed. Too hot to smoke. Too hot for cocktails. Just too hot. Emily lying down.

I've been thinking about my relationship with Jamie and I think I understand now what it meant. Jamie was my fantasy. She was my real-life porn. We had none of the day-to-day realities of a relationship and so in my mind, she was perfect. She always wore matching, sexy underwear, she didn't care if I left the toilet seat up, she didn't get annoyed by my 'man-tention span', the sex was incredible and frequent, she always looked stunning, she didn't fart in bed, she didn't have moods or make me go shopping at IKEA for five hours. Jamie was everything I wanted in my head, but it wasn't anywhere near real.

Maybe at first all relationships are about fantasy and illusion. During the honeymoon phase girls do wear matching sexy underwear, we let the little things go because the sex is incredible and frequent, we don't fart in bed and make each other do things we know they don't want to. However, once we get past that and the girls stop wearing the lacy black thong with matching sexy bra and instead reach for the period pants and we start trumping in bed like it's an Olympic sport, you reach the reality of relationships. It's about loving someone because of their faults and flaws. It's about living with them, despite all of their annoying habits, but knowing it doesn't matter because you will always love them regardless.

With Jamie the reality would have been very different from the fantasy because, like all girls, she would eventually have started wearing her big pants and I would have started farting for fun because that's just what happens.

WEDNESDAY, August 11th, 8.00 p.m.

Home. Emily asleep. Eating a bagel. Drinking tea. The heatwave broke today. The BBC weatherman did something very brave and said he'd predicted it, despite only yesterday saying it would last another week!

Baby doctor appointment today with Dr Proops. The man gets to see more of Emily's vagina than I do (a terribly sad but true statistic). Everything was fine with the baby. Emily also asked him to examine her breasts because they were a bit tender. It was strange because I hadn't seen much of them myself lately and I got a bit excited. They're enormous!

On the way home, Emily announced that tomorrow we're babysitting Steve and Fiona's brood of Js. Normally this would have set me on course for deep depression, followed by anxiety, followed by alcohol, followed by being in trouble with Emily, but not today. Today I saw it as an opportunity to show Emily that Harry Spencer is a new man!

THURSDAY, August 12th, 9.00 p.m.

Home. Exhausted. Emily asleep. Longest day ever. Happy.

What a day. We arrived at Steve and Fiona's late morning. James was going down for his nap. Joseph would go down in about an hour and Jane would be awake for the whole day. The newest member of the group, Jasmine, wasn't on a schedule yet and so we would have to play it by ear with her. It didn't seem too bad. Steve and Fiona looked exhausted. Steve barely registered our arrival. Would we be this tired in a few weeks? Would I look as bad as Steve? Would I smell as bad as Steve? As soon as we arrived they bolted. They were going to her parents for the afternoon to sleep.

It started well. Emily read books with Joseph and I watched *Toy Story* with Jane while Jasmine slept. We were in bliss. Outside it was blustery, but we were indoors and everything was going great. After an hour, Emily put Joseph down and it was peaceful. This wasn't so bad, I thought to myself, but I should have known. I should have prepared myself for what was to come. It all started with Emily.

'I'm going to take a little nap,' she said.

It didn't seem like a bad idea. Three of the Js were happily asleep while Jane was busy watching *Toy Story* with me. What could possibly go wrong?

'OK, no worries,' I said and so off she went to the spare room for a quick power nap. I was safe on the sofa with Jane. *Toy Story* had at least another hour left. However, as soon as Emily was gone Jane turned on me,

'Uncle Harry, can we make cakes? I want to make cakes.'

'I don't think that's such a good idea.'

There was no way we were going to leave the safety of the sofa and makes cakes. No way.

Ten minutes later and we were in the kitchen making cakes. I don't know how it happened. Jane started crying and I caved. Twenty minutes later we were in the middle of stirring cake mixture, there were eggs and flour everywhere, cracked eggshells on the floor and that's when Jasmine woke up and started screaming.

'Don't do anything until I get back,' I said to Jane.

'Of course, Uncle Harry.'

I went back into the lounge where tiny Jasmine was crying her little lungs out. I gingerly picked her up, hoping to hear Emily come trotting down the stairs but no such luck. Jasmine was still crying. I thought she was probably just hungry and I knew her milk was in the fridge. I just had to heat it up and so I headed for the kitchen. I was going to show Emily I could be responsible, grown up and a good father. That's when I heard the crash in the kitchen. I walked into a war zone. There were eggs all over the floor, spilt milk, flour everywhere and Jane was sitting in the middle of it, licking cake mixture off her fingers.

'I fell, Uncle Harry,' she said.

Jasmine was still crying.

'What the hell happened?' I yelled, which in hindsight wasn't a very smart idea, because this made Jane start crying. This was a disaster. For a moment, I thought about waking Emily up, but a part of me knew I had to do this on my own. This was my moment to shine. This was the moment I could show Emily I'd changed. I had to think quickly. I needed to get Jane cleaned up and Jasmine fed. I was a teacher, this should be a piece of cake. 'OK, Jane, everything's fine. Can you please clean up your mess while I feed Jasmine?'

'What do I get?' Cheeky little bugger.

'You don't get in trouble with your parents for making a complete mess of their kitchen.'

'Fine,' she said, rolling her eyes. She's going to be trouble when she's a teenager.

'Now, let's get you fed,' I said to Jasmine.

I quickly heated up Jasmine's bottle and before long she

was in my arms happily sucking on her bottle, while Jane tidied up the last of her mess. We had done it and just in time because Emily came walking into the room just as Jane threw the last eggshell into the bin and smiled like an angel.

'Everything OK?' said Emily with a yawn.

'Yeah, perfect.'

Emily looked around the room and smiled.

'It looks like you have everything under control.' I'd done it. I'd taken care of the kids on my own. Well, almost. 'Is that cake batter?' she said to Jane. Jane, wonderful girl that she is, had done a great job tidying up the kitchen, but not such a good job tidying up herself. She had chocolate cake mixture all over her shirt.

'Umm,' said Jane, looking at me.

'It's OK,' Emily said looking at me with a smile. 'You tried.'

The rest of the day was pretty much a success. Emily and I had a great time with the kids. Jasmine woke up, cried and we either changed her nappy or fed her. Jane, Joseph and James were all wonderful. We took them out to the park and all in all, we had a great day. Long, exhausting, but wonderful nonetheless. None of the kids were lost, died or said any of the major swear words. Emily even held my hand in the park.

SATURDAY, August 14th, 10.00 a.m.

At home. Lying on the bed watching Emily's belly. One day and counting.

Tom's due tomorrow and I'm starting to panic. It's odd because we've waited patiently for nine months and it always felt so far away, almost like it wasn't really happening, but now it's here. We're going to have a baby. Bringing a life into the world is like nothing else because it's forever. Once the little fella comes out, that's it. Our lives won't ever be the same again.

Since yesterday things have been a tiny bit better with Emily. We're talking and being slightly more affectionate, which wouldn't be hard considering I've had more physical contact with our postman during the past two months.

Emily's ridiculously large and uncomfortable. She can't even get out of bed by herself, poor thing. I'm spending my time rubbing lotion on her belly, helping her in and out of bed and making her food. It feels like I'm taking care of a very large, elderly relative. This is what the children of sumo wrestlers have to look forward to.

SUNDAY, August 15th, 9.00 a.m.
Due date

Emily couldn't sleep again last night because she was too uncomfortable. She really is bloody miserable. Fingers crossed the little fella comes today.

10.00 a.m.
Mum rang.

'Any news?' she said excitedly.

'Sorry, Mum.'

'Let me know as soon as anything happens.'

'Will do.'

2.00 p.m.
Mum rang again.

'Any news?'

'Not yet.'

'Let me know.'

'Will do.'

3.00 p.m.

Steve and Fiona rang.

'Any news? Has the water broken? Is she dilated? OMG! OMG! We're so excited.'

'Hello, Steve. Nothing yet.'

'Tell Emily we're thinking of her. Aren't we dear?'

'Hello, Harry, it's Fiona. We're so excited. Tell her we're thinking of her.'

'Will do.'

'And if you need anything.'

'Anything,' chirped Steve.

'Will do.'

'It's so exciting. Aren't you excited?'

'Very.'

'Well, we'd better let you go and take care of her. Call us as soon as anything happens.'

'Right, will do.'

'Anything,' said Steve.

OMG! I'm going to kill myself.

4.00 p.m.

Emily thought she felt something, but it turned out she just needed to go to the toilet.

8.00 p.m.

Still nothing. He's probably going to come during the night and wake us up.

9.00 p.m.

Mum rang again.

'Still nothing?' she said.

'Oh, shit, I forgot to call you. She went into labour two hours ago and he was just born.'

'What! Harry, no, how could you?'

'I'm joking, Mum. I'll tell you as soon as something happens.'

'Oh, Dear Lord, you almost gave me a coronary.'

'Sorry, love you.'

MONDAY, August 16th, 9.00 a.m.
Due day plus one

Still nothing. Emily getting very frustrated. She looks miserable. She is miserable.

'Why won't he come out?'

'It's probably nice and warm in there. I wouldn't want to come out either.'

'But the little bugger is killing me, Harry. He's sitting under my rib cage and kicking the shit out of me.'

'Let me have a word,' I said. I got down next to her belly, rubbed it and said, 'Hello, mate. I realise it's lovely and warm in there and you probably don't fancy coming out into the big wide world, but trust me, it isn't that bad. It seems terrifying at first. It's big, loud, colourful and full of really annoying people, but it's also full of people who will love you, make you happy and make life worth living. Plus, at the moment, your mum's really bloody miserable and she'd really appreciate it if you would come out.' Emily giggled above me.

'I hope that works, otherwise we're going for an Indian tonight.'

10.00 a.m.
Mum rang.

    'No news yet, Mum.'

    'Is she feeling anything?'

    'Annoyed, frustrated, tired, angry.'

    'That's not what I meant.'

    'I know.'

    'Just call me. Your father and I are on tenterhooks.'

2.00 p.m.
Ben rang.

    'Any sign of the sprog yet?'

    'Not yet, mate.'

    'Tell Emily we're thinking of her.'

    'Will do, thanks.'

    'And Katie said to try watching *Neighbours* while eating a Vegemite sandwich. It's supposed to help.'

    'Seriously?'

    'No, I made that up. The best thing is a good shag.'

    'Yeah, well that isn't likely unless she gets really desperate.'

    'She married you.'

    'Thanks for the support.'

4.00 p.m.
Nothing. Emily wants to go to Wimbledon Tandoori for a vindaloo. We're going to smoke the little fella out!

9.00 p.m.
That was frighteningly impressive. Emily finished a whole vindaloo curry. I had one bite and almost died. She is a trooper.

    'Well, something's definitely coming out tomorrow,' she said on the way home.

Let's hope it weighs about seven pounds with a full head of hair.

TUESDAY, August 17th, 7.00 a.m.
Due day plus two

Still nothing. Emily getting more frustrated. She looks more miserable. She is more miserable.

Another sleepless night. Emily rolled around like a beached whale while I lay there being tossed around like a pebble in the surf. It was hellish. I woke up at five o'clock this morning (after about two hours of actual sleep). Emily's still in bed, although what she's doing I have no idea.

As terrified as I am of being a father, nothing can be as awful as the waiting. I actually wish it was term time so I had an excuse to leave the house. As it is, I feel terrible for leaving her for a moment just in case something happens. It's like we're in jail and little Tom is the prison guard.

8.00 a.m.
Mum rang.

'No,' I said before she even spoke. 'We're going to the doctor today.'

'Just checking. Do you know the way to the hospital, Harry?'

'Yes.'

'The quickest way?'

'No, I only know the longest way.'

'There's no need to be sarcastic.'

'I'm sorry. I love you.'

'I love you too.'

10.00 a.m.
Emily just called down so I could help her get out of bed.

'Why did we buy such a high bed?' she said.

'We didn't. We bought a regular-size bed, but now you're the size of Belgium.'

'Thanks, that really helps.'

7.00 p.m.
Dr Proops examined her and said she wasn't remotely dilated.

'Nothing to worry about yet,' he said casually.

It's alright for him: he doesn't have to live in the same house as her. Getting desperate.

FRIDAY, August 20th, 9.00 a.m.
Due day plus five

Still nothing. Emily miserable. Me miserable. Raining.

10.00 a.m.
Dad rang.

'Hello, Son.'

'Hi, Dad, how's things?'

'Yeah, good. Just thought I'd see how things were doing . . . you know . . . with Emily.'

'Did Mum make you call?'

'Yes.'

'You can tell her we're still waiting.'

'Righto.'

4.00 p.m.

Ali came over this afternoon. He brought an ancient Indian potion that was supposed to help the baby slide right out. It smelled awful.

'What's in it?' asked Emily.

'If I told you, you would never drink it,' said Ali.

Emily was so desperate she downed it in one. Hopefully it does the trick.

11.00 p.m.

What a night! Emily and I just had sex! It was odd, a bit uncomfortable, difficult, but we did it!

It all started at about eight o'clock. Emily and I were downstairs watching telly when she turned to me and said, 'Harry, I need to get him out. We need to have sex.'

My first thought was, yes, of course, how quickly can we get upstairs and undressed (not very quickly as it turned out), but then I had another thought.

'No.'

'What?' Emily said incredulously.

'We can't have sex just because you need to. We need to have sex because you've forgiven me, because you want me, because it's time to move on. Are you ready to move on, Em?'

Emily looked at me in shock. I don't think she knew what to say. Luckily, for me she soon did.

'Yes, I think so.'

'Are you just saying that because you want to get him out of there?'

'No, I mean it. I was waiting for something to happen and it just did.'

'What, me turning down sex?'

'Exactly. I know how desperate you are and the fact you said no proved something to me. I love you, Harry.'

'I love you too.'

We looked at one another and smiled and then we went upstairs and had sex for the first time in months.

Before I move on, a quick word on having sex with a vastly pregnant woman. It wasn't just difficult, but like trying to fit a square block into a round hole, while being repeatedly pushed away by a giant inflatable ball. OK, so I'm being a bit dramatic, but it wasn't easy. There were also the geographical distractions. No one ever mentioned to me that when a woman is on the verge of delivering a baby, things unexpectedly move. I'd spent the last thirty-two years with the same old vagina map. I knew where I was going, what to avoid and what to find, but now everything had adjusted and things weren't in the same places. I was left fumbling around in the dark, hoping to stumble upon something that felt familiar. Luckily, I eventually did, but it was more through luck than actual judgement.

Emily lay there, naked, giant, while above her I tried to position myself in such a way that I could get myself in, while avoiding the belly and have sufficient room to actually thrust in and out. Obviously, due to the physical constraints and the laughter, it wasn't the greatest sex we ever had and it didn't last very long, but it didn't matter because it meant so much more than ever before. It meant that despite everything that has happened this year, Emily and I are going to be OK.

4.00 a.m.
The bed's soaking wet. We're soaking wet. Her water broke. We're off to the hospital! Sex worked! Tom's coming!

MONDAY, August 23rd, 9.00 a.m.

At the hospital. Emily and son asleep. Knackered. Happy. Overwhelmed with love.

Where do I begin? I was asleep when suddenly my dream got very aquatic. I woke up and realised why. Emily's water had broken and we were both drenched. It was very surreal.

'Are you wet?' she said.

'Very, you?'

'Soaked. I think my water broke.'

'He's coming,' we said in unison.

The next hour was a bit hazy. Despite being ready, having our hospital bag packed and knowing the quickest route to the hospital with my eyes closed, we were frantic. Probably because the idea of having a baby at home or, worse still, on the way to the hospital was terrifying. We did, however, get to the hospital safe and sound.

We checked in, got our room and then we waited. The nurse checked Emily out and she was dilated but not enough. She said it could be a while. It was at this point we had to make the decision. Did we call our parents now or wait. We decided to call them. Emily was worried that little Tom would come suddenly and her parents would miss it. An hour later and both sets of parents were waiting with us.

Dr Proops came and went, nurses looked, took her vitals, left and came back and did it all over again. Coffee was bought, drunk and still we waited. Emily's contractions were coming and gradually getting more and more intense. Eventually, after nearly three hours, Emily had the epidural. We weren't allowed to see it, but I saw the needle and almost passed out. It was enormous. It had the desired effect though and suddenly the pain went away and she looked very serene.

'Pauline wouldn't approve. We didn't try meditating, yoga, beating on bongos or anything,' I said to Emily.

'Fuck that,' said Emily. 'Just give me the drugs.'

It took a while, but eventually, nine hours after being admitted, it all started to kick off. Dr Proops came, nurses came and it was time to start pushing. Both dads left the room (Emily's orders) and so it was just me, Emily and the mums.

'Push dear,' said my mum.

'You can do it, honey,' said Emily's mum.

'I love you,' I said, holding her hand tightly.

It got very emotional. There was lots of grunting, huffing, puffing, sweating and swearing. During a momentary pause and feeling brave, I left the safety of the head end and ventured south to watch proceedings at the business end. It was like something from a sci-fi/horror film. It wasn't the same vagina I'd seen up close and personal on many occasions. I quickly re-joined Emily, giving her my support where she needed it and where I could stomach it.

'I can't do it. It's too hard,' said Emily between grunts.

We all encouraged her on. Her grip on my hand got tighter and then a miracle. His head suddenly appeared. The mums gasped and started crying. I leaned forward and sure enough, there he was.

Our baby.

My son.

Tom.

'Keep going, almost there,' I said to Emily between sniffled tears.

'Don't you start bloody crying,' said Emily.

Ten minutes later, one huge push and suddenly out he popped. It was incredible. It was awe-inspiring, beautiful and I was already madly in love with him. Everyone was crying.

I cut the cord and then Dr Proops gave him to us and Emily cuddled him on her chest. It was magical. The most wonderful moment of my life. Both dads were quickly called in and even they melted. My dad, the very definition of emotionally redundant, had tears in his eyes. For the first time in my life, I saw the soft core of my father exposed. He looked at Tom and looked so proud and so happy. Then Derek, tough ex-copper and often hater of yours truly, started crying and gave me a hug and I knew then we'd done something incredible.

The next day was another blur, but people came and went. Steve and Fiona (minus Js), Rory and Miranda, Ben and Katie, Ken and Kara, Stella from Kingston upon Thames, all stopped by. The grandparents milled around, all holding him and looking as proud as I've ever seen them. Emily and I have slept a little, but mainly just sat and gazed at our little bundle of joy. Then, late on Sunday evening, Emily turned to me and said,

'You know, I'm not sure he looks like a Tom.'

'What do you mean?'

'He just doesn't look like a Tom. He doesn't have that certain Tom-ness.'

'What are you saying?'

'I think we should call him William.'

'After my granddad?'

'Yes,' Emily said and I started crying again.

So, just like that, Tom became William, Emily and I were parents and nothing else in the world seemed to matter anymore.

11.00 a.m.
Watching William and Emily sleep.

He's beautiful. I had nightmares he was going to be horren-dously ugly, with an unfortunate-looking birthmark in the shape of a penis on his forehead, but he's perfect. I'm sure all new parents think that (even the ones with the really hideous kids), but he truly is gorgeous.

Unfortunately, the only trouble with William is that noth-ing is wrong with him. Dr Proops came by and said we can go home this afternoon. Just to put that into perspective, since he arrived we've been in the safety, care and comfort-able surroundings of the hospital, seconds from help, support and a whole ward full of nurses and doctors. This afternoon, we will have to go home, alone, miles from the hospital, safety, care and support and be by ourselves. It's terrifying to say the least. Not that we can't do it or that we've needed lots of help, but taking a baby home is scary because what if something goes wrong? What if the house is too cold or too hot? What if he won't stop crying? What if he won't eat? What if he gets sick? Plus, I've really been enjoying the hospital canteen. The food is excellent and they bring a little menu around each day so we can pick out what we want. It's like being in a very sterile hotel. I don't want to leave.

WEDNESDAY, August 25th, 7.00 p.m.

Home. Exhausted. Hungry. Smelly. Emily feeding William.

We haven't slept for more than a couple of hours since he was born. We're both completely and utterly knackered. We've barely eaten and I haven't showered in nearly three days. We're both running on autopilot. We float around the house taking care of William, occasionally mumbling to each other. I don't know how I'm going to stay awake during Ben's stag party.

THURSDAY, August 26th, 8.00 a.m.

William pukes, does tiny (but smelly) poos, sleeps, wakes up, screams, eats and demands our complete attention. I love him so much. Emily's exhausted. I've given her the day to sleep. I'm taking William to my parents' house (along with small bottles of milk Emily pumped). I'm tempted to try some.

9.30 a.m.
It tastes slightly sweet and watery. Not as creamy as cow's milk but not unpleasant.

9.00 p.m.
What a great day. I slept properly in my old bedroom. Mum took care of William and absolutely loved it. I took a shower and changed my clothes. I feel human again.

I got home about an hour ago. I stopped off on the way and got us dinner. It's strange because while Emily and I were locked away with William, the world kept on going about its business. People were still going to work, shopping, living and doing everything we weren't. It's also good to see Emily looking vaguely normal again. We had dinner, watched telly and actually had time for a cuddle while William slept next to us. It was absolute bliss.

FRIDAY, August 27th, 11.00 a.m.

Text from Rory.

*Decided to give fatherhood a bash. If
you and Picasso can manage it, maybe
I can too!*

Hooray!

SATURDAY, August 28th, 7.00 a.m.

Ben's stag party. Already exhausted after another restless,
fitful night's sleep. Emily off to her parents' for the weekend.
I was concerned she wouldn't want me to go on Ben's stag
party and I offered not to go, but she's fine. I'm excited to
spend some time with Ben and Adam, although the thought
of being awake until the early hours of the morning terrifies
me. Off to get ready for a day of action, followed by an
evening of drinking!

SUNDAY, August 29th, 11.00 a.m.

Ben's flat. Seeing double. Head sore. Body aches. Throat
sore. Partially naked. Body next to me (possibly/hopefully
Adam?). Sunny.

Never again. I know I've said that before, but I wasn't a dad
before. I'm going to need at least three or four days to recover
but I don't have that anymore. We did have a wonderful time
though. The day of outdoor activities was fantastic. We drove

into deepest, darkest Surrey (I didn't know it got that deep and dark), to a lovely old mansion where we indulged every boyhood fantasy (the clean ones at least. Miss Garibaldi, my old French teacher wasn't there dressed in a netball outfit). We played paintball. We did archery, abseiling, rode off-road three wheelers and attempted clay pigeon shooting (I shot everything but the bloody clay pigeon). We returned to civilisation for the evening, where the drinking and fun really began. Here are the abbreviated highlights (from my rather precarious memory).

6.00 p.m.: Covent Garden with Ben, Adam, Bano, Ben's dad Gordon and Ritchie. Started drinking at the Punch and Judy.

6.05 p.m.: Covent Garden. Bano started chatting up a group of girls who were on a hen night.

6.10 p.m.: Bano last seen heading outside with the bride.

6.45 p.m.: No sign of Bano or bride.

7.00 p.m.: Girls from hen group started crying when they realised that neither the bride nor Bano were coming back soon.

7.30 p.m.: Text from Bano: 'With bride hotel cu l8r x'.

8.00 p.m.: We left the Punch and Judy and headed off towards the next pub. On the way, Ben's dad Gordon thought he saw Ann Widdecombe and wanted to say hello.

8.05 p.m.: Turned out it wasn't Ann Widdecombe, but a cross-dressing man on his way to a cross-dressing club. Gordon was very disappointed. Cross-dressing man was very annoyed. 'Ann fucking Widdecombe? It took me two hours to get ready you cheeky fucker!'

8.40 p.m.: We bought Ben a yard of ale. Ben drank yard of ale to gallant cheers and thumps on the back. All very impressed.

8.45 p.m.: Ben returned from toilet after throwing up a

whole yard of ale. More gallant cheers and thumps on the back.

9.00 p.m.: Text from Bano, 'Leaving hotel c u soon bride was filthy x'.

9.45 p.m.: Somewhere in Soho. Bano back in the fold and suggested we go to a lap dancing club.

9.46 p.m.: Everyone declared Bano a genius and we headed off to lap dancing club.

10.15 p.m.: At lap dancing club. Tits everywhere. We paid for Ben to have a lap dance. More gallant cheers and thumps on the back.

10.25 p.m.: Ritchie was spotted giving his card to a lap dancer. Gallant cheers and thumps on the back until we realised she just needed some financial advice.

10.30 p.m.: We paid for Ben's dad to have a lap dance. Even more gallant cheers and thumps on the back.

10.45 p.m.: Thrown out of lap dancing club because Bano didn't adhere to the strict no hands on the tits rule.

11.30 p.m.: Club somewhere near Soho. All very drunk. Danced like idiots, including Gordon, who unbuttoned his shirt!

11.45 p.m.: Girl started snogging Gordon!

12.00 a.m.: Ben declared he loved us all very much.

12.01 a.m.: We declared we all loved Ben very much.

1.15 a.m.: I'm asked to leave after falling asleep on the corner of the dance floor. We all left together.

2.00 a.m.: All of us sitting in a kebab shop stuffing our faces with London's greasiest, dirtiest, spiciest and best kebabs. Despite falling asleep earlier, I managed to finish a large kebab with v. hot chilli sauce. Bano tried to chat up the girl behind the counter, until her dad started shouting at him, 'She's only fourteen! Dirty bastard! Dirty bastard! Fourteen!'

2.45 a.m.: To bed. Alone, drunk, chilli sauce all over chin, hugging pillow. A great day!

september

SATURDAY, September 4th, 7.00 a.m.

'Love you, Em.'

'Love you too, Harry.'

'I'm so glad we're back to normal.'

'Me too.'

'It got a bit weird there for a while.'

'It did.'

'Deidre St Cloud was a nutter. Admit it.'

'She was a bit eccentric.'

'Fucking barmy as a fruit cake.'

'OK, fine, she was barmy, but I was only trying to help.'

'And that's why I love you so much. And Pauline, what was wrong with her?'

'Now she was barmy.'

'But I thought you loved her. You were going crazy with those bongos.'

'I only wanted to go because I knew you'd hate it. Call it payback.'

'You fiendish little minx. I suppose I deserved it.'

'You did. You do know we can't have sex for at least another six weeks.'

'Unfortunately, yes.'

'But that doesn't mean I can't do other things for you.'

'Things like?' I said and then Emily smiled and slid down towards my groin. 'But William's in the room.'

'He's asleep.'

'I know but it feels weird.'

'You don't want me to do it?'

'I didn't say that.'

7.30 a.m.

'Shouldn't you be getting ready? I thought you had to be at Ben's by nine.'

'I'm waiting for the orgasm coma to wear off.'

'And how long does that normally take?'

'I don't know, ten to twenty minutes. I should be alright soon.'

'He's gorgeous,' said Emily looking across at William asleep in his cot.

'He is. He looks like you, you know.'

'Do you think so?'

'Definitely. A smaller, boy version of you, but he's definitely all you.'

'He has your eyes.'

'And my penis. Have you seen the size of that thing?'

'Harry, that's your son we're talking about.'

'Sorry.'

'You know we still have to decorate his bedroom.'

'We have plenty of time though. He's going to be sleeping in our room for a couple of months. I'll get to it soon.'

'Do I have to remind you how long it took you to clean out the shed?'

'I'll start on Monday.'

'Thank you.'

'I'm going to jump in the shower.'

'Orgasm coma gone?'

'Nearly, but I think I have to risk it. I can't be late for Ben's wedding. I'm the best man after all.'

'Joint best man.'

'Right, joint best man.'

11.45 p.m.
Hotel room. Eating salted peanuts. Drinking a beer. Watching
Emily and William sleep. Distant rumbling of music from the
wedding in the background. Very happy.

I finally got to Ben's just before nine o'clock this morning.
When I got there Ben was sitting on the balcony smoking,
while Adam and his dad were watching the telly.

'Morning,' I said walking in cheerfully.

'He's got cold feet,' said Adam. 'We've both spoken to him,
but he won't listen to anyone. Maybe you could have a word.'

'Of course,' I said and headed straight out to the balcony.

I couldn't believe he was getting cold feet. I knew how
much he loved Katie. He was happy with her. He loved
Australia. What could possibly have made him get cold feet?

'You,' said Ben.

'What? Why?'

'Because of what happened between you and Jamie. That
could happen to me too.'

'Why do you say that?'

'Because if it can happen to you, it can happen to anyone.
I always thought you and Emily were perfect. You were always
so happy together and if it can happen to you, what's stopping it from happening to me?'

'Nothing. That's the point though, mate. It doesn't matter
who you are, who you're with, how happy you are, mistakes
can happen, but it isn't the mistakes that destroy you, it's how
you deal with them. Emily and I are great now. We're as happy
as we've ever been. We bounced back because we are a great
couple. Just like you and Katie. I've never seen you so happy.'

'She is incredible.'

'And you'd be a fool to throw that away because you're
worried you might slip up and make a mistake. You of all people

should know you can't make decisions based on what might go wrong, because if you do that, you'd never do anything.'

'I know, but what if I meet someone else? What if I meet someone I like more?'

'That might happen. It probably will. You know how I feel about Jamie, but at some point we have to make a decision. Stick or twist. Do you love Katie?'

'Of course.'

'Do you fancy her silly?'

'Have you seen her?'

'Well, yes, she's gorgeous. Could you live with her?'

'We have been.'

'And does she have any annoying habits?'

'Of course, plenty.'

'But any you can't get over?'

'No, it's all silly stuff and besides, have you seen her?'

'And how's the sex?'

'Phenomenal. The best I've ever had.'

'And does she make you a better person?'

'A million times over.'

'So you love her, fancy her, can live with her and the sex is incredible and she makes you a better person. You're ready to get married. Now, come here, let's have a man hug and then you can get married. Deal?'

'Deal.'

Another minor disaster averted.

The next few hours passed in a whirlwind, but at two o'clock, an hour before the service, we were all in the pub across the road from the church having a last-minute drink. Ben is my best mate and it was wonderful to see him so happy. Ben and I played a game of pool and it felt like the end of an era. This was it. We were grown-ups. This used to be the norm. Saturdays in the pub, watching football, playing pool, drinking, before going to a club to try and pull a girl, but almost always failing, a greasy late-night kebab to heal the pain of failure, before home to play Playstation and then eventually to bed alone. That was then and this is now.

Now I have a wife and a baby to go home to at the end of the day. Ben was about to get married and would no doubt have kids himself one day. I would always miss those days but times change, people change and we can't long for something that doesn't exist anymore. The only thing to do is to embrace the present. Plus, there's nothing sadder than a single, middle-aged man at a nightclub, trying to pull a girl half his age. I don't want to be That Guy and neither does Ben. We were moving on together.

A couple of pints later and we headed to the church. Despite the three pints and a whisky chaser, Ben was a bag of nerves, while I was just focused on not losing the rings. As it turned out, the wedding was perfect.

Katie showed up on time and looked absolutely gorgeous, the organ player (despite looking dead), was fantastic, while the vicar did a great job of not being too religious and I didn't lose the rings. When it came to the 'I do's neither of them forgot their lines. Emily and William were sitting near the back of the church, in case they needed to make a hasty exit, but luckily William slept through the whole thing. Bless him.

They left the church to rapturous applause, before we all threw confetti over them outside (much to the vicar's annoyance). The weather was perfect, the couple was perfect and nothing was going to ruin this day. Not even Bano, who seemed determined to sleep with all of the bridesmaids and if not the bridesmaids then their mothers!

Then it was time for speeches. Adam and I had reached an agreement. We were going to do our version of good cop bad cop. Adam was going to do the good speech. He was going to recount happy childhood memories, tell Ben how much he loved him, etc. I, on the other hand, was going to do the bad speech, including embarrassing stories, any sexual/sheep references and drunken escapades. Luckily, I had lots of stories about Ben. After Adam had everyone in tears, it was my turn.

'Dearest Ben,

'You are my oldest friend, my best friend, my mentor, my inspiration and without you my life wouldn't be half as happy as it is today (wait for the crowd to get all soppy). However, a best man's speech without embarrassing sexual stories just wouldn't be a speech, which reminds me of that time when we were fifteen (wait for giggles).

'Ben was a bit of a late developer when it came to girls. A number of girls had tried to kiss him, but he thought the idea grotesque. That was until Julie Healey entered our lives. Julie was gorgeous, had breasts and for some reason quite fancied Ben. One day at school, she made it known she wanted Ben to kiss her and so Ben, never having kissed a girl before, decided to go for it. It was his big moment. They were going to meet behind the bike sheds after school. I went along for support. We waited for Julie and then, just as we thought she wasn't going to come, she arrived with her best friend in tow. By this point, however, Ben was so nervous and so afraid that as she walked towards him expecting a bit of tonsil hockey, Ben threw up all over her. She was covered (wait for huge laughs to die down). Ben had to wait another six months for his first kiss.

'Luckily, his first sexual experience went much smoother. Her name was Daisy. She was lovely, everyone said so. She had something magical about her. Maybe it was her fluffy, white coat, or her little hoofs, but as sheep went, Daisy was a beauty (hearty laughs all around).

'Seriously, Ben, you are an incredible man and Katie is the luckiest woman alive. Without being too sentimental, you are like a brother to me. I love you. I wish you weren't moving so far away, but whether you're two miles away or ten thousand, we will always be close.

'Katie, take care of him and if you ever break his heart, you'll have me to answer to. I wish you both all the happiness in the world. Ladies and gentleman, please raise your glasses to the happy couple. Ben and Katie!' (Lots of cheers, whistles and clapping).

Two hours later and Ben, Adam, Ben's dad Gordon, my dad, my mum (well pissed) and me were dancing like idiots to 'Come on Eileen'. We were sweating, kicking our legs in the air, pretending we knew the words and almost injuring other dancers in the process. As it was, I think I only ended up injuring myself (tight groin).

We sang, we danced, we drank, we smoked, talked late into the night, until eventually I found myself sitting with Emily and William. Emily had her head on my shoulder and William was asleep in my arms.

My wife and my son.

My whole world.

I'd made mistakes. I'd put this in jeopardy, but I had come out the other side and I think for the first time in my life, I feel complete. Maybe I needed Jamie to make me appreciate what I had. Maybe Jamie needed me so she could move on. Today we're happy, but tomorrow's another day and who knows what it will bring. I know one person who definitely doesn't know what the future holds. The BBC weatherman. He predicted it would rain today, but it's been the sunniest, driest day of the year. It's time he was fired. Seriously.

acknowledgements

Mum and Dad, for always encouraging me to follow my dreams.

My big Sis for being my big Sis. Apologies for the lack of vampires.

Simon, Darren, Steve, Malcolm and Stuart B, for always being my best mates.

Stuart Wilkinson, co-founder of the post-Dada lyricists, co-creator of the funniest joke of all-time and an important resource about teaching. Thanks mate.

Rupert, Kate, Peter, Richard, Mark, Liz, Simon, Alison, Johnny, Carrie, Lauren and everyone else at university who stopped me from studying and encouraged me to go to the pub instead. If I had worked harder, I may have got a proper job.

Gurmeet Matu, a great bloke from Scotland.

My daughter Charlotte and son Jack for giving me the inspiration to write a book about fatherhood.

Lastly, to everyone else I've ever met, because without all of you I wouldn't have reached this point in my life in exactly the same way.

Jon x

Watch out for Jon Rance's sweetly funny and touchingly honest second novel,

HAPPY ENDINGS

This is a novel about people just like us.

Kate wants to go travelling before she reaches the big Three-O, while her long-term boyfriend, Ed, just wants to settle down.

Jack is desperate to be a published writer for many reasons, but mainly to save his relationship with fiancée Emma.

Emma wants to be an actress more than anything in the world, or at least that's what she thought . . .

Told uniquely from four perspectives, this is a story about love, growing up and, of course, the search for a happy ending.

HODDER

Do you wish this wasn't the end?

Join us at www.hodder.co.uk, or follow us on
Twitter @hodderbooks to be a part of our community
of people who love the very best in books and reading.

Whether you want to discover more about a book
or an author, watch trailers and interviews, have the
chance to win early limited editions, or simply browse
our expert readers' selection of the very best books,
we think you'll find what you're looking for.

And if you don't,
that's the place to tell us what's missing.

We love what we do, and we'd love you to be part of it.

www.hodder.co.uk

@hodderbooks

HodderBooks

HodderBooks